W9-DDB-623

THE GARDEN OF
SMALL BEGINNINGS

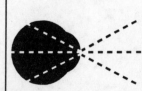

This Large Print Book carries the
Seal of Approval of N.A.V.H.

THE GARDEN OF SMALL BEGINNINGS

ABBI WAXMAN

THORNDIKE PRESS
A part of Gale, a Cengage Company

GALE
A Cengage Company

Farmington Hills, Mich • San Francisco • New York • Waterville, Maine
Meriden, Conn • Mason, Ohio • Chicago

LIBRARY OF CONGRESS CATALOGING-IN-PUBLICATION DATA

Names: Waxman, Abbi, author.
Title: The garden of small beginnings / by Abbi Waxman.
Description: Large print edition. | Waterville, Maine : Thorndike Press, a part of Gale, Cengage Learning, 2017. | Series: Thorndike Press large print women's fiction
Identifiers: LCCN 2017018220| ISBN 9781432842307 (hardcover) | ISBN 1432842307 (hardcover)
Subjects: LCSH: Widows—Fiction. | Women illustrators—Fiction. | Single mothers—Fiction. | Gardeners—Fiction. | Los Angeles (Calif.)—Fiction. | Domestic fiction. | Large type books. | BISAC: FICTION / Contemporary Women. | FICTION / Family Life. | FICTION / Romance / Contemporary. | GSAFD: Love stories.
Classification: LCC PS3623.A8936 G37 2017b | DDC 813/.6—dc23
LC record available at https://lccn.loc.gov/2017018220

Published in 2017 by arrangement with The Berkley Publishing Group, an imprint of Penguin Publishing Group, a division of Penguin Random House LLC

Printed in the United States of America
1 2 3 4 5 6 7 21 20 19 18 17

For my husband, David, who is my friend, my hero, and my woobie.

For my sister, Emily, who is the person I write for . . . the person for whom I write . . . oh, she knows what I mean.

And for my mother, Paula Gosling, who told me I was a writer before I could read. Now she can say she told me so, which mothers love to do.

ACKNOWLEDGMENTS

If there's a special place in hell for women who don't help other women, then I hope there's a corollary spot in heaven for women who do. Or free parking. Something.

These women made this book possible: Leah Woodring, who loves my children and backstops my life so I have time to write. I would be lost without her, often literally. Charlotte Millar, who listens to me complain and takes my side, even when I'm clearly in the wrong. Shana Eddy, the sweetest and smartest woman in Hollywood, who believed in me early and often. I will be forever in her debt. Naomi Beaty, Hilary Liftin, and Semi Chellas — three amazing writers who made suggestions and encouraging noises. And finally, my agent, Alexandra Machinist, who is almost too elegant and incisive to be real, and yet is.

There came a time when the risk to remain tight in the bud was more painful than the risk it took to blossom.

— ANAÏS NIN

PROLOGUE

It's been more than three years since my husband died, yet in many ways he's more useful than ever. True, he's not around to take out the trash, but he's great to bitch at while I'm doing it myself, and he's generally excellent company, invisibility notwithstanding. And as someone to blame he's unparalleled, because he isn't there to contradict me, on account of being cremated. I talk to him a lot, though our conversations have devolved from metaphysical explorations of the meaning of death to generic married conversations about what to have for dinner, or who's on the hook for the lost tax returns.

When he died in a car accident, fifty feet from our front door, I seriously considered dying, too. Not because my heart was broken, though that was true, but because my mind was completely boggled by the logistical challenges of living without him.

However, it's just as well I didn't, because he would have been waiting for me in heaven, and man, would he have been pissed. He'd have made eternity feel like forever, I can promise you that.

I was driving along, letting my brain spiral aimlessly, when my phone rang. It was my sister, Rachel.

"Hey, Lil, are you on your way to get the kids?" Just the sound of her voice made me smile.

"I am. Your knowledge of my daily schedule is embarrassing for both of us." I flicked on the indicator, slowed a little for the light, and made a turn. All with the phone illegally wedged under my ear. Sometimes I astound even myself.

"Can you pick something up for me on your way back?"

"Am I coming to your house?" Maybe I'd forgotten. It wasn't impossible.

"Well, you might have been. How do I know? Anyway, I haven't seen the kids for a couple of days, and you know how they pine."

I laughed. "I can honestly say they haven't mentioned you once."

She laughed back at me. "You know, one day you'll accept they love me more than you, and your denial of it isn't helping any of us move forward."

I pulled into the carpool line, doing the silent eyebrow raise and smile of greeting through the windshield at the teacher on duty. "Look, I'll admit they're fond of you. What is it you need, anyway? Something fundamental, like milk, or something more typical, like lubricant and a Duraflame?"

Suddenly a small palm smacked the window, making me jump and leaving a smear. Its owner, Annabel, peered in and narrowed her eyes. Her younger sister, Clare, stood behind her, gazing spacily around. Behind both of them, the teacher smiled tightly, telegraphing long-suffering patience with an undercurrent of threat if I didn't get my ass in gear. I hurriedly hit the door-open button. I'd hate for her to drag out the death ray on my account.

My sister was answering me. "I need a pound of bacon, some Parmesan cheese, spaghetti, eggs, a loaf of bread, and a bottle of red wine. And butter, of course."

"I'll call you back." I straightened my head, dropping the phone on the floor. "Do you need help or can you get her in, Bel?"

"I got it."

Annabel was only seven but had the gravitas of a forty-year-old career diplomat. She'd been born that way, calmly mastering breast-feeding, crawling, eating solids, and whatever else I threw at her. She regarded the world resignedly, as if we were exactly as we'd been described in the brochure: a little underwhelming, but what can you do? She buckled Clare in, struggling with the straps.

"Too tight?"

Clare shook her head.

"Too loose?"

Clare shook her head, her large brown eyes fastened trustingly on her older sister. Annabel nodded at her, turning to climb into her own seat, fastening her own harness with the self-assurance of a test pilot on his fiftieth run, rather than someone with no front teeth and a Dora barrette in her hair.

"Good to go," she informed me.

"Clare?" I wanted to make sure the little one hadn't lost the power of speech since breakfast. Presumably, I'd have gotten a call from the teacher, but with all these budget cuts . . .

"Good to go, cheerio." OK, smallest planet heard from.

I scrabbled around on the floor for my phone and called Rachel back. I put it on speaker this time and yelled at it as it lay in my lap. After all, now I had the kids in the

14

car. Safety first, people. Rachel picked up before it even rang on my end. She's a very busy woman.

I watched for a gap in the traffic as I yelled at the phone. "Hey, why didn't you say bring me the fixings for pasta carbonara? And why can't you stop on *your* way home?"

"Because I like to give you little riddles to solve, little challenges that keep you on your toes. Otherwise, your brain will atrophy, and then who will help the kids with their homework?"

"Are you cooking for us, too?"

"I certainly can. I'd be happy to. Why are you shouting at me?"

"I'm not shouting at you, the Bluetooth's broken. But I'm glad you're making dinner." I took a left.

"Are we going to the store?" asked Annabel. I knew she found the store irritating but was balancing that against the possibility of sudden candy.

I nodded.

"One other thing," added my sister. "You'll have to tell me how to make it."

"And then are we going to Aunty Rachel's?" asked Clare.

I nodded and then shook my head. My sister was doing her Jedi-mind-trick "These aren't the droids you're looking for" thing.

"Wait, Rach, let me ask you this: If I'm buying the groceries and making the dinner, why aren't you coming to my house?"

There was a pause.

"Oh, that's a much better idea. Thanks! I'll see you later on." She started to hang up.

"Stop," I interrupted. "If you're coming over, you can pick up the groceries. I've got the kids, remember?"

"Oh, yeah. OK." She hung up.

I looked at Clare in the rearview mirror. "No, honey, Aunty Rachel is coming to our place."

Both kids looked happy to hear it. They really did like her better than me. And why not? She could turn a request for a favor into an invitation to dinner and make you feel good about it.

Preparing Your Garden

As soon as your soil is soft enough to work, turn it over with a fork and leave it alone for several days.

- Cover the soil with a 1-inch-thick layer of compost. Don't skimp.
- Use a spading fork to loosen up the soil. Mix in the compost. Rake out stones and other crap, leaving the soil smooth.
- A 10 × 16 foot plot is a good size for a beginner. If that's too daunting, start smaller. Remember, one pot on a balcony is still a garden.
- Your seed packets have a world of information. They'll tell you best conditions and times to plant. Not sure? Ask someone at the garden center, or call your local agricultural extension. Gardeners love to grow other gardeners.

CHAPTER 1

I'm an illustrator, which sounds romantic, as if I spend my days under a spreading tree, dapple-splashed with sunshine, a watercolor tablet steady on my knee. Actually, I spend my days slumped in an office chair, destroying my posture and working on a computer. There is sunshine, of course, this being Southern California.

I love doing traditional illustration, the pencil and paint stuff, and I wish I had more time to do it, but when I left college, the job I found was illustrating school textbooks. I took the job expecting it to be a good starting place, but it turned out to be a great big comfy chair of a job, with a good salary, benefits, free coffee, and all the second-grade textbooks I could ever want. Eighty-two percent of American school children use Poplar Press products, and have done so for nearly a century. I love it. I learn all kinds of interesting stuff, and I draw and create things kids look at and, presumably, doodle little hats and mustaches on. Once, Annabel brought home one of my textbooks — *Kids in History, Fourth Edition* — and I saw that dozens of kids had used it, each of them adding new details to my historical figures I never would have imagined. Who knew Martin Van Buren was so well hung?

There are four of us in the creative department, plus a full-time writer, three fact-checkers, and a general assistant who's been there forever and who actually runs the whole place. She looked at me as I walked through the door that morning, and pursed her lips.

"Checking sent back your whale penis, Lilian."

I raised my eyebrows. "Rose, how long have you been waiting to say that?"

She didn't flicker. "I got in at seven, so a couple of hours, I guess."

I kept walking. "Tell them they'll have their penis back in the morning."

She coughed. "I already told them they could have it back later."

I stopped and turned. "Why did you do that?"

She was looking at the magazine she'd hidden beneath her desk. "Because then I could say, 'We'll have your penis back at the end of the day, but it will be hard.' "

"I can see how that would be difficult to pass up."

She shrugged. "In the maelstrom of tedium that is my day, I grab what rays of sunshine I can."

My office mate Sasha looked up as I walked in. "Hey, did Rose tell you about the penis?"

"Yes, she did. Did you still need me to help you with your biology book?"

"The development of the chicken egg? It can wait."

"OK, thanks."

Sasha shrugged. "The chicken should probably come first anyway . . ."

Let me be clear: The creative department of Poplar Press is not usually a comedy mecca. Often it is very dull, especially if we're updating a chemistry text or something. But it does have its moments, and there is the coffee.

I sat down, opened up the whale-penis file, and stared at it. It's not a whole file of whale penises (penii?); it's just one relatively small illustration in a veterinary-medicine textbook, and I'd been a little suspicious of why it was even included. Yes, it was important to be thorough, but how many vets were going to need to operate on a whale penis? It's not like the last time you took your parakeet to the vet you couldn't get into the waiting room on account of the impotent whale sitting nervously on several hard chairs. Or a young whale couple, holding hands and looking enviously at the baby animals in cardboard boxes all around them, occasionally shooting each other supportive glances and clearing their throats. I checked my e-mail: The fact-checkers had sent it back simply because one of the labels was misspelled. How did they even catch that? I picked up the phone and punched in a number.

"Fact-checking, Al here."

"Al, it's Lili."

"Hey, Lili, sorry about your penis."

I shifted in my chair. "Jesus, what is it with everyone this morning? You're all beside yourselves about the penis."

"As it were."

"So here's my question, Al. Are you sure there's a mistake? My input from the editor agrees with what I have, so what do you have there, an encyclopedia of penises? PenisCheck 2000?"

I could hear him grinning. "I cannot divulge the sources of the fact-checking department, you know that. I'd have to kill you, and then we'd lose our best illustrator."

I turned to Sasha. "Your boyfriend just said I'm the best illustrator."

We could both hear Al yelping. Sasha shrugged without turning around.

"Tell him now I've seen Moby's gear, I've lost all interest in him anyway."

"Al, she's leaving you for a cetacean."

"Again? That whore. No, but seriously, our guy at the aquarium caught the typo, and we checked with the editor, and his original content was wrong. No big deal, just checking the facts. We see a fact, we check it. It's our job."

"Oh, well, OK, then. I didn't know you had a tame whale guy on call."

"Again, I cannot reveal my sources, but how else do you think two scruffy guys with liberal-arts degrees proof all this stuff, if not for a fat, fat Rolodex of smart people with very narrow fields of focus?"

"You make a good point, Al." I hung up, fixed the word, and re-sent the document to Rose. In the cover note, I wrote she could stick the penis in fact-checking's in-box, which I knew she would appreciate.

My phone rang. Rose. "Upstairs wants to see you."

I frowned. "Am I getting fired?"

23

She clicked her tongue. "No clue. Why don't you gather your balls in your right hand and go upstairs and find out for yourself?" Rumor has it Rose was the mistress of the first Mr. Poplar, and was installed in the art department, as it was originally called, to hide her from his wife. Seeing as that would make her around eighty, and she is not that, I doubt it, but clearly she has embarrassing info on somebody. Otherwise, they would have fired her long ago. She has people skills like lions have gazelle skills. I sighed and headed upstairs to face Roberta King, my general manager.

Roberta King was probably around my age, but we had as much in common as a roller skate and a race car. (This isn't the best analogy for either of us but was something my dad always said and it springs to mind. He died last year, but I am keeping him alive by stealing his best material.) Roberta and I had met maybe half a dozen times, at work activities that sought to build community through trust falls and other excruciating experiences, and all I could remember about her was that she had looked as uncomfortable as I had felt.

I was wearing my working-mother-at-work

ensemble, consisting of a long skirt over boots (with two different socks underneath, but the skirt covered them), a long-sleeve T-shirt that I had slept in, and a V-necked and somewhat stretched sweater from Target. Roberta was wearing a suit. She smelled of flowers. I smelled of waffles.

However, she was smiling at me as if we were old friends, which of course meant I was about to get fired.

"Hi, Roberta. Rose said you wanted to see me?"

"Yeah, hi, Lili, come on in. Take a seat." She pushed her chair back from her desk and crossed her legs, indicating that this was a casual, girl-to-girl type of thing. I sat at an angle, like you do, and crossed my legs, too.

"How are the kids?" Ooh, a personal question.

"They're good, thanks. You know . . ." Shit, I had trailed off. Why was this difficult? I was a woman, she was a woman, we both worked in publishing, ovulated, perspired, ate ice cream and felt guilty about it, read *People* at the checkout, wondered what people thought of us. We should be able to be relaxed.

"Two little girls, right?"

I nodded.

"And one dead husband?" OK, she didn't say that. I just added it in my head. People often ask, when they don't know you, "Oh, and where's your husband?" Or, "And what does your husband do?" And it's very hard not to reply, "In heaven, hopefully." Or, "Oh, he mostly just rots." But anyway, she didn't mention him, which meant she remembered he was dead and was being polite and thoughtful. Bitch.

"So, Lili. As you know, things are a little tight in publishing right now. Education budgets are getting cut all over the country, and that's having a direct impact on our business, of course. Poplar's trying to stay ahead by branching out a bit."

I laughed. She paused, frowning a little. I blushed. "Sorry . . . I thought you were making a pun . . . Poplar . . . branch . . ." I swear a tumbleweed blew through the office and bounced over a ridge in the carpet.

Roberta cleared her throat. "Fortunately, an opportunity has presented itself. The Bloem Company is one of the largest seed and flower corporations in the world." I nodded. Even I had heard of them, and I don't know a daisy from a doorknob. "They produced a series of flower guides, and they're going to add a series on vegetables. They've asked us to publish them, because the small press who released the flower guides has gone out of business."

I nodded and put on my intelligent listening face, adding a little between-the-eyebrows frown for extra focus. I was actually just waiting to hear my name, like a dog.

"We'd like you to illustrate them."

I nodded again, but she had stopped talking.

"Well, that will be . . . fun." I was puzzled. What was the fuss about? Why was she pulling me into her office to tell me about a job? Normally we get briefed on new projects downstairs, in a short meeting, and then they arrive via e-mail.

Roberta started up again. "It's a very big job."

"Well, there are lots of vegetables in the world."

"Yes. And the Bloem people want to cover all of them. There will be several volumes, plus an addendum."

"I love an addendum."

"And we want you to do it by hand, not computer. Watercolors, pen-and-ink, charcoal, whatever you like. Bloem wants to create something artistic and lasting. While at the same time capitalizing on the rebirth of interest in slow food, organic gardening, and the back-to-the-land movement." She was

27

nervous about something, I could hear it in her voice. She suddenly looked at me and blurted out, "I'm afraid I did something terrible. Truly, truly terrible."

I was surprised, because I hadn't thought she was that kind of girl, but I got ready to be shocked.

"I said you'd take a gardening class." She cleared her throat. "A vegetable gardening class."

"I'm sorry?" I frowned. "Did you say a gardening class?"

Roberta blushed. "I was on the phone with the woman from Bloem, and she mentioned that one of the Bloem family sons was teaching a class on vegetable gardening, here in Los Angeles, and I said you'd take it."

"The class?"

"Yes."

"On vegetable gardening?"

"Yes." She spoke more slowly, as apparently I wasn't getting it. "I said you'd take a class on vegetable gardening." She said it the way someone else might have said, "And you'll be slowly dipped in battery acid, toes first."

"I don't mind taking a gardening class. It sounds like fun." I paused. "Unless it's a three-year commitment and requires a lot of heavy lifting?"

She shook her head quickly. "It's Saturday mornings, for six weeks. We would of course be compensating you for your time." I half shrugged, and she leapt on it. "And giving you extra vacation days."

I would have done it for nothing, but there was no need to tell her that. "Sounds fair."

She shuddered. "I would have taken the course myself, but I simply couldn't."

I altered my opinion of her, subtly. "Why?"

"I hate worms." She visibly shivered, and may even have gone pale. It was hard to tell under her perfect makeup. "I had a bad experience as a child. I can't even stand too close to soil, you know, just in case."

I had to bite my lip not to ask for details. What qualifies as a bad worm experience? I imagined her running along, tiny and cute in coordinated Baby Gap, tripping, falling, her little braids twisting in slow motion as she hit the ground, skidding, coming face-to-face with a worm . . . that pulled out a gun and shot her? That bit her on the nose? I mean, honestly, they don't even have mouths. But you can't say that kind of thing to people. You can't mock their fears openly. But I made a note to do it later, in private.

She still looked worried. "So will you do it?"

I shrugged. "Of course, happy to. I'm sure it will inspire my illustrations." I didn't add that I could always get up close and personal with a carrot in the produce department, but she seemed to think this class would help the project, and who was I to argue?

She relaxed, visibly, and stood up. Her clothes fell perfectly, not a wrinkle. Maybe she had some little guy under the desk, steaming her as she sat. Mine kind of stuck where they were, as if someone had wadded them into a ball and thrown them at me.

"Excellent. The class starts this Saturday. You can bring your kids."

I said thanks, and she said thanks, and we both shook hands and said thanks again, and then she added something.

"We're very worried about the future of Poplar. But I know you'll make a good impression, do wonderful work, and save the company."

"No pressure, then." I tried to soften my sarcasm with a small smile.

Her first genuine smile since I'd entered her office appeared. "I know you're up to the task."

I tottered out and headed back downstairs.

I went to the tiny kitchen and poured an enormous coffee. My mug said, WORLD'S

GREATEST DAD, which I supposed was applicable, although I picked it because it was the size of a bucket. Rose had put a sign above the coffeemaker: IF YOU TAKE THE LAST OF THE COFFEE, PUT ON A NEW POT, OR I WILL MAKE YOUR LIFE . . . CHALLENGING. She meant it, too. Sasha forgot once, and Rose connected all her outward-bound calls to the CEO's office, which meant five times in a row the guy picked up the phone and there was Sasha. Eventually the CEO suggested she not forget to put on more coffee next time.

Back at my desk, I called my sister.

"Can you babysit the kids every Saturday morning for the next six weeks?"

There was a pause. Then she said, "Yes, if you don't mind dropping them at my house and running the risk that naked people might be there. Or trained animals."

I laughed. "Come on, your private life isn't that exciting."

"That's what you think. Note the use of the word *private*."

"So that's a no, then?"

"Do I have to commit to the full series? Can't I do it as needed?"

"This is as needed. Work has asked me to do a gardening class, and it's every Saturday for the next month and a half. I'm illustrating a book on vegetables, and they think it will help if I learn how to grow them."

"They might be right."

"I doubt it. I did a great job on *Monasteries of 14th Century Europe,* and I'm not a monk, nor French, nor dead for five hundred years."

"Good point. Can't you take them with you?"

"I could, but I thought they'd rather hang with you."

"How about I come to the class, too, and help you with the kids there?"

I actually took the phone away from my ear and looked at it.

"Are you OK? Gardening? Really?"

She sighed. "I'm feeling oppressed by my job today. I have spent the last two hours on the phone, yelling at people I will never meet, but who hold the fate of my company in their slippery hands. A very important item has been lost in transit, which I am having a hard time with."

"Wow, you really are pissed. You just ended a sentence with a preposition."

"Eat me."

"What was it?"

"Oh, you know, the usual. A priceless, thousand-year-old statue of a horse."

"Well, maybe it's just in the wrong box or

something."

"It's life-size. And on its back is a naked woman holding aloft the headless body of an eagle. But apart from those minor distinguishing features, it's easily missed."

"OK." I paused. "I have no response to that at all. Good luck with your missing horse." We hung up. Honestly, our conversations were getting more and more like an old married couple's every day. Apart from the headless-eagle part, although I always say you never really know what goes on in someone else's marriage.

"We're what?" Annabel looked skeptical in the rearview mirror.

Yet again, back in the car. I should buy myself one of those beaded seat covers that are supposed to be good for your back, but I'd end up with the pattern permanently embedded in my ass, and the last thing I need back there is more texture.

We were heading home after school. Or at least we would be, once the carpool line inched its way out of the school parking lot. The thing about carpool lines is that teachers use them to indicate how much they like your kids, and, by extension, you. I might be reading too much into it, but how else can I explain the fact that I might be at the front of the line and able to see my kid sitting there, picking her nose with all the subtlety of Howard Carter in a pyramid, and have teachers hunt high and low for children to take to cars way behind me? Cars containing parents who send in cookies more frequently, or even at all. Parents who remember to send thank you cards after birthday parties, or put clean clothes on their kids more than once a week. They're always nice to my face, these teachers, but they say things like, "Oh, Annabel is so unique." Or, "Clare said the funniest thing again in class today." Or, "She has an amazing vocabulary, Mrs. Girvan. Honestly, I'm not even certain a tiger *has* a clitoris."

I answered the question calmly. "We're going to learn how to grow a garden."

"I already know how to grow things." Clare was excited. "We do it at school."

I looked at her, quickly, over my shoulder. "You do?"

She nodded. Annabel confirmed. "The little kids have a garden in the playground. We see them out there digging in the dirt."

"I kissed a worm." That's the thing about Clare, she's shy.

"Did he kiss you back?"

She laughed. "Mom! Worms aren't he's. They're both girls *and* boys!"

Huh. Score one for the Los Angeles public school system.

"Yes, they're hermaphrodites," Annabel clarified.

"No, they're boys *and* girls." Clare wasn't going to let her sister one-up her.

We were nearly at the street. "Well, anyway, we're starting this weekend, and it's going to be fun. Aunty Rachel is going to take the class with us."

"Can I get back to you?" Annabel apparently needed to consult with her people.

"Well, I'm doing it." Clare didn't need permission from anyone.

We parked in front of the house, and I let the kids out, stepping back to avoid the small cascade of car crap that fell out when the door slid back. You could always tell where I'd parked: granola-bar wrappers, a small, bent straw from a juice box, a grubby wipe. Mommy droppings. I imagined a Native American tracker crouching low on the sidewalk: "Middle-aged, plump woman, heading south, surrounded by young." He would straighten and shake his majestic head pityingly. "Moving slowly."

As I shut the car door, I noticed broken car-window glass in the gutter and instantly wondered if it had been there since my husband's accident. It hadn't, of course, but images of that day often flickered into my mind without being invited. Broken glass. A car door slamming suddenly. Coffee spilled on the street, still steaming. The sound of emergency voices distorted by static.

They had come very quickly when Dan had been killed, although I hadn't heard the sirens. I was standing in the kitchen, replaying the argument we had been in the middle of, as it happened, saying all the things I had meant to say. It had been a hissing morning argument, where we'd gone to bed angry, woken up still angry, and then had to put it on infuriating hold while he took the kids to school.

"I'll be back," were his last words, but not in a pleasant, don't-worry way, but more in a Terminator, this-argument-isn't-done way. Not that it mattered. It wasn't true anyway, and never would be.

I cut back to today and watched the kids get out of the car in that jumping-falling way little kids do, then I reached into the backseat to get backpacks, art projects, and stray shoes. I could hear our Labrador, Frank, barking as I walked to the door, and he greeted us enthusiastically, checking the kids for food, then scooting his fat butt across the rug.

"Frank has worms again, Mom," announced Annabel, Child Veterinarian, turning on the TV.

"Maybe he just has an itchy bottom," suggested Clare. "It happens."

I sighed and started emptying the dishwasher. The dog has worms. Clare needs a filling in a baby tooth because I'm a bad mother and give her sugar. My sister wants dinner. Meanwhile, I haven't had a haircut in five months and have started to resemble Cousin Itt. Cousin Itt was a blonde, of course, whereas I am more of an indeterminate brown, but still. I caught sight of my reflection in the kitchen window and for a minute thought I was my mother. Fantastic.

An hour or so later, my sister walked in. "You're starting to look a little like Cousin Itt, did you know that?" She put the grocery bags on the counter and picked up Clare, who was squealing about the dog and his worms. "Wait, who has worms? You have worms?" She looked at Annabel. "Do you have worms, too?"

"Yes." Annabel was expressionless, engrossed in the TV. "Hundreds of worms."

I put water on for the pasta and started making dinner. I thought about the times I'd watched my mother chopping onions, the radio playing, an empty tomato can holding her wooden spoon on the counter, the smell of melting butter permeating the air. I wondered if she'd been as under-whelmed as I was. Every day around four o'clock I would start making dinner for the kids, which meant for me, too, because otherwise I would eat alone, or not at all, and then they would eat (if I was lucky), take a bath, get into their jammies, have stories, and go to bed. When Dan had been alive, he would arrive in the middle of it, full of adult thoughts and complaints about his work, which at least provided some visual interest and the possibility of polysyl-labic words. Now Rachel was often here, which worked, too, but sometimes I found myself singing the *Curious George* theme song under my breath in a way that prob-ably indicated brain-cell death.

Rachel leaned against the counter and examined me. "You're pissed about the Cousin Itt thing, right? I'm sorry. That was thoughtless. Besides, it's not Itt so much as it is Morticia. I can still see a slice of your face. And it's a good slice."

I looked at her silently, poking my wooden spoon at the bacon, breaking it apart. She was lovely, my sister, both to look at and as a person. She was single, but not celibate, largely by choice. She had been married once, very young, and had taken a pledge not to do that again. Taller than me, thinner than me (which was forgivable, seeing as she didn't have kids), with better hair and firmer thighs, she nonetheless made it clear that she put the kids and me above her own plans. I worried sometimes that the sad circumstances of my life had curtailed her freedom. I said as much, once, and she pointed out that the sad circumstances of my life were also the sad circumstances of her life.

"Hey, my brother-in-law, who I really loved, got killed in a car accident, and my sister went insane for a while, so I had to take care of her kids. That happened to me, remember? You are just a bit player in the drama that is Rachel Anderby's Life, starring Rachel Anderby, written by Rachel Anderby, directed by Rachel Anderby. In my life, you're simply a supporting character. Lili, the kids are billed above you."

But I knew it had cost her something, to be available for me, and I knew that she knew that I knew, and that if it ever came to kidney donation or taking a bullet, I was her girl. Mind you, she did have a hectic social life these days, and was even, on occasion, busy for an entire weekend.

I drained the spaghetti.

"So, what are you doing on Saturday

afternoon?" I asked her. "After our thrilling new gardening class."

"A date, what else?" She was folding the napkins into swans, a trick she had learned one summer waitressing at a theme-park restaurant. At the time, it had seemed as though the entire three months had been one long, drunken orgy of seasonal workers in the sun, but the napkin origami had made it all worth it. Otherwise, it would just have been fantastic and frequent guilt-free sex with other happy young people, and who needs that?

"With whom?" I raised my eyebrows but kept my tone neutral, a trick I had learned one summer interning at a publishing house (no sex, no origami, but loads of free irony and all the bookmarks you could carry).

"A new guy."

"From work?" Rachel worked at an international import-export firm that specialized in art and artifacts. She was the head of logistics for them, and could routinely be overheard on the phone saying things like, "Well, the sarcophagus can overnight in Cairo, then, but it better be in Budapest before Tuesday, or the Pope's going to throw a shitter." She often met men through her work, but she never dated anyone who worked for her company. She was a bit of a slut, to be honest, but a slut with rules.

"Kind of. I met him at an opening."

"Cute?"

She grinned at me. "No, repulsive, with knock-knees and a squint. I thought it was time to broaden my horizons."

"Nice."

"Mommy?"

I looked down. Clare had appeared. "Yes, honey?" I tucked a strand of hair behind her ear, smoothing her cheek. The physical perfection of a small child is sometimes too much to deal with. Did the kid even have pores?

"I want to paint."

"Not now, sweetie. Dinner's ready."

"But I really, really want to." Sadly, the physical perfection is often paired with immense self-interest. The strand of hair popped out, and I started to reach for it again.

"I hear you, honey, but now is not a good time. Maybe in the morning."

"No. Now." Clare was hungry, apparently. She ducked her head away, not letting me tidy her hair.

"Go tell your sister to come and sit down for dinner, OK?"

She debated throwing a fit about the painting, the struggle between hunger and rage apparent in her puckered brow. Rachel intervened, picking her up and carrying her, upside down, to get Annabel. I tossed the drained spaghetti; threw in the egg, cheese, bacon, butter, and onions; and stirred it fast to cook the egg. Carrying the pan across to the table, I beat the kids to it, and by the time they sat, their dinner was steaming on their plates. I gave myself a small round of applause because no one else was going to do it.

Rachel looked up at me. "You can join me on my date, if you like. I'm sure this guy has a friend." She put a forkful of food in her mouth. "Actually, I hope he has more than one, but the squint could be putting people off."

I frowned at her. "Don't be silly." I never talked about dating in front of the kids, which made it easy to avoid the topic completely, as they were always there. I wasn't ready to date, the kids weren't ready for me to date, and, in fact, I was planning on not dating until they finished college. I would encourage them to take a year off first, to tour Europe. Plus there was the strong possibility of several years of post-graduate studies. I was safe for at least two decades, at which point my lady parts would have fused together like Barbie's anyway.

I got drinks for everyone, a plate for myself, and finally sat down.

"Mommy," Annabel said. She was twirling spaghetti around her fork, a freshly acquired skill. Often the twirling went on much longer than it needed to, but these things take practice.

"Yes, sweets?" I reached for extra cheese.

"Did I tell you I have a boyfriend?"

I flicked a glance at Rachel. "Nope. Who's that?"

"James."

OK, at least it was a kid I knew. An actual kid, not an imaginary kid.

"Really? I like James. He's nice." I filled my mouth with spaghetti and thanked God for the Italians. Spaghetti, pizza, ice cream. If they weren't so busy making love and whizzing around on Vespas, they'd probably rule the world.

Annabel made a face.

"He's silly. But he's my boyfriend."

"Does he know it?"

She looked scandalized. "No! Of course not!"

Rachel looked at Clare.

"Do you have a boyfriend, too?"

"No, I'm married." Clare had a mouthful of spaghetti, but she smiled around it.

"Oh yeah?" Rachel kept eating. "Who are

you married to?"

"Frank."

Frank banged his tail on the ground, hearing his name.

"Huh. Did you know your husband has worms?"

Clare nodded.

Annabel was patient but firm. "Clare, you can't marry the dog." She put down her fork.

"I did. It's done." This was one of Clare's favorite things to say. "It's done" covered a lot of things, like drawing on the wall, peeing on the floor, eating candy. It's done, nothing can be changed, it's over. She was all about closure, that one.

"But people can't marry dogs."

"Why not? I love Frank."

Annabel nodded. "Yes, so do I."

"And people who love each other get married."

Annabel nodded again, although Rachel opened her mouth to object. I frowned at my sister, and shook my head, subtly.

"So the dog is your husband?" Annabel was skeptical and turned to me. "She can't marry the dog, Mom."

"Bel, she's too young to really marry anyone. But if she wants to say that she and Frank are husband and wife rather than mutt and kindergartner, who are we to rain on her parade?"

She looked at me, thinking.

"Look," I continued. "Last week she spent three days pretending the bathtub was a coral reef infested with deadly eels, and you let that one slide." I smiled at Annabel. "She's only five, after all."

"Although," Rachel chimed in, "Frank's nearly eight, a much older man."

I looked at her. "Yeah, that's the worrying part, the age difference."

"But it's silly." Annabel was really not having it.

"So? Lots of things are silly, honey, and usually that's a good thing."

Clare misinterpreted her sister's unhappiness. "Hey, you can marry Henry if you like." Henry was our rabbit. He lived in the garden, in a hutch, and I have to admit that more than once I totally forgot he existed.

Rachel laughed. "Wait, I want to marry Henry, he's supercute." This was undeniable.

"He's a bit short for you, isn't he?"

"He's very fluffy." Annabel was entering into the spirit of the thing, finally. "He has very big ears, like that boyfriend you had at Christmas."

Rachel snorted. "How do you remember

these things? I barely remember that guy."

Clare was on a roll. "And Mommy can marry Jane." The cat.

Annabel lost her smile again. "Mommy can't marry Jane. One thing, Jane is a girl, and girls don't marry girls . . ." Rachel opened her mouth to correct her, but Annabel was getting louder. "Two, Jane is a cat, and cats don't ever get married, and three, Mom is already married to Dad, and you can't marry two people at once."

"Who wants dessert?" I said, chirpily, getting to my feet.

"But Dad is dead," said Clare, firmly.

I started clearing plates, noisily. "How about ice cream?"

"Yes, but they're still married." I pulled open the freezer in a hurry.

"But he's dead. It's done."

Annabel started to flush, which was not a good sign. "Yes, but they're still married, so she can't marry anyone else. Ever."

I gave it another shot. "Ooh, who wants chocolate sauce?"

Clare frowned back at her. "But what if she loves someone? She can marry them."

"Marshmallows?"

Annabel stood up, and I realized this was about to go south. Luckily, so did Rachel.

"Bath!" she yelled, leaping up and grab-

46

bing Clare.

I picked up Annabel, who was starting to shake. Often weeks would pass when she wouldn't mention her dad at all. But other days she would just crumple. Clare often set her off, because the whole thing meant less to her. She'd been less than a year old when Dan died. To her, Dad was just a word, something other people had, like a horse, or measles.

As Rachel headed to the bathroom, blowing raspberries on Clare's tummy, I sat down with Annabel on my lap.

"Honey, I love you and Clare and Aunty Rachel. I'm never going to marry anyone else, OK?"

She was crying a bit now, and just nodded. I rested her head against my shoulder and stroked her head.

"I'm always going to love your daddy, OK? No one else will ever be your daddy — just him. And I will always be your mommy."

"And Aunty Rachel will always be my aunty?"

I nodded, against her hair.

"And grandma . . ."

"Will always be your grandma, yes."

"And Frank?" More tail banging under the table.

I smiled. "Will always be Clare's husband, yes."

She laughed, finally, and I carried her to the bathroom.

ESSENTIAL EQUIPMENT

All new activities are excuses for shopping.

You'll need these basic supplies:

- *Garden gloves*
- *Fork*
- *Rake*
- *Hoe*
- *Hand cultivator or trowel*
- *Watering can or hose*

But if you don't have money or room for these things, just buy seeds and use your hands. The plants don't care.

CHAPTER 2

The next day, Clare had an afternoon play-date. Samantha was in her class at school, collected Littlest Pet Shops, and could rattle off the names and evolutions of three hundred Pokémon, ergo they were best friends forever. In this way, little girls are like grown men: They only need one or two things in common to become official buddies. Fishing. Golf. An interest in breasts. Unfortunately, Samantha's mother and I couldn't even find two things in common, so I just dropped and ran. Not a mortal sin in mothering terms, but probably a faux pas. I don't care. If they want to drum me out of the Mother of the Year club, fuck them. It's a stupid club, anyway.

Rachel called me just as Annabel and I were getting close to home.

"I was going to offer to pick Clare up from her playdate and bring her home."

"You're back again tonight? Two nights in

a row?" I paused. "Is the hazmat team at your house again? Or that guy who's convinced you're married?"

"My ex-husband? No, I just prefer the conversation of the kids to the silence of my apartment and the taste of my own cooking."

I waited. She was an honest woman, she couldn't lie.

"OK, the taste of takeout pizza. But, of course, if you just want to be sarcastic, you can pick up your own goddamned kid yourself."

But she did, of course, and I was grateful. There was a price to be paid, though, and once the kids were asleep, Rachel launched into her campaign to reinvigorate Lili's love life.

We were collapsed in front of the TV in my living room. We weren't watching it, but it was on, the constant companion of modern life. God forbid we'd sit in silence with our thoughts. When Dan was alive, we would often spend hours not saying a word. It was bliss.

"So, you haven't had sex in nearly three years, right?" Rachel had pulled her socks off and was examining her toes.

I shrugged, trying halfheartedly to throw Lego pieces into a bucket in the corner.

"More than three years, if you count the last year of my marriage. I was pregnant, then I had a baby."

She frowned at me. "Presumably, some married people have sex all the time?"

"Sure, on TV."

"You're not selling it."

"I'm not trying to."

I ran out of Legos to throw, just when I was getting good at it, and moved on to My Little Pony figures. Different bucket, and you have to compensate for the mane when you calculate trajectory. My house was tidy once a week, when the cleaning lady came, and for about twenty minutes. It was decorated in "early childhood education," with an underpinning of "young married couple try to create a peaceful oasis." Calm colors and natural fibers mostly, covered in a patina of finger paint and plastic animals. As if a toy store and a Zen monastery had fought, with the toy store getting the upper hand and the monastery passively resisting. As it would, presumably.

Rachel was lying on the sofa, halfheartedly doing sit-ups. I was shocked.

"Are you exercising?"

"No, I'm trying to reach the remote."

"Ah."

"Yup." She found it under her butt and

started flipping through the channels. She settled on a cooking show and went back to her toes. "Do you have any nail polish?"

I got up slowly. I used to be able to leap to my feet. I used to be able to stand up and sit down without thinking about it. Now if I sat in one position for more than five minutes, I seized up. I felt like the Tin Man: *oil . . . can . . .*

I crept into the kids' room and fetched a little basket. "There are five shades of pink, three purples, some gold, some glittery, a green that smells of mint, and a miniature music stand that presumably went with something at some point . . . that's it."

She raised her eyebrows. "Is this Annabel's collection?"

I nodded.

"When did you last paint your toenails?"

I shrugged. "Who's the president?"

She sighed, despairing of me. "You used to be vain, for crying out loud! I used to make fun of you for spending hours in the bathroom every morning. You color co-ordinated your eye makeup with your shoes."

"I got married. I had kids. My husband died. I let myself go."

She frowned at me. "You're still totally gorgeous. Underneath all that . . . scruff."

"Gee, thanks."

"You know what I mean. You and Dan were like the arty-hipster prom king and queen. Golden couple. Yearbook hotties."

"OK, keep your hair on. I was cute. Dan was cute. I get it."

"And you're still totally hot. You're just hiding out in a middle-aged-mom costume." She had leaned forward on the sofa, the better to underscore her point, and if I'd wanted to, I could have punched her in the nose. I considered it.

"Wow, Rach, that's motivating. Let's change the subject before my last remaining shred of self-esteem unravels."

She glared at me for a moment but gave up and started painting her toenails different colors instead. I pulled out my sketch pad and began drawing her. She was beautiful, despite her tendency to micromanage my personal life. Long dark hair, all thick and wavy in a way mine wasn't, the face of an angel and the brain of a very successful tax accountant, or something. Great figure, strong and full, which she did absolutely nothing to maintain. Not to worry, she'd fall apart once she had kids.

"I'm just saying you need to get back out there, and let someone get back in there."

She was focused on her toes, but I wasn't fooled.

"No, I'm good, thanks. You've always been the one who needed to leap from one dick to the next, like a logrolling contestant."

There was a pause. "How do you mean?" she asked.

"You know . . . when they've got all those logs in the water and they have to keep going from one to the other really fast so they don't fall in the water and get crushed."

"No, I meant about me. The logrolling simile was bizarre, but I knew what you were referring to."

I sighed, and tried to include her forehead frown lines in my sketch. "I just meant you like to have a boyfriend. Sometimes several. Apart from the brief period you were married." We both turned our heads and pretended to spit on the ground. It was a family tradition when anyone mentioned her ex-husband. "You've never dated anyone for very long."

"And that makes me a cock-hopper?"

"Is that a thing? An actual term?"

"It could be." She put the little brush back in the jar and put on her earnest expression. I'd seen it many times before. "Look, this isn't about me and my healthy sex drive. It's about you and your apparent disinterest in meeting a guy. Or a girl. Or two girls and a guy, whatever. Dan has been gone for a long time now. You're still young and attractive and funny and sexy, and it's time you got out there and lived a little."

"Rachel, he didn't move to Nebraska to live with a cocktail waitress named Lurlene. He died. Killed suddenly in a horrific accident that I basically witnessed. It's a shock to have your soul mate ripped off the planet like that. It takes time to recover. I haven't recovered yet. Let it go."

I didn't want to get angry with her, because I understood she meant well, but this conversation was always exhausting. I got up to go check on the kids, hoping she'd get my less-than-subtle hint and change the subject.

It worked. When I got back, she had finished her nails and was ready to move on. "Hey, in other news, I totally forgot that Alison asked if she could babysit sometime."

This was something that mystified me. People I barely knew would offer to babysit my kids. Of course, they didn't know them as well as I did. I looked around: Frank was on the armchair, and Rachel was lying on the sofa. I sat on the floor. "Why on earth would she want to do that?"

"Because for many people children are

fun. Presumably, you thought they would be fun, too, or did you conceive them as a condition of your parole? I know Dan wasn't all that keen, so it must have been your idea."

This was partially true. Dan had maintained a public face of indifference to the concept of babies before Annabel was born, but from the minute we found out we were pregnant, he was into it. He would lie next to me, whispering to the bump, answering random questions he said he could hear. "No, it was Secretariat," he would say. Or, "Just eat whatever you can find." Or, "Yes, you can have a pony."

"Well, Alison should come and meet the kids before she volunteers."

Rachel sighed. "Lili, she's met them about fifty times. Alison is the receptionist at my office. She babysat them loads when you were in the nuthouse and I had stuff to do."

"It wasn't a nuthouse. It was a hospital."

"With locks on the doors."

"Well, yes."

"And lithium and Thorazine and people who thought they were Amelia Earhart."

"That was just one guy."

"Whatever. You're trying to change the subject. When was the last time you and I went out on the town? When was the last time you had a little too much to drink and did something embarrassing?"

"I repeat, who's the president?"

She reached for her phone. "That's it. I'm calling Alison. Let's go out tomorrow night."

"Friday night? Surely you have plans?"

"Yes," she said, "I'm taking my sister out. She's a spinster of this parish, and getting bony."

I shook my head again, more firmly. "No, Rach. I don't want to."

But she was talking, and I found myself letting her arrange things with Alison. I could always back out at the last minute.

She hung up the phone. "Now, that's all done. No backing out at the last minute. I know you're thinking of it."

"Me? No way."

How to Grow a Beet

Beets are fussy about the pH of their soil, which isn't unreasonable, as they're buried in it. Use a pH kit and shoot for 5.5 to 6.

- Be generous with aged manure before planting, and make sure you've got plenty of phosphorus . . . but not too much nitrogen. Too much nitrogen and you'll end up with lots of leaves but only very, very tiny beets. Cute, but disappointing.
- They also like soil above 50 degrees.
- Plant seeds 1/2 inch deep and 1 to 2 inches apart.
- When you're ready to harvest, run out and buy some goat cheese. Nothing better than beets and goat cheese.

CHAPTER 3

On Friday, I left work early because I had an appointment with Ruth Graver, my grief therapist. At this point, she was really just a therapist, as the grief had subsided to a kind of dull roar, as if the monster in the closet had a toothache and wasn't coming out right now, but I still went to see her a couple of times a month. I had always assumed the therapy, which had started when I left the hospital, was supposed to get me to a point of acceptance about Dan's death. I wasn't there, not even close, despite Dr. Graver's best efforts.

"And why do you think Annabel got upset?" Ruth Graver was a no-nonsense dark-haired woman who looked almost as intelligent as she actually was. She had the air of someone who, following an alien invasion and the annihilation of half the planet, would be organizing the resistance and handing out blankets. For all I knew, she was privately a speed freak with tattoos over 80 percent of her body and an obsession with the early music of Frank Sinatra, but at work she was as cool as a cucumber.

I recrossed my legs. "For the obvious reason, I guess. She doesn't want me to replace her daddy by marrying someone else."

"She said you're still married to him."

"Right. It doesn't make sense to her that death changes one's marital status. It doesn't make much sense to me, either, to be fair."

"In your mind you're still married." Her voice was neutral, of course. No judgment here, Lilian. Just turn the handbag of your soul inside out and shake it.

I nodded. "Not just in my mind, but everywhere. When I have to fill out a form and the choices are single, married, or divorced, I check 'married' and write in 'widowed.' Why isn't that box there, anyway? Bureaucracy is normally so all-encompassing. If I were a Native Alaskan or a speaker of Urdu, I'd have a little box, but as a widow, I'm supposed to revert to single overnight." I found I was picking my nails, and stopped.

Graver's office was decorated in "classic mid-century therapist," and as she waited

61

in silence for me to continue my diatribe, I gazed at the familiar things on her shelves. A small pot a child had made by coiling clay, a miniature Eames chair that matched the one she sat in, joke action figures of Einstein and Poe. I knew nothing about her, although I sometimes tried to get her to tell me about herself. She wouldn't, which was annoying.

I realized I still hadn't said anything, and smiled.

"Why are you smiling?"

"Because it gives me something to do with my mouth. I'm tired of hearing myself complain." I started picking my nails again. "I'm tired of people asking me questions, and looking hopeful when they see me with a man, tired of little pauses in conversation when I say I'm fine, as the entire world waits to see if I'm going to start seeing someone." My throat felt tight, but with anger. "If Dan had survived the crash but been a vegetable, silently drooling in a hospital bed somewhere, nobody would be encouraging me to date, right? Well, let's just pretend he's Bertha Mason-ing somewhere and I'm not a free woman, because I really don't feel free."

She said nothing, but the wrinkles at the corners of her eyes deepened. Concern. I knew that look well. I looked at my watch and smiled wider.

"Time's up, Dr. Graver. See you next month."

I left, imagining her sitting there motionless, gathering dust until I next appeared.

I had already tried, and failed, to get out of dinner that night, but Rachel had set her phone to go straight to voice mail. And she even had the nerve to change her message so it said, "If this is Lili trying to cancel dinner plans, don't even bother to leave a message, because I'm going to ignore it. If it's anyone else, I'm all ears." *Beeeeep.*

The other irritation was that the kids were excited Alison was coming over. Strangely, as Rachel had said, they knew who she was and felt she was an excellent babysitter.

"I won't be here," I had reminded them, trying to upset one of them so I would have an excuse not to go out.

They nodded. "Alison has pink hair," Clare volunteered. Ah, yes, now I could visualize her. Maybe I should have pink hair. It seemed to be so positively received.

"I won't be putting you to bed." Desperate measures.

They nodded again. It was Friday, going to bed was a more fluid concept, and there was no school the next morning. They were blasé.

"When she reads, she does all the voices," added Annabel.

"I do all the voices," I reminded her, somewhat hurt, the TV remote in my hand.

"Yes, but all of hers are different." A pause. "Can you press PLAY now?"

When Alison showed up at five, she brought her pink hair and was wearing a miniskirt over the top of tartan leggings, with a T-shirt that said, TRANSCEND THE BULLSHIT. She pushed me toward the bathroom.

"Rachel said I should force you to take a shower and get all dressed up. She'll be here at seven to get you."

"Did she give you a dress code?" I was joking.

"Sexy casual."

Puzzling. Alison pulled a piece of paper out of her jeans and read it out.

"That black top with the laces, a little undone, the nice bra I gave you for Christmas, jeans and boots; plenty of makeup; hair up in a loose knot."

We looked at each other.

"She also said to touch up your toenails in case you took your shoes off."

"You have to wear shoes if you're going

outside. It's the law," Clare chimed in.

"I'm not sure it is the law," Annabel said, looking at Alison. "Mom says it is, but sometimes I think it's not."

Alison frowned. "Laws are just the prevailing rules of the hegemony; question authority." Then she looked at me, quickly. "If that's OK with you?"

"Oh sure," I said, trying to remember what hegemony was. "Question away."

I walked off. It was an incredible luxury to have two hours to myself to get ready, and I decided to just accept it. The kids were fine, I was fine, the dog and cat were fed. It was OK to take some time for myself and . . . I realized I was rationalizing taking a shower.

I considered my face critically as I put on my makeup. I had reached the age at which less makeup was starting to look better than more. Too much tended to get stuck in wrinkles. I honestly thought an exception was going to be made in my case. That my great complexion would last forever and my apparent invulnerability to cellulite was a genetic gift. Neither had been true, and having two kids had done the same number on my body that it did on every woman, not counting the airbrushed set. It was unfair, but there it was. I looked good when I was done, if your boundaries were generous. Slim-ish, young-ish, somewhat sexy, if you can be sexy when you're totally disinterested in sex.

Rachel whistled when she came to pick me up. "Oh yeah, that's what I'm talking about. You look great."

Annabel and Clare were giddy with the novelty of it.

"You look like a princess, Mommy," said Clare, skipping about. "And you smell like Macy's!"

Annabel was more discerning. "An evil princess, though, because regular princesses don't wear black all over."

"But her hair is like a regular princess, because it's up."

"Yes, but it's got no ribbons or anything, so that's more like an evil princess."

"Yes, but she doesn't have a short guy with her, and evil princesses always have a short guy." Clare's voice was getting louder; this was about to turn into a fight. Time to leave.

Once we were outside, I was overcome with excitement.

"I'm outside," I said to Rachel. "In the dark!"

She laughed. "I know! It's thrilling!" She pretended to look around. "Where are the kids? Oh wait, they're not here!" We clutched each other and giggled.

Yup. The Anderby sisters were living the dream.

I might not have a rip-roaring sex life, or any sex life at all, but one pleasure is still open to me, and that's eating. Once I'd accepted I was going out for dinner, I had suggested a restaurant where each and every tiny dish made me want to die a little. The menu offered a range of "small plates" that were rich, fattening, and tasty. It's kind of sad how excited I was as we pushed open the big wooden door and greeted the hostess.

Twenty minutes later, I had butter running down my wrist and was happily licking it off when Rachel's eyed widened at someone behind me.

"Hey! Charles! How are you?" She stood, presumably to greet this Charles person, and I quickly wiped butter off my chin and turned around.

Charles was tall, good-looking and, I assumed, trying to get into my sister's pants. This was common. Most of her male friends or acquaintances were somewhere on the Rachel Anderby acquisition spectrum. Not that she doesn't have male friends she has no intention of sleeping with — of course she does, she's not a machine, for crying out loud — but she has eclectic taste.

I watched them to see where he fell on the chart and decided that she hadn't slept with him yet, but that he still held out hope. He was smiling at me and shaking my hand as she introduced us, but he swiftly went back to watching her.

"Can you join us?" Rachel said, which surprised me. I moved my chair around, and Charles sat down, somewhat apologetically.

"I don't want to interrupt you ladies." He was across from me, and I noticed him re-arranging the cutlery in a slightly nervous fashion. OK, he definitely hadn't slept with her yet.

"Not at all," Rachel replied, turning to me. "Charles is visiting from our London office."

I smiled at him, wondering how long I needed to wait before starting to stuff my face again. "How nice. How long are you going to be in Los Angeles?"

He really was handsome. "About six months, Lilian."

"Please call me Lili. Only my mother calls me Lilian." I reached for the tiny plate of bacon-wrapped dates, assuming they would talk shop and I would peacefully eat more than my share, when Rachel's phone rang. Normally she turns it off at dinner, so I raised my eyebrows at her when she answered it.

"Sorry," she mouthed, heading out the door, "it's work . . ."

And there I was, my mouth full of hot date, so to speak, all alone with Charles. As I watched out of the window, I saw Rachel hang up the phone and hail a cab. She didn't even look back.

Traitor.

I broke the uncomfortable silence. "When did this get set up?"

He colored slightly. "This morning."

"Did she tell you I wasn't interested in meeting anyone?"

"Yes, but to be honest, I had told her the same thing, and she rolled right over me." He smiled. "She said she thought it would be good for both of us to . . . I think the word she used was *practice*."

His English accent was charming, but I was still annoyed. "Practice ambushing people?"

He looked contrite. "I didn't realize she wasn't going to tell you I was coming to dinner." He rearranged the cutlery one more time. "I wouldn't have agreed to an ambush." He coughed; the poor bastard

69

really was uncomfortable. "Not at all sporting."

I laughed suddenly. "Not quite cricket?"

He shook his head. "Not in the least."

I called the waitress over, and turned to him. "Are you actually hungry?"

He nodded. "Yes, famished. But it's totally OK if you just want to get the check. I understand. I believe she left her credit card details with the restaurant in case you stormed out and refused to pay."

I laughed. "Oh, then that was an error on her part." I smiled at the waitress. "We'll get two of everything, please."

She hesitated. "All the vegetable dishes?"

"No, two of everything on the menu. Just start at the top and keep going."

Then I turned back to Charles and smiled. We were both victims here, and he had a very pleasant face. "OK, Charles. Why don't you want to date?"

"I'm still in love with my ex-wife. And you?"

"I'm still in love with my dead husband."

And from that point we got on just fine.

I arrived home just after midnight and called Rachel. I knew she would be up, waiting for a report, and if she wasn't, well, she was now. I opened the conversation with a proven winner.

"What the actual fuck were you thinking?"

She remained calm. "I'm sorry, who is this?"

I wasn't having it. "That was a totally bullshit move, as you well know." I was undressing, and threw my bra so it hung over Frank's head. It's the little things that keep me amused. "What if I'd punched your friend in the nose? I could have set back Anglo–U.S. relations for weeks."

She was unapologetic. "You wouldn't. You're too considerate." She paused. "Unlike me."

"I charged over a thousand dollars to your credit card."

"How the hell did you manage that? It's not an expensive restaurant, and you don't drink more than a glass of wine, ever!"

"True, but everyone else in the place did, and we all drank a toast to you."

She paused. "Fair enough. I knew the risks when I came up with the plan. Did you sleep with him?"

I sighed. "Of course I didn't fucking sleep with him. We're both in love with other, totally unavailable people. His ex-wife left him for some young guy she met online, and my husband is dead, as you may have noticed." I flicked out the bedside light.

"Don't do it again, Rachel."

"I can't promise. I want you to be happy."

"I am happy. Don't do it again, or I'll call Mom and tell her about the badminton player."

She sucked in her breath. "That was over a decade ago!"

"And yet I believe Mom still knows his parents."

There was a silence. "OK. You win. No more fix-ups."

"No more pressure."

"OK." She sighed. "See you at the class. Maybe you'll meet someone there?"

I hung up on her. Honestly, she was beyond help.

THE CHEMISTRY OF SOIL

Plants need nitrogen, phosphorus, and potassium for healthy growth.

- Nitrogen is vital for leaves and stems, and promotes the dark green color we admire in broccoli, cabbage, greens, and lettuce.
- Phosphorus promotes the strong and early growth of roots and shoots; the baby- and toddler-hood of the plant. It's also necessary for setting blossoms and developing fruit, and is important for those edibles that develop after the flowers have been pollinated — cucumbers, peppers, tomatoes, et cetera.
- Potassium makes plants vigorous and strong, resistant to stress and disease, and tasty to boot. Carrots, radishes, turnips, onions, and garlic would be lost without it.

CHAPTER 4
THE FIRST CLASS

Saturday was sunny and clear, as it is most days in L.A., and we actually managed to be at the botanical garden at ten. It was originally some rich guy's estate, and has only been open to the public since the fifties. But they did a wonderful job with it, and it looks like it's been there forever. Plus, it has peacocks.

Rachel was meeting us there, and as we stood outside waiting for everyone to arrive her car pulled up, blaring music, and she got out with sunglasses on and an enormous cup of coffee in her hand.

"Well, I guess the celebrity quotient is here now," muttered an older lady with an unfortunate sweater.

"Looks like she's still drunk," remarked another, somewhat similar older lady.

It was unlucky that Rachel picked that moment to stumble a little, but she did, and it's not like I could yell over, "Hey, the two old bats on my left think you're hammered, so watch it." Besides, she was still firmly on my shit list.

As if this wasn't awkward enough, Annabel turned a wonderful shade of pink, and spoke up.

"She's not a celebrity. She's my aunty, and she's very nice, and she was born with one leg longer than the other, so sometimes she trips and has to wear ugly shoes, and it's not nice to talk about someone behind their back." Then she glared at them with her arms folded. At that moment, Rachel reached us and realized she'd walked in on something.

"Hello, all, what did I miss?" were her exact words. I was at a loss, but Clare leapt into the breach, of course.

"The woman with the sweater with the happy cat on it said you were a celebrity, and then the woman with the sweater with the sad moose on it said you were drunk, and then Annabel told them off, and now you're here and no one's saying anything anymore." Clare finished this up with a hug for Rachel, who hugged her back and said, "Wow, I'm glad I missed it, and hey, what about those Dodgers?"

"Last night's game was outstanding." This from a young woman who looked all business, with her long hair pulled back very tight. "Manny continues to bring his classic game."

"Which is why," continued a young, stoned-looking guy, who may have been old enough to vote, but I wouldn't bet on it, "the Dodgers finally have a chance of reclaiming some of their former status."

Another man walked up in the middle of this careful conversation between the politest fans of baseball in the world, and I reached shakily for Rachel's cup of coffee.

"Good morning, everyone. I'm your teacher, Edward. Have you all managed to introduce yourselves yet?" Ah, the teacher, the Bloem-family son. I regarded him over the rim of my coffee cup, and realized I was surprised. I had imagined an old dude in clogs rolling a huge wheel of Edam, but this guy was tall, about my age, and looked friendly enough. No cheese. I felt heat on the side of my face and turned to see Rachel squinting at me, meaningfully. She knows my type. I shook my head and frowned at her, and then quickly turned back to pay attention and impress the client with my dedication. Not that he was the actual client, but hey.

"Sort of," said the young woman.

"Actually," said the woman with the sad

moose sweater (a side note, the moose wasn't sad, he just wasn't knitted very well), "I owe this little girl an apology, and we haven't been introduced yet." She knelt down so she could look properly at Annabel, who was still pink and pissed off.

"What is your name?"

"Annabel Girvan." She was standing her ground, her light-up sneakers firmly planted. Only her twisting fingers gave away her shyness.

"How old are you?"

"I'm seven."

"Well, my name is Frances Smith, and I am fifty-seven, which makes me literally half a century older than you, and yet you are completely right and I am completely wrong. It's very rude to talk about someone behind their back. And besides, it's obvious we were wrong about your aunty, both because she's clearly not drunk, and also because you shouldn't judge other people before you know them."

Annabel stuck the knife in. "My mom says it's wrong to judge people ever."

Frances smiled, "Well, she's right, and actually my friend and I were just making idle conversation. Will you accept my apology?"

Annabel nodded. Frances actually had the

balls to look up at Rachel. "And will you accept it, too?"

Rachel shrugged and smiled. "To be honest, I didn't hear any of it, and I'm kind of stoked you thought I was a celebrity, drunken or otherwise. But yes, of course."

Frances stood back up, a lot more smoothly than I would have, and after another pause that redefined the word *awkward,* Edward continued.

"It is unclear to me what happened, but I am often confused by Americans, so let's pretend everything is fine and go to look at the garden."

Seeing as this was my approach to life in a nutshell, I followed him willingly. Annabel held my hand the whole way, while Clare whittered away to Frances Smith, the traitorous little rat.

As we walked through the botanical garden, it was like an episode of *Gilligan's Island* or something. Giant leafy plants arched overhead, birds cackled at their good fortune, and the air was filled with the scent of flowers and the sound of insects freaking out with excitement. Then we turned a corner, cut across employee parking, and arrived at our destination. An abandoned lot. The space seemed enormous to me, like a field or something, and it was very plain, covered in scrubby grass and devoid of anything taller than a dandelion. In one corner there was a shed-type thing, like a small garage, and there were a few large cardboard boxes, but it wasn't what I had expected. All around the field was a fence, and beyond that the rest of the botanical garden bloomed and waved in the breeze in a mockingly verdant sort of way.

Edward the teacher stood there, shoving his hands in his pockets and then taking them out again. Maybe he was nervous, or maybe his dick itched, who knows. I wished I had a doughnut. I was feeling somewhat light-headed, and the sun was threatening to keep shining for the foreseeable future.

"It seems we have all made the trip successfully, so welcome to our future vegetable garden. The botanical garden has generously given us space for this course." He waved his hand about. "As you can see, there are two main areas, and a couple of smaller ones. The name of the course is Vegetable Gardening 101, so it was decided we would start with the very, very basics. Some of you may not have fantastic gardens of your own. Some of you may just have dirt, or a patch of shrubby grass or something." He actually looked at me when he said this, and smiled a little. I tried to look grown-up, and probably failed. "So we're going to start from ground zero, so to speak, and make a vegetable garden from scratch."

One of the class, an older guy with a gray mustache and salt-and-pepper hair spoke up. "So we're going to dig up all this grass?" He looked around at the rest of us. "I'm not sure this is a class so much as a free labor pool for the botanical garden."

Edward laughed, although the guy didn't seem all that amused. "Well, yes and no. We're going to dig, but it's going to be more fun than you think."

The guy made a humphing noise like a walrus but didn't argue further. I got the impression he was just waiting for a chance and narrowed my eyes at him. This class has to be a success, I telepathed. The future of my job depends on it.

"First, we are going to introduce ourselves, and then we are going to get started. I will start, and the celebrity will follow." Ah, so he had caught the drift of the weirdness earlier. "I am Edward Bloem, and I am a professor of gardening, I suppose you could say. My family business has been flowers and gardens for centuries, and luckily for me there is nothing I like better." He nodded at Rachel.

Rachel shrugged. "I'm Rachel Anderby, I've never gardened in my life, mostly because I work for an art importer, which is a very indoor job, and I'm here to keep my sister and nieces company. I am not a celebrity, although I often imagine what I would say on *Ellen.* And I wasn't drunk this morning, but that doesn't mean I won't be next time."

Several people laughed, including Frances Smith, and then her happy-cat-sweater friend spoke next.

"My name is Eloise, like the little girl in the storybooks. I've gardened all my life, but only in window boxes or containers. My partner and I just bought a house that has a real garden, and we knew Dr. Bloem by reputation and came along so he could give us ideas."

We all turned and looked at Edward, who had the good sense to look down in a humble way.

"Reputation for what?" asked the young man, curiously.

"For being a master gardener." Eloise looked surprised, as if everyone in the world but us knew this. "And of course, Dr. Bloem is one of the leading authorities on humus, internationally."

"The spread?" The eagle-looking guy was lost.

"I think of it more as a dip," interjected Rachel.

"*Humus* is a term for one of the major components of soil." The tight-haired young woman spoke clearly, shutting us all up. "Basically, it's decomposed matter. Leaves, animal remains, broken-down bark, that kind of thing."

Frances chimed in, "It's what everything becomes, eventually."

Rachel couldn't be stopped. "And it's yummy on a pita chip."

Edward cleared his throat. "It is possible we could move on?"

Frances went next. "I'm Frances Smith. I never really gardened, but I watched Eloise, and now I need to step up my game. We're both teachers, by the way."

Teachers. *Lesbian* teachers, we all thought, or at least I thought, and felt that little pique of interest and support I always felt when I met lesbians or gay men, or interracial couples, or anyone, in fact, who lived a life that seemed more interesting and less mainstream than mine. Which was most people.

Next up was the young gardening expert. She looked as if she could kill someone with one of those ninja neck-snapping moves without blinking. Maybe it was just that her hair was too tight.

"Hi, my name is Angela. You can call me Angie, because everyone does. I've had a lot of indoor plants because I've never lived anywhere except in an apartment, and I'm taking this course because it's unlikely I'll ever get a chance to have a big garden like this. Plus the free part doesn't hurt. Plus I like vegetables. I didn't realize you could bring kids, so next week I'll bring my son, who is five." One of those polite, well-spoken ninja neck-snappers. Then she smiled, and her face completely transformed, revealing that she was young, pretty, and happy. Two seconds later, it was gone, the sun back behind the clouds, but we'd seen it.

Edward spoke up. "Next week we will be joined also by a student teacher named Lisa, who will be taking on the children's garden. She's not here this week because we won't be doing any planting yet, but she'll be here every week after this. In fact, we have room in the course for a few more people, so spread the word."

Then eagle guy. "I'm Gene. I retired this year from banking and have barely spent more than five minutes outside in the last twenty years. My wife is worried I'll keel over and die of boredom without a job, so she enrolled me in this course to give me a hobby. I have no idea about gardening at all, and am probably the least healthy guy for ten square miles, so if you ask me I'm more likely to keel over and die lifting a spade, but happy wife, happy life, right?" He said this whole thing without a smile, and I got a sense of his whole life from it. A workaholic, a patient, elderly wife, and both of them scared shitless about what happens now. I wondered if he'd retired or been laid off.

The young guy told us his name was Mike, and he was here because he'd been at the botanical gardens the week before and saw a poster for the class and signed up on a whim. "I like to do all kinds of things," he said, shifting from foot to foot. "I skateboard, snowboard, mountain bike, surf, run, play in a band, but I was standing under a tree last week, just being in nature, you know, which I dig a lot, and realized I don't do anything slow and mellow. Then I turned around to leave and there was the poster for this class right there in my face. It was like a sign from the universe, you know what I mean? So I went with it, and here I am." He grinned around expansively. "None of you cats are anything like me, so it should be cool to hang with you guys and expand my mind, right?"

I would have thought that hanging out with a bunch of middle-aged folks, not counting Rachel, Angela, and the kids, would be pretty mind-numbing for a young person, but I am wrong so often and on so many different topics, I was prepared to be wrong on this one.

Then I realized every one of them was looking at me. I jumped a little, and swallowed.

"Uh, I'm Lilian Girvan, Rachel's sister, and these are my kids, Annabel and Clare. I'm here because I'm illustrating a book on vegetables and my company kindly sent me to this class so I could learn more about them."

Clare chimed in, "Plus, she doesn't have anyone to play with since Daddy died."

Silence. Sounds of birds singing. I smiled like an idiot and waited for the green grass to part and swallow me up. But it didn't.

"Well, splendid," said Edward, possibly a touch too loudly. "Let us get started."

He unrolled the large roll of paper he was carrying and laid it on the ground.

"This is going to be our garden plan.

Right now it's a blank slate, but before you begin any gardening, you need to know how it will all fit and work together. Vegetables love to grow, but you need to think about what each kind needs, in terms of sun and space, and if you strategize enough in advance, you cannot really go wrong." He talked like a children's book from the fifties, which was strangely endearing.

He sat on the grass and spread the paper in front of him, motioning for us to join him. With varying degrees of elegance, we did so. I could see that the kids were getting a little antsy, though, so I told them they could run around. They took off like grey-hounds. Edward was talking about dividing up the space.

"I want to organize the garden into large plots. One for root vegetables, one for salad, one for climbers, and one for berries. We're going to grow a large variety of different things, and by the end of the summer we should be able to prepare a big meal using just our own produce. We're also going to donate the rest of our harvest to the local food bank. It's a community garden."

He looked around at us. "We'll work in teams, and each week we'll rotate to the next area. That way you'll learn about all the various plants we're growing." He looked at Annabel and Clare, who had stopped racing around and were doing their usual things: Annabel was looking serious and focused, as if she were expecting a pop quiz at any minute, and Clare was singing and looking at a dog she could see in the distance. "It would seem we will only have a small number of children this time, although we should allow for one or two more, I expect, so let's put a children's garden right here." He leaned over and drew a smaller square in the middle. "If we put them here, then we can keep eyes on them while they garden, and it will be harder for them to wander off in that way children like to do." He sat back. "Each plot will be relatively small, because we're going to use intensive organic methods." He was sketching, not very well. I was tempted to offer to do it for him, but that might have seemed pushy. "We need to make paths." He sketched some walkways in a basic grid. "And we need a space for the composters and worm bins."

Angie looked at the rest of us. "Did he just say worm bins?"

Eloise nodded. "Not earthworms, smaller worms. They make excellent fertilizer."

Mike. "The worms?"

Eloise. "No, their pee."

Angie. "Worm pee."

Edward. "Worm pee — or worm tea, as we call it — is one of nature's miracles."

Rachel couldn't help herself. "I know that when I get down on my knees every day, I always kick off my gratitude list with worm piss. Those miniscule bladders just give and give."

Edward looked up at her and frowned in an "English isn't my first language and I'm not sure if you're joking or not" way, but then turned back to his plans. Not everyone gets Rachel, or understands that she simply can't stop herself from making jokes. With a mother like ours, we both developed a strong line in sarcasm as self-defense.

Edward leaned back on his haunches. "We also need to consider the position of the sun in relation to our plants."

"Isn't it, generally speaking, right above us?" Mike laughed.

"In the middle of the day, yes, but of course it rises in the east and sets in the west, and as it travels overhead it creates shadows which must be considered. There is almost no natural shade here for our plants, which is both good and bad. Anyway, we will talk about this more once we start actually putting seeds and plants in the ground. For now, we need to get to the earth." He pulled a walkie-talkie thingy from his pocket, and pressed a button.

"Bob, we are ready for you over here." Edward got to his feet, stretching. He was very tall and well built, and why I was noticing this I have no idea.

"Normally you would dig your own beds and paths, but then again normally you wouldn't be starting with a space of this size. These days we can cheat a little."

Right on cue we heard an engine noise, and turned to see a man driving a small tractor toward us. The children squealed, and we all grinned.

"It is much easier," continued Edward, raising his voice, "to use a large machine to dig up the ground, though a rototiller is not a precision instrument, clearly. We will have plenty of work to do ourselves."

The tractor came pretty close and stopped, and Bob, with the face of a Greek god and the bashed-up hands of a plumber, wandered over. This was the problem, or joy, of living in Los Angeles: The best-looking people from all over the world came to Hollywood, seeking their fortune and some measure of fame. Back in Buttfluff, Maryland, they were constantly being told they should be a movie star. They were the prom king or queen, or 4-H glamour girl, and they got off the plane expecting to be mown down by paparazzi. Instead they discovered that the guy who rented them a car, the girl who pulled them a latte, and the dude at the dry cleaner's were all better-looking than them. And could probably sing and dance in two languages. You were constantly walking down the street and spotting the most beautiful creature you'd ever seen in your life, then turning a corner and seeing three more. It was insane. Anyway, here was another perfect example, driving a very small tractor and working at the botanical garden while he waited to be discovered behind a marigold. I personally would have thought there were more populated places to go wait in, but hey, maybe he liked the tractor.

I glanced at Rachel. The drunken celebrity had lowered her sunglasses and was regarding Bob thoughtfully. I knew that look. I saw it on the dog's face whenever there was beef cooking. I looked at Bob, feeling sorry for the little cutlet, but he was looking back at her, with the nonchalance that only serious good looks can carry off. I sighed inwardly. I had thought a gardening class might be drama-free, but apparently not.

Edward was talking. "And now, who wants to drive the tractor?"

■ ■ ■ ■

However long I live, I will never forget the sight of Clare driving the tractor. Yes, she was sitting on Bob's lap and he was working the pedals, but she had her hands on the steering wheel and was doing all of the important squealing.

She had been the first to stick up her hand when Edward had asked for volunteers, and to my surprise he had called her up.

"You are the perfect person to start, as there is nothing at all you can do wrong at this point."

Bob grinned and took her from Edward as he handed her up.

"I'm going to put this seat belt over you, all right, but the most important thing to remember is that you must stay sitting down, OK?"

Clare nodded, obviously somewhat scared of being so high up.

Angie looked at me. "Aren't you worried she might get hurt?"

I nodded. "Yes, but I'm sure Edward and Bob know what they're doing." I looked at Edward. "You know what you're doing, right? She's not going to fall off and get crushed?"

He looked at Bob who, somewhat un-reassuringly, shrugged.

"Do you want me to take her off?" Edward asked. "If Bob loses his mind and flings her in front of the tractor, it will definitely not be good." It was a funny image, and I started to laugh, then realized I was the only one.

"Let her do it." I turned. Gene, of all people, had spoken up. "She's just experiencing what generations of children did on farms throughout American history, and besides, what is life without a little excitement and risk?" He still wasn't smiling, mind you, which further underscored his Sam the American Eagle appearance. But he made a good point.

"I won't get down, anyway." Clare sounded unwavering on this. I looked at Rachel. She turned up her palms. Annabel spoke up.

"If she's doing it, I'm doing it, too."

"Oh, go ahead. But if you drop her, I will turn you into humus on the spot."

Bob laughed. "Fair enough."

And lo and behold he set off, Clare squeaking with excitement. So what if I was derelict, as she lay in the emergency room getting her leg set, or her kidney removed, she'd probably forgive me.

Once Clare had driven two loops, the tiller tearing up the grass behind them, Bob stopped in front of us.

"Who's next?"

"Can I sit on your lap, too?" Rachel was shameless.

Bob smiled and nodded.

And as they set off, with much the same amount of squealing and laughing, it was clear he had no idea his goose was totally cooked.

Gardening turned out to be fun, but harder work than I had thought. Once the ground was mostly cleared, apart from broad strips of grass as pathways, we paced off the four main plots and placed flags and string along the plotlines. Our time was soon up, and Edward assured us that things would be further along when we returned the following week.

"It's a little naughty, but there isn't really time in three hours to do what we need to, and if we leave the ground like this for a week, we'll spend the next session weeding. So over the week, Bob and I will build raised beds in the plots and get things ready. Your homework is to do research and decide what vegetables you'd like to include. I'm going to send you a list to look over, too, so make sure your e-mail is on the sign-in sheet. While you're at it, look up the term *potager,* which is the type of garden we are creating. Basically, it means a garden in which vegetables, flowers, and herbs are grown together, making it efficient." He frowned at himself. "I'm sorry, I have a tendency to lecture. I find the whole subject of gardening fascinating." He coughed, politely. "You know, it has been suggested that gardens like these, attached to cottages or smaller houses, started after the Black Death of the fourteenth century killed so many people there was suddenly enough land for everyone to have their own garden. I like to think that it was also in response to that stress, that in times of great difficulty, growing food is comforting, as well as practical."

He paused. "I'm doing it again, aren't I?"

It struck me that "Mommy, what's the Black Death?" was in my future.

He carried on, ignoring my inner monologue. "Anyway, Bob will be making it very easy for you, but you'll still have plenty to do. The few purchases you might want to make are a good pair of gardening gloves, a wide-brimmed hat, and plenty of sunscreen." He waved his hand. "We have no shade here, which means you run a high risk of getting gardeners sunburn, which is painful."

He turned away from us and pointed at the back of his neck, which was, indeed, very brown. "Back of the neck, top of the shoulders, forearms, and hands. And, one unforgettable summer when I was young and silly, the soles of my feet. I was too cool for shoes, but not smart enough to sunscreen my feet."

We laughed. Mike chimed in. "When I first started surfing, I was pretty dumb, too, and I burned the backs of my knees. Man, all I could do for, like, four days was lie in a hammock and cry, while all my friends caught some righteous curls."

"Lying in a hammock doesn't sound so bad," Frances said, smiling.

"It isn't if you're supposed to be at, like, school or something, but when the alternative is surfing . . . it's torture." He was very earnest, our little Mike, but it was possible that he lived entirely in a dream world. Certainly Angie was looking at him in a very confused way, even though they were the same age, more or less. I wondered again about what Rachel had said, about the kind of people who would be drawn to this class. I didn't sense any actual insanity, not yet anyway. Maybe it was like that saying in poker: If you don't know who the sucker is at the table, it's probably you. As we walked back toward the gate of the botanical garden, I fell in alongside Angie.

"Your son is five?"

She nodded. "I only have him every other weekend, because I share custody with his father, but maybe he will cut me some slack and let me bring Bash to class every week."

I looked at her. "It probably wouldn't matter if he only came every other week. It's not like they're grading us."

She smiled. "True, but I'll tell you something. I grew up in your classic projects, east L.A. I never saw so much green, like we see here, until I was in my teens. Literally. The only trees I'd ever seen were those crappy ones on the street, surrounded by dog shit. Just running around on an enormous piece of grass, like your kids were doing today, is something Bash doesn't get to do very often. So I'm going to bring him every week." She smiled at me sweetly. "Even if I have to shoot his shithead father in the nuts."

Sunday has always been my favorite day. I let the kids gorge themselves on TV, lolling around in the living room in their jammies, calling Frank to deal with spills, while I pretend I'm living in turn-of-the-century Paris, shockingly slender, young and unencumbered. When Dan was alive, he would walk to the corner with Frank for the *New York Times,* and we would scatter it around, competing over which of us got "The Week in Review" and the magazine. Now I read the news on my computer, then spend an hour looking at before and after pictures of celebrity plastic surgery. I don't even know why. I start out reading something worthy and intellectually interesting, like the fate of the world's water, or transgender politics in Hungary, and always end up back at Meg Ryan's face. She's like a black hole.

Eventually I got up to see if I could bug the children into giving me something to do. They waved me away, and after standing in the living-room doorway for a while, secretly watching *Phineas and Ferb,* I decided to go and evaluate the backyard. Maybe I could create a vegetable garden that would feed us all. Or keep chickens, or something. I sat on the kitchen steps and drank coffee, listening to the sound of the Los Angeles morning (helicopters, rap songs through car windows, hipsters riding bicycles to farmers markets, ringing their stupid little vintage bells). Frank pushed past me and stumbled down the three or four cement steps. Finally, he thought, finally she's discovered the hidden cache of organic sausages I've dreamt so much about. After sniffing about for a minute, which is all it takes back there for a thorough inspection, he threw himself down glumly and sighed a sigh that literally blew a leaf around. I knew how he felt, because I wasn't sure it would ever be possible to grow anything out back. It was sunny right then, in the morning, but there was a sea of weeds that looked ready to take up arms if we tried to unseat them, and a squirrel regarded me balefully from the one small tree we had. The squirrel was an urban creature, impossibly fat and round (there was a McDonald's around the corner, and he probably had a collection of Happy Meal toys to rival Clare's), and he was thwacking a metal pipe into his palm, warningly. OK, that isn't true, but he was definitely a menacing squirrel, and not the shy and darting woodland creature one hears about in the kids' books. I have a friend who used to feed the squirrels that came to his deck, in a Snow White kind of way, and one day, daring to reach out to pet one of his tiny dependents, he got bitten to the bone and had to have rabies shots. I repeat, to the bone. When Tennyson said, "Nature, red in tooth and claw," I kind of assumed that nature was going to keep the redness to herself, so to speak, but it seems as if we've been implicated in some way and any minute now the animals are coming for us. It would serve us right, I expect (see earlier reference to McDonald's).

I leaned my head against the door frame, closing my eyes and trying to imagine a tiny oasis of greenery in the garden. Did I want flowers? Vegetables? Long, tangled vines of jungle fruit with chimpanzees hooting and throwing bananas? I started to drift off, which is something I have noticed about my life — I used to have energy, but then I had kids. Now I run at a constant sleep deficit of about two hours a night for the past seven years, and if I close my eyes, I fall asleep. I found myself dreaming of vegetables so shiny and beautiful they could only be Hollywood vegetables, professional vegetables with agents. I stood in my picture-perfect garden with a reed basket over my arm, my hair in long braids with red ribbons on the ends, picking runner beans. One of the kids (like mine, but clean) was standing by, gazing up at me with admiration, marveling at my mastery of Mother Nature. Propagation porn. I opened my eyes. The reality was a mostly concrete backyard, a tiny lawn huddled at one end, with several muddy Polly Pockets half buried in the flower beds, looking like the victims of a war crime. I could see enough candy wrappers to suggest my kids were importing treats from the outside, and very little that looked like it had actually grown there. I sighed. As with all other porn, reality and fantasy weren't even distantly related.

How to Grow a Tomato

Stick your tomato plant in the ground and admire it: Tomatoes are susceptible to compliments. Water generously.

- Watch for predatory bugs: They're sneaky.
- If the weather is particularly dry, find some flat rocks and place one next to each plant. The rocks pull up water from under the ground and keep it from evaporating into the atmosphere.
- If using stakes, prune plants by pinching off suckers so that only a couple stems are growing per stake.
- Try not to eat all the tomatoes off the vine, and be cautious: A sun-heated tomato can be explosively juicy.

CHAPTER 5

I had barely sat down at my desk the next morning when the phone rang. It was Roberta, from upstairs.

"How did the class go?"

"It was fun, thanks." I unpacked my breakfast of champions: a cinnamon cruller the size of a baby's head and a triple latte. Better living through chemistry.

"No worm incidents?"

"None worth mentioning. Only sighted in the distance." I was a little impatient to bite the cruller, I have to admit.

I heard her shiver. "And the Bloem son? Did you speak to him?"

I frowned a little. "Yes, of course. He was the teacher. I could hardly avoid it."

"Do you think you made a connection?"

I thought about it. "Uh . . . sure?"

She sounded pleased. "Excellent. Did he mention Poplar?"

I tried to be good, but she was cockblocking me and my cruller. "Well, yes. He asked if I wanted to go to work for Littleman's Press, as they were offering to do the encyclopedia for less than us, *and* plant fourteen thousand trees to replenish the earth." Littleman is our biggest competitor, and the friendly rivalry between us was occasionally less than friendly.

She sucked in her breath. "Absolutely not! We will totally outplant them! Tell him we'll plant twenty thousand!"

I went ahead and took a bite of cruller, just to make her suffer a little more. "I'm joking. He didn't talk about it at all. I mentioned that I was illustrating a book about vegetables, but I didn't mention who was publishing it. Do you want me to?"

There was a silence as she pondered the political implications. "Perhaps. If it comes up organically."

I chuckled, appreciatively.

"Why are you laughing?" She sounded worried.

"I thought you were making a joke . . . you know, organic, gardening . . ." I trailed off.

"Poplar is counting on you, Lili," Roberta said. "Please take this seriously."

"OK, Roberta." I licked my fingers after I hung up the phone, and wondered if it was me who was unfunny, or her. I decided it was her and continued with my day.

After work, I went to the grocery store. Leah, our babysitter, was with the kids at home, so I dawdled around the aisles, picking up inappropriate food and random crap. When I got out of the hospital Leah was there, hired by Rachel, using Dan's life insurance money. She makes my life possible, and I'm not even slightly joking. When I'm standing at the pearly gates, assuming I don't go the other way, Leah is the person I'm going to give a special shout-out to. Yo, Petey, I shall say, that girl Leah, she's fab. Make sure she gets a good cloud. She picks up the kids from school on those days I can't, brings them home, gives them a snack, starts dinner, helps with homework, and basically eases the whole transition. That way, when I walk in the door, the house is an oasis of calm. A sanctuary of sanity in an insane world. A welcoming harbor of peace.

Tonight, after the grocery store, for example.

"Mother, Annabel said that boy cats have boobies, so I went to find Oscar and found him, but he doesn't have boobies, and then he scratched me and Annabel laughed."

There were heated tears accompanying this speech, and it was delivered in a tone of voice that made the dog scratch at the back door and whine.

I came the rest of the way through the front door and carefully closed it behind me. The villain of the piece was right there.

"Mom, Clare is totally making it up. She was the one who said that cats didn't have boobies, that only mommies had boobies, and I said, 'What about mommy cats?' And that was when Oscar scratched her. Honestly, I had nothing to do with it."

Leah was leaning in the kitchen doorway, palms up in the air.

"Sorry, I opened the fridge door during a period of peaceful silence and by the time I closed it everyone was crying."

Oscar was the neighbors' cat, but he regarded property lines as one more example of man's perfidy and spent as much time in our place as theirs. He and our cat, Jane, had an understanding. They were both fixed, so I assume it was just paw-holding and mutual grooming, but who knows.

"Is Oscar OK?" My dad had been a lawyer, and he'd raised me to clarify liability before anything else.

They nodded.

"Is he in the house?"

Clare shook her head. "No, he was asleep in the backyard, and I flipped him over so I could look at his boobs, and he scratched me and ran away."

Annabel looked at her. "Well, if I came over to you while you were sleeping and flipped you over, you'd probably be annoyed, too."

"You laughed at me. She laughed at me, Mom, when I was bleeding all the way to death!"

Leah shook her head subtly.

"To death?" I asked, putting my purse on the floor and trying to shake off the kids so I could put down my keys. "Any coffee, Lee?"

"In the pot, just made it." Coffee isn't just for mornings in my kitchen. I've been known to get up for a crying kid in the night and wash down an aspirin or two with cold coffee. It does nothing for me. In fact, I only know how dependent I am when I skip a cup or two and fall to the ground with an apparent aneurysm. I heard coffee makes you fat. It's a small price to pay for consciousness.

"Look, ladies." I knelt down to look them in the eye. "Let's get this straight. All mammals make milk, you know that. Mommy mammals make milk to feed their babies.

Cats are mammals, therefore girl cats have boobies. Oscar is a boy, therefore no boobies."

"But he has nipples." I guess he hadn't scratched her that quickly.

"All male mammals have nipples, no one knows why, probably just to keep their fur done up. Let it go. Next, it is never a good idea to wake a cat suddenly. They get irritable. If you bug a cat and it scratches you, that's your tough cookies, OK?"

I took a breath and turned to Annabel. "However, it is totally uncool to laugh at your sister for getting scratched, so apologize please."

She mumbled.

"In English."

She mumbled again.

"Audibly."

"Sorry, Clare."

"OK, this episode is over. Let's go see what Leah has killed for dinner."

And then I took off my coat. Five minutes in and a crisis dealt with. Gosh, parenting was rewarding.

Leah had apparently slaughtered a chicken, cut it up into little irregular pieces, and breaded it, all in the hour since they'd gotten home. She's very productive.

"I was thinking with baked beans and a

string cheese, then fruit for them to ignore, maybe a yogurt on the side for them to take one bite of." Yes, she clearly understands my children.

I got myself a cup of coffee. "Great. Annabel, did you set the table yet?"

"I was going to let Clare do it, to apologize for the laughing."

"That's very giving of you."

Carrying my coffee, I went to my room to get changed. I hadn't done anything to my room at all since Dan died, and his side of the bed had become Frank's. The old dog was sprawled out as I walked in, doubtless covering the quilt with tiny worm eggs, or whatever. His leg was twitching as he dreamt, so I left him to it. Dan and I had gotten him as a puppy, at a street adoption, and he had seen me through cohabitation, marriage, parenthood, and now grief. He was what I referred to as a Los Angeles Garbage Hound, mostly Labrador. He was yellow, plump, and slow. I aspired to be more like him, his approach was so effortlessly Zen: love nice people, eat appreciatively, nap frequently, be patient, and say yes to everything. I carefully hung up my work clothes and put on my real clothes. Sweatpants, an old Halloween T-shirt that for some reason took five pounds off me (it had stretched in the wash in some unfathomable way and hung just right), and slipper socks. Thank you, Target, sanctuary to those of us who wander your aisles in aimless search for the one thing we came in for and the forty-two things we didn't, but which, at that price, we could not resist. How we love you. I turned to leave and Frank roused himself, dropping off the bed with a thud that reverberated through the floor, followed by a pause as he wondered if he'd survived the impact and checked that all his legs were working. I feel the same way every morning, to be honest. I scuffed back to the kitchen, and he wandered sleepily behind me.

While the kids were eating, Leah gave me the rundown.

"Annabel has math homework, half of it is done, due Wednesday. Clare has to do reading, but that's it. Annabel was invited for a playdate on Friday, after school."

"Where?"

"Charlotte's house."

I reached for the house diary, a large blue calendar we kept together.

"It's in there already." Leah was nothing if not organized. Actually, she was lots of things, plus organized.

I frowned at her in mock indignation.

"How did you know I'd be available to drive her? For all you know, I could have had plans."

She laughed. I waited. She kept laughing. I kept waiting.

"No, really?" She suddenly looked worried. "You have plans?"

"Nah, just messing with you. We have gardening class in the morning, but that's it."

She smiled patiently at me, then looked at her watch. "Oops, gotta run. Class."

She kissed the kids, ruffled Frank's hair, and headed out the door. Nobody ruffled my hair.

I sat down and stole a nugget from Annabel's plate.

"Nuggets aren't really good food, you know." She waved her own nugget at me. "You should eat vegetables and things like that. They help you grow."

"I don't really need to grow anymore, sweetheart. I'm done growing."

"Yeah, but you still need nutrition. We learned about it at school. Otherwise, you'll get curvy and your hair will fall out."

I frowned.

"Do you mean scurvy?"

"That's what I said. You'll get it and your

hair will fall out. You need to eat more limes."

"Thanks, sweetness, I'll bear it in mind."

Clare was helpful as ever. "Her hair is already falling out. I see it in the shower. Lots of hair, and it can't be ours because we don't take showers."

Super. Now I'm balding.

"Maybe it's Frank's," I suggested, getting to my feet and going to look in the fridge. "Maybe he's secretly taking showers." I pulled out the fixings for a ham sandwich and set about making it.

"He can't turn the faucets."

"No thumbs."

He was standing there, looking back and forth between them, hearing his name, counting the nuggets in and out. Sometimes, after the kids have gone to bed, I find him still there, patiently waiting. Somehow he knows there is still half a ketchup-y nugget left on a plastic plate above him, and dammit, it's his by law (this would be *Labrador v. Toddler, U.S. 1978*). He's too polite, and too old, to get up on the table for it, and he has faith I will eventually come along and give it to him. He moves around the house like a landlocked beluga whale, stately and impervious. He watches me closely. Maybe he thinks I'm going to discover a platter of steak lying around, or a seam of peanut butter running through the walls. His perpetual optimism puts me to shame.

"Can I have ice cream?" asked Clare.

"Did you finish your fruit?"

"Yes. Mostly. Some."

"Then yes. Can you get it yourself?" I'm trying to teach self-reliance, and ice cream seemed like a good place to start. The fact that I had literally just sat down is irrelevant.

Clare got up and pulled open the freezer door, whereupon several bags of frozen peas fell on her. "Avalanche!" she cried, stepping back. I asked Annabel to go help her, which, of course, she refused to do. I often wonder what happened to my check to the charm school. It never got returned.

I stuffed the peas back in the freezer, pulled out the ice cream, put a small scoop in a bowl, offered it to Clare, was rebuffed, put another small scoop in the bowl, offered it, was rebuffed, added chocolate sauce, and had it finally accepted.

As she sat back down, I slowly licked the ice cream scoop and sucked a dribble of chocolate sauce from my knuckle. Yup, as I said before, parenting is deeply rewarding.

Later that night, after the kids were asleep,

my phone rang. I looked at the clock: 11:00 P.M. Only one person called that late.

"Hi, Mom."

"Hello, dear, how are you?" She was drunk, but I wasn't sure yet how drunk. The fact that she'd coordinated herself to use a phone this late suggested not too drunk, but once she'd mastered speed dial, even that guideline had become less reliable.

"I'm good, Mom, just heading off to bed actually."

"This early?"

Here's the thing with my mother: She thinks she's twenty-seven. She was a model, and started really, really young, like thirteen. At thirteen, she had to pretend to be sixteen; at twenty-four, she had to pretend to be eighteen; at thirty-five, she had to pretend to be twenty-seven; and then she just stayed there. It was entirely possible she had managed to actually forget her age. She was raised in England, by a woman my father described as the biggest bitch in the British Empire, and he never said anything bad about anyone. My grandmother had specialized in that most British of skills, sarcasm, and my mother had grown up thinking that was how you spoke to everyone. As a professional narcissist, she had also been completely incapable of seeing anyone else's point of view, but she listened to my dad with a reverence bordering on childlike. Rachel and I were never sure what our dad had seen in her, beyond her physical beauty, which was considerable. But he saw something, because he surrounded her with love, and his genial good humor and warm intelligence was a bubble that protected her and everyone around her from her inadequacies and bitterness. Now that he was gone, things had gotten a little difficult.

"Yes, Mom. I have to get up in the morning, remember? To take the kids to school, go to work, all that good stuff."

She sighed, and in that sigh I detected approximately three scotch and sodas. About par for the course; she was unlikely to burst into tears, or accuse me of anything.

"I was calling to see if we could do brunch this weekend? I haven't seen my grandchildren in so long." She sniffed. "I'm not getting any younger, you know. You won't have me to kick around for much longer."

I rolled my eyes. "Mom, you're sixty, you work out every day, and eat like a bird. You're healthier than any of us."

A pause. I'd distracted her with a compliment, which never failed. "I still want to see the children."

I remembered the gardening class, which

instantly paid for itself a hundred times over — ignoring the fact, of course, that it was completely free. "Actually, Mom, Saturday brunch isn't going to work for a while. How about we do a dinner here one night?"

"You eat so early, Lilian. Like a farmer or something. Civilized people eat after eight, you know."

I just waited. This was a very old argument.

"Why can't we do brunch? Are you seeing someone?" Whiny and nosy all in two sentences. She was a master.

"No."

"Why on earth not? You're not getting any younger, either, remember. And your beauty has always been fleshier than mine, and flesh doesn't last as well as bone structure, sadly."

I counted to five. I thought about my kids. I scratched Frank behind the ears.

"We're doing a class on Saturday mornings for the next six weeks, that's all. We'll schedule dinner instead, OK? I've got to go to bed now, Mom."

More sniffing. "Well, maybe Rachel will have brunch with me. She has a more interesting life anyway."

"Rachel's doing the class with me, Mom. Sorry."

"What kind of class is it? Is it something I'd enjoy?"

I got up and started turning out lights. "No, Mom. It's a gardening class. You'd be outdoors. You know, in the sun."

Easy win. "Oh no, I couldn't do that." I mouthed the words along with her, as I headed to my room. "Not with *my* skin." I hung up and shook myself, like a dog with something in its ear. As my head hit the pillow, I let her words wash off me. As a child, her little daggers had cut deep, but now they just bounced off all my shiny scar tissue. Lucky me.

That night I dreamt about Dan again. We were young, and he was holding my hand as we walked across the street. I could feel his knuckles under my fingers, felt his hand tightening as he paused to let a car pass. My sleeve rustled against his jacket, and I could smell his skin and see the corner of his mouth, smiling. I was just a little step behind him, looking down, when his hand pulled away and I was alone in the middle of the street. He was over on the sidewalk, and as I frowned a train came along and obliterated him, pushing his body ahead of itself so suddenly I could still see the image of him on my retina. Then he was holding my hand again, and I tried to hold on tighter but it all kept repeating, the hand, the pull, the train. I woke up and lay there for a moment, trying to remember every detail of how it felt to hold his hand, trying to remember the smell of him.

Eventually I got up and went over to the closet. Frank lifted his head but put it down with a sigh when he saw what I was doing. He'd seen it before. In the closet, in large Ziploc bags, were Dan's clothes. Not all of them, but most. Some bags I had never opened, some I opened a lot. I pulled one out now, holding a T-shirt I could remember him wearing maybe once a week our whole lives together, and yanked it open. I held it to my face, breathing in deeply, inhaling the only physical thing left of him, the smell of his unwashed clothes.

I'd been doing a big load of laundry the day Dan was killed, and I regretted it bitterly. When I'd come back to the house that very first night, the kids and Frank were safely at my mother's house, and the whole place was dark. In my purse I had the hospital statement detailing the efforts to revive my husband, the enormous bill for pointless services rendered. In the dark, I walked into our bedroom and started double-bagging everything I could find that wasn't clean. As I padded around on feet bandaged from running across broken glass in the street, I remember, there was an enormous pressure in my skull, the synapses in my brain apparently snapping one by one. Every time I took a breath, it hurt, the air sharp and acrid, tearing apart the soft tissues in my lungs. My whole body pounded with every pulse, as if I were hanging upside down, the blood pooling in the backs of my eyes. But it was vitally important that I did this one last thing, capture the last molecules of Dan left on Earth — the skin cells, the tiny atoms of sweat, the microscopic traces of shaving cream — before they evaporated and left me with less than nothing. Luckily, when Rachel found all the bags after I'd been hospitalized, she'd realized at once why I'd done it and put them all safely away. In the years since then, I had rationed myself, let some of the air out only when necessary. And now, as I inhaled the faint scent of my husband, turning my head and closing the bag when I needed to sob, I still wished I had died instead of him. He'd be so much better at grief than I was.

How to Grow Broccoli

Plant in the fall, if your climate is warm, mid- to late summer most other places.

- Space your plants 12 to 24 inches apart and allow 36 inches between rows. Broccoli likes to take off its corset and spread out.
- If you get too many seedlings, be ruthless when thinning. The needs of the few outweigh the needs of the many.
- Try and keep the soil moist. Broccoli needs to be kept moist. *However,* do not get developing heads wet when watering. They will come to life and terrorize the neighborhood. That's not true, but they won't like it.

CHAPTER 6

The next day, after school, the girls and I visited the bookstore and picked up a plant guide (along with the inevitable seven books featuring princesses, horses, fairies, and a certain yellow square guy who lives in a pineapple and who shall remain nameless). On the one hand, I don't want to spoil my children, but on the other hand, I like that they get excited about books. Yes, those books are often about characters they see on TV, and they get more excited about candy, but still, it's enthusiasm for the written word. Plus, I can deduct all book purchases from my taxes because, hey, I work in publishing. So it's virtually free. This creative math used to drive Dan mad.

"How can you spend $50 and claim you saved money?" he would say, and wave the credit card bill at me. It was one of the things we actually got annoyed with each other about.

"Because it would normally have been $80, so I saved $30. Why can't you see that?"

"Because we didn't need the fucking books/clothes/art supplies/dog toys/paraffin wax heater in the first place!" Then he would go off on his whole tirade about too much stuff, too much clutter, while stomping about through a small sea of his own dropped socks and consumer electronics. I bitterly regretted wasting time arguing with him. If I could exchange the time I spent picking up socks and complaining for one more kiss, or even for five minutes of sitting together silently, drinking coffee in the living room, I would do it in an eyeblink. The bedroom floor stayed clear of men's socks and boxer shorts now, and it probably missed them as much as I did.

Once we got home, Clare wasn't interested in the book about plants.

"I'm going to plant strawberries, I already said." She headed off to her bedroom, Frank close behind.

"And nothing else?"

"Nope. Strawberries." The bedroom door closed. I wondered at which point her charming single-mindedness would turn into OCD.

Annabel was more interested, although

she, too, was up for strawberries.

"Is it just vegetables, or can we plant flowers?"

"Whatever you like, I think."

"Can you plant flowers in a pattern?" she asked. She was flipping through the flower guide.

"Sure, I guess. I don't think they'll put up a fight." I was making coffee while she sat at the table.

"I want to make a heart in red flowers with blue flowers around it."

"Okeydokey. So, let's look for red flowers and blue flowers."

We flipped, she picked blue violas ("painted porcelain" they were called, a pale blue with darker blue edges, very pretty,) and something called a "chocolate cosmos," which was more burgundy than red, but still, it's her garden.

"Are they actually chocolate?" asked Clare, who had come back for a snack for herself and a rawhide chewy for Frank.

"No, but it says here that they smell of chocolate."

"Hmm." She'd fallen for that one before.

They went off to play, and I started looking through the book for myself. There were beautiful photos of vegetables growing in that organized yet organic way they do in

122

photographs, and I have to admit it was very appealing. I was looking, too, for flowers for our back garden. The book was helpful, clearly laying out the information about what kind of soil each plant liked and how much sun was ideal. I realized we had several different kinds of environments in the garden — some shade, some sun — and it was hard to keep it all straight.

I think better when I'm drawing, so I grabbed one of the kids' sketch pads and started on a rough plan of the garden. There was a nice shady part at one end, which might be a good place for the kids to play when it was hot. I sketched in a bench nearby, so I could sit and watch them, or read. Maybe a hammock would be better . . . I got up, rootled around in the "art area" (corner of the living room, a bucket of pencils and broken crayons and markers with missing lids) for a bit, and came back with colored pencils, an eraser, and more paper. I started drawing a garden I didn't even know I had in my head. I went back for the garden book, and began looking by color, making notes as I went. I lined the back fence with salvia (kind of a blue-purple color) with something called Scabiosa "summer berries" (kind of pinks and purples, including one that was almost black —

so cool, a gothic flower) in front.

I closed the book and rested the paper on it, just drawing the garden. I put in a flagstone path that wandered across the tiny lawn, ending up at the shady end, and drew the kids, kneeling down in the corner, playing with something. The bench — I had decided against the hammock, as apparently this imaginary garden of mine was more "English cottage" than "Hawaiian exotic" — was simple and tucked into a grove of lavender. Before I knew what I was doing I'd drawn in a pond, with a heron standing in it (*Aquatic Birds of the Pacific Coast,* 2006, 3rd ed.). I kept drawing happily, coloring and shading, until Annabel touched me on the shoulder. I leapt about nine feet in the air, which is hard from a seated position.

"Eek, you scared the crap out of me. Could you be a little more clompy?" I stood up and stretched a little, holding my pad.

Annabel frowned at me. "Mom, I called you, like, five times, including once from right behind you. You were in a world of your own, like Clare."

Huh, interesting. I smiled at her. "Sorry, honey. I was thinking about the backyard."

"Can I see what you drew?" I handed her the pad and went to look in the fridge to see what marvels awaited us for dinner. Ooh, pork chops. Be still my beating heart.

From behind me I could hear Annabel turning pages. "Is this supposed to be our garden?" She sounded somewhat skeptical.

"Sure, why not? Remember, the teacher said all gardens had possibilities."

"Yeah . . ." She still didn't sound convinced. "Is that why you drew him in?"

I paused. I hadn't drawn him. She showed me the picture.

"See? You put him here, on the bench. But he isn't really tall enough. The teacher's very tall."

"Everyone is tall to you."

"And his hair is darker than this. But I guess he can sit on the bench, seeing as he's teaching us how to make the garden." She started to walk out. "Can I keep this picture, or do you need it?"

I looked at her. "You can keep it if you like."

She smiled and wandered out. I stood there a moment, not sure what I was feeling. It wasn't Edward on the bench. It was Dan. I hadn't even known I was doing it, really, but when she turned the picture toward me, I saw it right away. Dan, with his foot crossed over his knee, a book open on his lap, hanging out near the kids, same as always. I felt guilty, suddenly, for changing things without his input. Not that he'd given a flying dog's crap about the garden.

I sighed, and started the dinner. Frank was under the table, so I asked for his counsel.

"Tell me, Frank," I said, making his tail thump. "Is it OK if I plant a garden, even though I can't get Dan's input on it, and even though he won't see it?"

Frank pointed out that I didn't know for certain that Dan couldn't see it. In fact, if heaven was above us, as was traditionally held to be true, then he would get a great view of it.

"Maybe, in that case, I should follow Annabel's lead and write something in flowers that only he can read." Well, him and the ten thousand news helicopters that buzz low across the Los Angeles sky all the time. Frank asked what I would write.

"I don't know. Maybe, 'I Love You'. Or, 'We Miss You.' Or just, 'Hi, there.' "

Frank laid his head on his paws. How about *Fuck You For Dying, You Bastard,* he suggested.

That evening I sent an e-mail to Edward Bloem, listing the flowers we had picked out. I also impulsively scanned and sent him the drawing I'd done, having retrieved it from Annabel's room. I wrote:

Dear Dr. Bloem,
Here are the flowers that Annabel would like to plant for the class. She says she would like to make a heart shape — is that possible? If not, let me know so I can prepare her emotionally for the disappointment. Clare wants to grow strawberries, and I can't get her to go beyond that. However, I was dreaming about flowers for my garden at home: I drew a plan and have included it attached to this e-mail. I don't suppose you could take a look and let me know if I'm delusional or not? Yours, Lilian Girvan, mom of Annabel and Clare.

Then I sent it off and sat there for a moment, wondering when I had morphed into "Lilian Girvan, mom of Annabel and Clare," rather than just Lilian. Dan had called me Lil, Rachel and my parents called me Lili. I suddenly remembered the experience of giving birth to Clare, when the nurses just called me Mom and Dan Dad. As in, "More ice chips, Mom?" Or, "Get out of the way, Dad." They didn't say that last bit, of course. Dan spent the whole time Clare was being born sitting on a chair eating an enormous doughnut. Every time I pushed, he was there, next to me, but when the mists cleared, he would be back on the ugly chair, chewing. Three seconds after he cut Clare's cord, he reached into his little bag, pulled out another doughnut, and handed it to me, crumbs on the baby be damned. And that is what makes a great husband. Appropriate application of baked goods.

Ping. New mail.

Dear Lilian,
This list looks fine, and Annabel can plant flowers in any shape she wishes. If she's fortunate, they will come up neatly, but you should prepare her not for devastating disappointment but the need to moderate her goals. Nature sometimes decides to go her own way, and resists straight edges in general. But it should be pretty, I think. Your drawing is beautiful — you are an artist, I see. But to know if it will work or not, I would need to see the garden itself. Maybe I can come to your house after class and take a look. It would be a pleasure to give my opinion.

Yours,
Edward Bloem

Huh. Well, that gave me something to think about.

As I sat there, thinking about it, Rachel called. She sounded stressed.

"You told Mom I was taking a class with you?"

I frowned. "Yes, because you are. She was trying to insinuate that you were the better daughter because you would go for brunch with her on the weekend, and I was trying to preemptively stop her from harassing you by telling her you weren't available." I paused. "That was wrong?"

She sighed. "No, of course not. But she just called and told me I was wasting my life hanging around with you and the kids instead of going out and hunting for a husband." She paused, and answered the obvious question. "Yes, she was hammered, but she mostly is, right?"

I sighed back at her, supportively. "Bitch. Did she also manage to get a dig in about being out in the deadly sunshine?"

"Of course. Every ten minutes in the sun . . ."

"Is six months on your face, I know." I went into the living room and started kicking small toys toward the baskets. My lower-body workout for the week. "You know, I have no idea where she even got that from,

I've never heard anyone else say it. I think she made it up."

"Or maybe some early magazine editor told it to her and she fastened onto it like a crab. Who knows?"

"Don't let her get to you, Rach. You know she lives in a dream world."

"I know." There was a silence. "She's just . . ."

"I know." Now I was silent. There wasn't anything to say, really. Our father used to say our mom was like a child. "She sees things very simply," he would say. "She takes great joy in small things, and lives very much minute to minute." He liked that about her, because he himself was very cerebral, worried about the future, about money, about the state of the world. Our mom couldn't give a rat's ass about the world, as long as most of it was looking at her. I could see, as an adult, that their relationship worked because she didn't complicate his life. He could fix her bad moods with gifts of jewelry, flowers, flattery. For him, she was easy. Unfortunately, like most narcissistic, childish people, she looked on other children as either followers or competition, and by preschool Rachel and I had our labels. It had taken Rachel a lot of bad experiences, and a lot of good therapy, to get where she was. My breakdown had been an annealing, a hot forge of character that finally showed Rachel how strong she was. But even now the old witch could catch her alone, or late at night, and kick a few foundation stones out of her battlements.

We slipped into old rhythms.

"Ignore her, Rach. She's an idiot."

"I know."

"You have a great life. You're beautiful, smart, far more capable than she ever was. She just can't take it."

"I know."

I finished in the living room and wandered down the hall to check on the kids. "She's just getting old."

"I know."

"Wrinkled and droopy."

"I know."

I pushed open their door and looked at them, sleeping in a tangle of sheets and stuffies and special blankies, faces like angels. "She doesn't know anything about your life."

"I know." Her voice broke. "So why do I still let her get to me?"

I closed the door on my own daughters, praying with every strand of my DNA that this wasn't a conversation they would ever have. Knowing that long after my flawed and piss-poor mother died, my sister and I would still be having it. When you dig a deep enough conversational groove, it's awfully hard to see your way out.

How to Grow Carrots

Make sure your soil is fluffy and free of stones; carrots have a hard enough time pushing through as it is.

- Plant seeds 3 to 4 inches apart, in rows that are at least 1 foot apart. Side note: No need to pull out the tape measure for this stuff, just eyeball it. They're not going to get pissy and refuse to grow just because you're an inch out. Unless you plant those fancy multicolored carrots; they take that shit really seriously.
- Mulching will help to keep the ground moist, speed up germination, and protect the roots from too much sun. Use wood chips, shredded rubber bits, or the tiny shoes of dolls. If you're like me you have enough lying around the house to mulch a freaking field.
- Once plants are 1 inch tall, thin so they stand 3 inches apart. Snip them with scissors, instead of pulling them out, to prevent damage to the roots of other plants.
- Carrots taste much better after a couple of frosts. Following the first hard frost in the fall, cover carrot rows with an 18-inch layer of shredded

leaves to preserve them for harvesting later.

Chapter 7
The Second Class

On Saturday, we arrived at our part of the botanical garden and for a moment I thought we'd gone the wrong way. Where the open field had been was now, clearly, a garden. Impossibly Handsome Bob was standing there, looking proud of himself, and he had every right to be. The children's garden was outlined in terra-cotta tiles and divided up like the spokes of a cartwheel. In the center of it was a larger, tiled area, making a sweet spot for them to work or play. Four cedar benches, just like the ones I had drawn for my home garden, were arranged around the cartwheel, making it easy to sit and watch the kids. The larger vegetable plots were more soberly outlined, with raised beds, two to a plot, with woodchip pathways between. Apparently, it had been quite a week.

Rachel had driven with us this time, as she was planning on coming to our house after. I had boldly written back to Edward that he was more than welcome to come over and advise me on the garden, and she wanted to be along for the ride.

"Besides," she added, her feet up on the dashboard, "I've barely seen the kids since last weekend, and who knows what damage you've done to their delicate psyches in that time."

I looked in the rearview mirror. Clare had completely painted her face with red marker that morning. When she'd walked into the kitchen, I had momentarily freaked out, because I thought she was covered in blood. It turned out she was being a ladybug, the better to get down and dirty with her strawberries. She was a method child. There really wasn't anything an amateur like me could do to a psyche like that, but I didn't say anything. Better to let Rachel think I had some influence. Annabel was just gazing out the window, presumably pondering the inherent mortality and futility of life. Then I realized she was singing the *Sponge-Bob* theme song, so probably not.

I thought about what Rachel had just said. "Hey, that's true. Where have you been?"

"Around, just not around your house."

"You're being secretive."

"I'm not. I'm avoiding the question, it's

entirely different."

Now that I saw Handsome Bob blushing as he looked at her, I thought maybe I could hazard a guess who she'd been around. But hey, she's an adult. I would quiz her later.

We were the first to get there, apart from Bob and Edward, who was off to one side, fiddling with some boxes, so we sat on one of the benches. It was surprisingly noisy in the botanical garden. Birds were yelling their heads off, bees were buzzing around in a beelike fashion, and butterflies were flapping about swearing and jostling one another for the good flowers, like tiny teenage vandals in garden-party frocks.

As ever, my kids were on the ball.

"The birds are much louder here than they are at home, why is that?" asked Clare. Along with her red face, she was wearing a polka-dotted Minnie Mouse dress — sorry, ladybug dress — and while it wasn't my first choice for gardening clothes, it was certainly *a look.*

Annabel answered her. "I don't think they're any louder. I just think everything else is quieter here." Annabel was sitting on my lap, wearing overalls and sneakers, being the more practical child. Only she and I knew she'd forgotten to put on underpants.

Clare frowned. "You mean they're always

singing this hard, we just can't hear them properly?"

"Yeah, you know, the cars are loud and stuff." Momentarily Bel rested her head on my shoulder, making me swoon. I'm like a teenage boy sometimes: Their hair! Their hands! The smell of their clothes! Other times, I just want to run for the hills. Clare looked thoughtful.

"Huh. That must be annoying for them. I don't like it when I'm trying to say something and no one is listening." She was very empathetic, Clare. A sweet kid. "No wonder they poop on the cars all the time. I would, too." Empathetic but vengeful.

The other people started to arrive. Frances and Eloise were today not dressed in similar sweaters, although they still managed to look alike somehow. I wondered if eventually I would have started to look like Dan, had we been together our whole lives. Then I wondered if Frances and Eloise had been together a long time, or if I was just making an assumption. I try not to judge books by their covers, but I do it all the time. Lack of imagination, that's my problem. Gene stumped up, and then blew us all away by smiling at us.

"Good morning, all!"

"Good morning, Gene," Eloise replied.

"You seem very chipper this morning."

He threw himself down on the bench across from us. "I am chipper. My wife, bless her heart, baked me a coffee cake before she had to go away for a bit. This morning I sat in the garden in perfect peace and ate half of it in one sitting. Delicious." He looked at us, his smile fading in case we thought he was a soft touch. "I like cake."

Angela appeared, with a small boy. It looked as if they were deep in conversation, but as they got closer, I saw it was a monologue.

"And then Orthobot turned into a flame-thrower and blew up the skyscraper, but then Dandobot showed up and turned into a crane and rebuilt it really, really fast, but Orthobot tried to kill Dandobot but didn't because then the evil robot sword monster came and tried to kill them both and they teamed up to beat him, and then they blew him up and it was awesome." If the kid breathed once in this whole speech, I would've been amazed.

Angela caught my eye and smiled briefly. "Wow, Bash, that sounds very exciting."

"No, Mom, it was *awesome.*"

And then he looked up and saw us all watching him, and he fell silent and retreated behind his mom. She grinned at us.

"Hey there. This is Bash, my son. Say hi, Bash."

He mumbled something. Bash. Great. Presumably because he was a destructive force of nature, like most little boys. Not that I'm biased or anything.

"Hi, Bash," piped up Clare, my little diplomat. "I'm going to grow strawberries in my garden. What are you going to grow?"

He shrugged, still silent.

"What school do you go to, Bash?" asked Frances, gently.

He shrugged.

Just then, Mike trundled up on a mountain bike. He did a daring dirt-track swerve to come to a stop, and the kids all made appropriate oohing sounds.

"Yay, peeps," he said, which I think is a form of greeting. Or maybe it was, "Yo, peeps." I don't remember exactly. The peeps I remember because Clare turned to me immediately and said, "Can I have some Peeps when we get home?" To which I replied that we didn't have any, on account of it not being Easter, and also on account of Peeps not being an actual food but a by-product of weapons-grade plutonium production. Actually, I just said no, but I thought all the rest of it.

"Splendid, you're all here." Edward had

come up behind us, and we turned at his voice. He was not alone. Not only was Impossibly Handsome Bob with him, but also a pretty, smiling girl.

"Everyone, this is Lisa Vellinga. She comes from Holland, too, and she's here to help the kids with their garden."

"I'm planting strawberries," someone said firmly.

Lisa smiled. "You must be Clare." She looked at the other two. "Which makes you Annabel and you Sebastian."

Oh. Bash, short for Sebastian. Ah.

She reached out, and Clare, of course, took her hand. "Let's go and see what we need to do to make the earth ready to put your plants in it." My two headed off dutifully, but Bash hung back. Angie firmly turned him to face her and knelt down.

"Bash, I'm going to be right here. You'll be able to see me the whole time, and you can get as dirty as you like, OK?" He nodded doubtfully, but walked over to where Lisa and my kids were waiting.

I looked at Angie, who was watching him thoughtfully.

"He's a little shy?"

She nodded. "He'll be fine once he settles, but he's slow to warm up."

Bash was standing with the others when

141

Clare suddenly touched his arm and smiled. She pointed to something on the ground, and they both knelt down.

"That's cute," Angie said. She was wearing her hair more loosely today, probably because having her kid around left her with less time, and in general she seemed softer and happier than the previous week.

"Clare's very friendly. Her teacher calls her the mayor of kindergarten."

We had been muttering quietly, but Edward raised his voice.

"Are you two attending? What if you miss something important and all your vegetables die?" His voice was stern, but he was grinning.

"Yeah," Rachel chimed in, "or worse, some dreadful weed gets started in your crappy plot and then ruins my beautiful Eden."

Mike laughed. "I was planning on only growing weeds."

"Weeds or weed?" Frances looked severe in that "I'm a teacher and you're a naughty kid" way.

"Uh . . . I meant weeds, on account of not really believing that I can grow anything, not to mention that weed is illegal, right?" He was wearing a T-shirt with a picture of bigfoot fighting the yeti, and I was finding it distracting.

"Actually, under state law, you can grow six mature or twelve immature plants, as long as you have a medical marijuana ID card."

We all pivoted to look at Eloise.

"Or at least that's what I hear." She looked at Frances, who raised her eyebrows a little, but said nothing.

Edward coughed. "This is diverting, but let's stick with vegetables and flowers and herbs. Edible herbs."

Gene spoke up. "I believe little Clare is planning on growing strawberries."

I laughed. "You caught that, did you?"

Edward pulled a list from his pocket. "OK, here are the assignments for today. Gene and Mike are together on carrots and cauliflower. Frances and Eloise are going to begin the salad garden. And Lilian, Rachel, and Angela are going to share the work on the other two beds: beans, squash, corn, peppers, peas, and tomatoes."

He suddenly raised his arms and spun around. "Part of the goal of this course is to teach you to see the natural world that lies underneath the city, to understand how seasons work and how the composition of the earth makes such a difference to how and what you can grow. So many of us have lost touch with the seasons, with the weather, with all the cycles of life that go on around us all the time. You can get fruit year-round, thanks to airplanes, and if you spend all day in an office building, you don't really notice if it's cooler outside than it was the week before. And of course, you poor Angelenos only really have one or two seasons, anyway. Hot, less hot. Some rain, no rain. Sad, really. So when you're digging and planting today, think about how what you're doing ties you to generations of people who've worked this land before you."

Just as he finished this unexpectedly poetic little speech, Clare burst out laughing. I looked over. The kids were already digging, each of them now sporting large floppy hats, and Clare and Bash were giggling. Rachel had noticed, too.

"Hey . . . I want a hat. And I want to dig, too. Let's go."

Edward smiled. "Yes, enough talking. As for the hats, I do have some, but they have a rather large company logo on them, so feel free to get your own. Now, go to your plots and literally stick your hands into them. Break up lumps of mud, examine them closely, and try to get a sense of its consistency. We're going to start by amending the soil and setting up any trellises or supports our vegetables will need. I'll come around and talk to each group in turn, OK?"

The kids were chattering happily, and grinned at us as we stood there.

"Sit on the ground, Mom," said Bash. "It's warm!" He was beaming.

Angie smiled and sat, looking up at us. "He's right, it's very warm." She stuck her hand in the ground.

Rachel sighed. "OK, dirty-butt time, I guess." She sat, somewhat gingerly, and after a moment I did, too.

I looked at the others. Eloise and Frances were nearby, and while Frances was already at work, raking the ground and breaking up lumps, Eloise was just kneeling there, her face up to the sun. She looked calm and peaceful. Maybe she was stoned.

Mike and Gene were talking to Edward. Impossibly Handsome Bob came by, pulling a flat cart piled with bamboo stakes.

"Hi, Rachel," he said, as cool as a cucumber.

"Hi, Bob," she replied, equally cool.

"I had fun the other night." Still cool, but his eyes were pretty hot. Angie and I weren't even pretending not to listen.

"Me, too." Rachel amped up the heat herself, then pulled a signature move by turning away, reaching up to pull her long hair into a knot, bending her neck gracefully. I'd seen this move work in 97.8 percent of situations in which it was applied. Bob's eyes narrowed fractionally, and he grinned at Angie and me.

"Delivery, ladies."

After he'd unloaded his cart next to us, he trundled off, never once addressing Rachel again. It was like watching a nature documentary. I spoke sharply to her.

"Rachel Anderby, when did you go out with Bob?"

"Hey, did I tell you I was going to grow lavender?"

Angie and I looked at each other. She tried.

"Rachel, did you sleep with Bob?"

Rachel suddenly looked up, into the sky. "Is that an eagle?"

We gave up. But we knew.

I bent down to see what treasures Bob had given us. Long bamboo poles and a bale of twine. Maybe we were going to be making kites later. Narrow black pipe with holes in it. It was all somewhat underwhelming, but whatever.

Rachel was chatting to Angela. "So, excuse me for sounding like a dickhead, but do you live in the projects, or whatever they're called these days?"

146

Angie nodded. "I live in East L.A., yeah. I'd like to say it has its good side, but it doesn't. I'm in nursing school at night. I'm going to get out as soon as I can and go live somewhere else, if Bash's dad will agree to it. Which he probably will. Or someone will shoot him, which will make the argument easier." She was smiling, joking, but then suddenly she remembered that I was a widow, and she colored.

"Shit, I'm sorry, I totally forgot your husband . . ."

I shrugged. "I forget him, too, sadly. Often for hours at a time I'll forget he's dead, and when I remember, it kind of sucks for a bit, and then it's OK again."

"How long has it been? Since he died?"

"It will be four years next month."

Rachel made a face. "Wow, that's funny. When you asked, in my head I said a year, but it really has been that long."

Angie looked at her. "You knew him, too, I guess."

"Sure. They were married for a long time, and we lived in the same city, so I saw them a lot. I miss him, too. He was hilarious."

Edward walked up. This week, the weather was warmer, so he'd lost the sweater and was just wearing a T-shirt and jeans. He was stronger than I had imagined a professor

147

might be. All the male teachers at art school had been weedy and interesting-looking, with facial hair that made a statement. Edward looked like a firefighter or something, tall and strong and coordinated. Not that I was evaluating him physically, because that would have been demeaning and wrong of me. Edward rubbed his hands together and grinned at us.

"Time to get dirty, ladies."

We all gazed up at him, and he blushed. "I mean, in the actual dirt."

He sat down next to us and stuck his hand in the earth.

"OK, so the soil is where all the magic happens, basically."

I spoke up. "I thought it was sunlight and water that mattered." (Fifty-seven basic biology textbooks, not to mention *Sesame Street* et al.)

He nodded, still working the dirt with his strong fingers. "Of course, you can't grow anything without them, but the soil is where the plants live, where they get their sustenance, and the health of the soil determines how well they do. All the water and sunlight in the world won't help them if the soil is too tight for their roots to spread out, or too loose and sandy for them to be able to stand upright."

We all nodded, looking serious and thoughtful. He continued explaining, in his formal way, with the cute accent, and I have to say I'm not sure I absorbed all that much. It was like a chemistry lesson at school. Potassium, nitrogen, something else, I forget, the nature of decomposition and ergo composting, worms were discussed . . . after a few minutes of concentrating, my mind started to wander and I just looked down at the dirt and played with it while his voice rolled over us. Angie and Rachel asked questions, and nobody bugged me. The sun was warm, the kids were engaged, and there was something nice about sitting in the earth, just breaking up lumps. I felt . . . what's that word . . . happy.

Suddenly Edward stood up again, and so did the others. Shit, I must have missed something.

"Hey, dreamy, time to wield a shovel." Rachel reached down and pulled me to my feet. "You OK?"

I nodded. "Sorry, I was just mellowing out."

Impossibly Handsome Bob had shown up again, and it was clear he wasn't afraid of playing with fire: He had gone back to the basic playbook and taken off his sweatshirt, revealing a tight T-shirt over even tighter abs. Rachel pretended not to notice, but I saw her hand clench involuntarily. Bob was pushing a wheelbarrow full of something dark, which he dumped next to us. It smelled. Or he smelled, but the former was more likely.

"Steer manure," announced Edward. "You can take it and dig it into your soil. It will add lots of excellent nutrients."

Bob handed out pitchforks and shovels. Then he trundled off, presumably to get more manure. It was like a Chippendales farming fantasy routine.

I was having trouble with basic instructions. "Dig it in? I hate to ask an obvious question, but what exactly do you mean?"

"I'll show you." Edward picked up the shovel, shoveled up some manure, threw it onto the nearest plot of soil, picked up the pitchfork, and started digging and turning over the soil. "Imagine you are a large kitchen mixer, just mix the ingredients together." He grinned. "Once the earth has been amended, we're going to lay in some drip irrigation." He indicated the black pipe. "And then build some supports. One bed is going to contain fava beans, green beans, corn, and squash, and the other will have tomatoes and English peas."

Well, at least he had ambition. Edward

smiled attractively at us all and walked off toward Frances and Eloise. We all watched his butt walk away, and then turned to the task at hand. And it was easy, to start with. But after about five minutes, I started to sweat.

I turned to Rachel.

"Is it me, or is this harder than I thought?"

She leaned on her fork, managing somehow to look like she'd been leaning on pitchforks all her life. All she needed was a gingham shirt and pigtails and she'd be Elly May Clampett.

"I think it must be you, to be honest. In what fantasyland did you think manual labor would be easy? Doesn't the phrase *manual labor* kind of give it away? If they called it *manual vacation* or *manual relaxation,* then I could see where you might get confused."

"Manual relaxation sounds like something a hooker would offer," chimed in Angie, who seemed impervious to effort and was nearly done turning in all her manure.

Fine. I started turning again and tried to pay attention to it as a meditative exercise instead of something that was making my back hurt.

"Mom?" I paused, glad of any distraction, to turn to Clare.

"Yes, honey?"

"I planted my first strawberry. Come see."

I jammed the fork in the earth and went to look.

Clare was yattering away, as usual.

"So first we stirred in all this yummy poopy stuff for the ground to make it happy, then we carefully made little holes in it with our hands, and then we gently put the little plants in it and tucked them into their beds. It was nice. The teacher is really nice."

The teacher, Lisa, was right there as she said this, and she smiled. "It is easy to be nice to Clare, I think." She reached out her hand, mud and all, and I shook it. "Your children are natural gardeners, Mrs. Girvan."

"Please call me Lili, and I'm happy to hear it, although God knows where they get it from." I looked down at their little pieces of garden. The earth was all fluffy, and a single strawberry plant was perfectly placed in the middle. Annabel was still working, and hadn't even looked up at me, which was a good sign she was enjoying herself. She had started with her central heart part and had outlined the shape with smooth pebbles. She was nearly done filling it in with seeds, and I could see a small pile of seed packets next to her.

"How come Annabel has seeds and Clare has plants?"

Lisa smiled. "Because Annabel wanted to plant seeds, and strawberries are best grown from small plants. They will spread out to fill the space over the next few weeks, and if we had planted seeds, we wouldn't have fruit by the end of it. We still might not, but the gardens will be here for several months, so she will be able to come back and eat the results of her work over the summer. Annabel had the choice of plants, too." Lisa pointed behind her: A flat of red and blue flowers was sitting a little ways off. "I brought both, because I didn't know her yet. She was quite clear that she wanted to grow them from seeds, so that's what she's doing. Let's hope they grow and flower in time."

I went back to my garden. Angie had taken pity on me and was turning in my manure, as hers was already done. I let her carry on, as I believe in honoring the desires of the individual, but I did lean on my pitchfork, helpfully.

Once our earth was ready, Edward wandered back to talk to us.

I was sitting on the ground, and he looked down and smiled at me. "Are you having

153

fun, Lilian?"

I smiled back. "My back hurts, but apart from that, it's super."

He laughed at me. "New things are sometimes painful, no? In this way, gardening is like life."

I made a face. "But sometimes, pain is your body's way of telling you to avoid something. Maybe I'm not made for digging."

Rachel chimed in. "Or maybe you are just being a wuss."

I looked at Edward. He winked at me. "Let us save the debating for another occasion, no? In this bed, we're going to plant the classic Three Sisters garden. I assume you know this."

I started to shake my head, but then it came back to me. "Three Sisters? It's a Native American thing, right?"

He nodded. "Yes, and it's a perfect example of companion planting, which is where you choose to grow plants together that somehow help each other to flourish."

"How romantic." Rachel sighed.

He smiled at her. "The Native Americans were experienced and efficient horticulturalists, rather than romantics, although it's possible to be both. The cornstalks act as supports for the climbing beans, the beans fix nitrogen in the soil for the corn and squash, and the squash provides mulch and root protection for the corn and beans. And then, just to make it all perfect, when you eat the corn and beans together, they form a complete protein." He grinned, "Thrilling, no?"

We all looked at him. I wasn't sure if *thrilling* was the word I would have used, but it was nice. He crouched down close to me and started making a mound of earth.

"Come, ladies, join me. We need to make two or three mounds about a foot tall and two or so feet across. Then we'll plant some corn seeds in a circle, and then you're done for now. We add the beans later, and the squash after that. While we're waiting for the corn to start, we'll be working on the other beds, which will hold plants that grow more quickly." He pointed. I could see muscles working under his T-shirt and suddenly realized I found him attractive. Clearly the sun was getting to me.

Rachel looked at her nicely manicured nails. "Didn't humankind invent a whole set of small hand tools for this kind of work?" I realized both the other women were just standing there, watching us. To be fair, I had already been sitting on the ground when he arrived, but still.

Edward shrugged. "Of course, but for what we're doing, the human hand really is the best tool, and it's nice to get a sense of the consistency of the earth. Trust me, it's just mud. It washes off."

Angie spoke up. "He's laughing at us."

Edward just smiled. "Humans have been growing food for themselves since the dawn of time. Indeed, many plants have developed a dependence on us, just as some plants require digestion by birds to activate their seeds. We do our part by planting seeds in healthy soil, watering them, weeding them, and leaving them in peace. They return the favor by growing fruits and seeds and flowers that we like to eat."

Then he picked up some of the bamboo poles and turned to me.

"Would you like to help me build supports for the tomatoes?"

"Sure." I brushed some of the dirt off my hands, and took several of the bamboo poles. He had five or six in his hand and stuck them in the ground in a loose circle. I followed his lead.

"We're basically making a tent shape, a cone, if you know what I mean. Lean the poles together and use the twine to tie the tops together. Weave it in and around to keep all the poles balanced and supported."

He was doing it, and his hands moved quickly. Suddenly he took my hands and moved them to the poles, handing me the twine. "I'll hold the bamboo, you wind the twine around. That work?" I looked up at him, and his eyes were warm and friendly. "You can't really make a mistake. Just do what feels right to keep the little teepee together."

I took the ball of green twine and tried to mimic his actions. I wound the twine around each pole and then onto the next. He was right. It just seemed natural. Pretty soon, my little cone of sticks was standing firm.

"How do we get the tomatoes to climb up it?" I frowned. "Do they even climb? I don't think I've ever seen a tomato plant."

He said, "Don't look now, but they're right behind you."

I turned slowly, to see a tray of spiky green plants. "They look pretty harmless."

He nodded. "They are. Tomatoes are one of my favorite things to grow. They're easy, they almost always set a lot of fruit, and as long as you keep the caterpillars off them, you can just stand there in the sun and eat your fill." He licked his lips, like a little kid. "Delicious."

"What's delicious?" I turned, startled. Annabel had materialized right next to me, having apparently acquired the power of teleportation.

"Tomatoes," answered Edward. "Do you want to help your mom plant some?"

"Sure. I finished my flowers."

He smiled at her. "Can I see?" She nodded and led him away. He turned to look at me as he went. "We're going to set up the irrigation first, so go grab some black pipe. I'll be right back."

I just stood there and watched them walk away, her little figure tiny next to him. Shaking myself, I turned to get the pipe.

It turns out setting up a drip irrigation system, which sounds all impressive and farmer-ish, actually involves digging troughs in rows along where you're going to plant your seeds and then burying pipe in them. We left pipe sticking out at the ends, for someone cleverer than me to hook up to actual water, and that was it. Then Edward looked at his watch and pulled a tray of tomato plants over.

"We have time to put these in the ground. Let's do it."

I let Annabel show me how to do it, and together we planted the tomatoes. Once I'd done one or two, I discovered that I liked it, and that furthermore tomato plants smelled good. Not a pretty smell, but an interesting one, peppery and green. I could smell it on my hands, and in the sunny air. I suddenly realized that all my senses were getting more of a workout than normal, and maybe that explained why my brain wasn't buzzing with its usual self-critical commentary. I was getting input from my hands, my eyes, my ears (listening out for killer bees, noticing the birds arguing about something, half listening to the voices of the rest of the class and the piping sounds of Clare teaching Lisa all about cat nipples), and my nose. I wondered why this was so relaxing when it was also so physically active. There was probably some metaphorical lesson to be drawn from it, but I was damned if I was going to hunt for it. For the first time in recent years I was going to stop thinking and just dig in the dirt.

How to Grow Cucumbers

Once your seeds are in the ground, protect them from pests by using netting, a berry basket, or a specially trained golden eagle. Whatever you have on hand.

- Occasionally put your finger in the soil to test the moisture level: If it is dry past the first joint of your finger, get out the watering can. If you can't pull your finger out, you're overwatering. Inconsistent watering leads to bitter-tasting fruit.
- Water slowly in the morning or early afternoon, avoiding the leaves. Water droplets on delicate leaves become magnifying glasses in the sun, burning the plant and really pissing it off.
- Spray vines with sugar water to attract bees and set more fruit.
- Cucumbers may not set fruit because the first flowers were all male. Both female and male flowers must be blooming at the same time. Be patient.

CHAPTER 8

After class had officially ended, we all stood around chatting. Gene continued to be in his strangely unsmiling yet obviously happy mood, which turned out to be kind of charming.

"So, Gene," I said. I had decided to investigate my classmates. "Do you have kids?"

He nodded. "Two, one about to graduate from college, and one about to have her first baby. It's very exciting. My wife is visiting her now. The house is very quiet without her."

"So you should come and eat at our house," piped up Clare, who had taken a fancy to Gene, possibly because of his support over the tractor riding. "My mom said she might order pizza for when we're working in the garden."

Gene smiled a little, which, as you might have guessed, was his notion of a mild

161

frown. "Oh, that's OK, but thank you, Clare. I'm sure your mom has plenty to do without additional guests."

"She's already having additional guests." Edward had arrived, along with Impossibly Handsome Bob. "Bob and I are going over to help her create a charming oasis in her back garden."

I smiled, a little bit embarrassed that he was telling everyone he was coming over. Rachel chimed in. "I'll be there, too, and I was planning on mostly standing in the bathroom, examining the zit that's appearing next to my nose. If you're there, you'll be able to do the work I could theoretically have done."

I looked around at everyone else. What the hell? "Actually, if anyone else wants to come and hang out and eat pizza and laugh at my garden, you're all welcome. Angie, Bash can hang out with the kids and play, if you like. The house is a mess, and all I was going to do was indeed order a couple of pizzas, but it would be nice." I shrugged, trying to convey a mixture of relaxed invitingness and casual no-pressureness. I'm generally a grumpy, reclusive person on the inside, but sometimes on the outside I surprise myself with my friendliness.

Amazingly, they all said yes. Edward was thrilled.

"I think with all of us there, we can do the whole thing this afternoon! It will be fun."

"And next week you can do mine." Angie laughed.

"Why not? It can be a project. We will do everyone's garden." Edward was serious. "Do you have a garden, Angela?"

She sobered. "No, I have a balcony. Actually, I have two balconies because I live next to my mother and we ripped out the separator a decade ago. But still, no earth."

Edward's eyes gleamed. "Great! A container garden. They can be wonderful."

Angie looked dubious and changed the subject.

I gave everyone my address, and we all headed for our cars. I admit I sped on the way home, in order to get home and clear the more obvious health hazards before they arrived. But apparently Eloise and Frances held the teacher land speed record, because they were standing outside the house when I got there.

Frances smiled at me. "We hurried so we could help tidy up a bit before everyone descends on you."

For a second I thought about pretending there was no need, but common sense prevailed. "That would be fantastic. It looks like a disaster area in there. You have no idea."

Eloise laughed. "We taught elementary school for twenty years apiece. We have every idea. You think two kids can create havoc, you should see what two dozen kids can achieve."

Frances nodded, following us into the house that didn't, for once, smell disturbing. "And when we started teaching there would often be thirty kids in the class, and the classroom would frequently devolve into an anarchist state." She laughed, which was reassuring, as it was probably utterly terrifying at the time.

Eloise looked around at my kitchen, which still had all the breakfast dishes out everywhere. "It's not too bad, actually," she said, which was patently untrue. "Why don't I load the dishwasher while you clear the surfaces, and Frances and Rachel and the kids can do a quick once-over everywhere else."

She opened the dishwasher and got started. She was so . . . capable. Then the doorbell rang, and I went to get it. It was Angela and Bash.

"Hey, I tried to get here fast to help you with cleaning up. Bash, run and find the girls . . ." He had already shot into the house. She turned and grinned at me. "I think he's in love with Clare."

I shrugged. "She'll break his heart, I'm afraid. She's a fickle pickle." I turned and led the way to the kitchen, passing the cleaning crew of Rachel, Frances, and now all three kids throwing things behind the sofa in the living room.

Angie laughed. "I see you already have a team in place."

I nodded. "Eloise is working on the kitchen, but it could easily use all three of us. Thanks for helping."

She squeezed my arm. "I swear, if everyone's coming to my place next week, I'm going to need my entire extended family to take off work and come clean. Otherwise, you'll never all fit." She looked around at my house. "I like your house. It's very cool."

I tried to see past the mess. It was a nice house. When Dan and I had bought it, it was a total wreck, but we had worked hard on it. (This was before the kids, obviously, although people do strip paint and sand floors with children underfoot, hard though it is to imagine. I would always be tempted to wall one of them up when no one was looking.) It was a Spanish-style, one-story house, with dark wood floors, white plaster walls, arched doorways, and lots of original woodwork. I had mostly painted the walls white, but inside the niches I had done bright blues, yellows, oranges, and the kids' room was colorful, too. Angie was still talking.

"Rachel told me you're an artist, and I can see that in the house."

I laughed, embarrassed. "I'm not really an artist. I'm just an illustrator."

"What's the difference?"

I thought about it. "An artist works from inspiration. An illustrator works by direction, illustrating a text."

She thought about it. "So the only difference is who you work for."

"I guess."

"Doesn't sound like a very big difference to me."

Rachel walked in, saving me from having to respond.

"It's all done, I'm having Eloise come to my place after. She's an angel of cleaning. She claims it's from not being able to leave work until the classroom was picked up, but I think it's a God-given talent."

"Like being an artist," said Angie, airily, and walked off toward the kitchen.

Rachel looked at me. "Did I miss something?"

I shook my head. "Not really. Here come the guys. Did they charter a bus?"

Edward, Gene, Mike, and Lisa were coming up the front path. Gene was carrying some tools, and Mike and Lisa were chattering away. I held open the door.

"Mike's going to teach me to surf," Lisa said. She seemed thrilled. "We're going today, after this."

I made an encouraging expression. "That's exciting. I guess there's not much surfing in Holland."

She laughed. "It is the North Sea! No one goes into it on purpose." Still chuckling at the idiocy of Americans, she and Mike headed off into the house.

Gene next. "You surf already, I imagine, Gene."

He frowned. "Not ever, but my wife would probably like me to try. She has big plans for me." I was starting to revise my opinion of his wife. She sounded a lot ballsier than I had originally thought. Edward stopped as he came in the doorway.

"Hello, Lilian."

I managed to say hello back without incident, but he wasn't done. "I realized on the way over that invading your house this way might not be comfortable for you."

I shook my head. "Hey, I invited everyone, remember? It's nice to have new people here for a change, and I'm too old to care what people think of my messy place. Mostly."

He frowned. People were frowning at me a lot today. "You are not old, Lilian. You are young and beautiful." And with this he turned and followed the others. I stood there like a mushroom, a young and beautiful mushroom, but a mushroom nonetheless. I couldn't even tell you that he was flirting with me. He was very serious and didn't smile as he said it, but still, he had called me beautiful, and it was nice to hear. Confusing, but nice.

I went to shut the door and nearly smashed poor Bob's face, which would have been painful for him and a loss to women everywhere.

"Oh, sorry, Bob! I didn't realize you were there."

He grinned. "Happens all the time. Edward asked me to drive the truck over with your plants."

Finally, my turn to frown. "My plants?"

"Yeah, plants for your garden, I guess. Shall I bring them through the house, or is there a side way?"

I showed him the side way, and where he could park the truck, then I looked in the truck and goggled. It was full of flowers, plants, shrubs, trays of moss and ferns, bags of soil and compost and mulch. Hoses, watering cans, bamboo stakes. Paving slabs, ornamental stones. I think I saw a birdbath as the truck pulled past me. This was too much. I went to have it out with Edward.

He was standing in the backyard with Gene and Eloise, pointing at things in an impressive way. He had a printout of my picture, for crying out loud. Everyone else, from the sound of it, was playing with My Little Ponies in the kids' room. Well, except for Frank, who was standing next to Gene and being patted. When Gene paused, Frank would stretch up on his tippy toes, which is challenging for a fat Labrador, to push his head back into range. Shameless.

As I got close, Gene turned.

"I like your dog," he said, and actually smiled a real smile. Frank does that to people, I'll give him that.

"Thanks." I wasn't going to be distracted. "Edward, why is Bob here with a truckload of plants?"

Edward looked surprised. "Because we are going to fix your garden, are we not? How are we going to do it without plants?"

I considered this. "I thought you needed to look at it first?"

169

He shrugged. "Surely, but then I thought I might as well bring a few things. If we can't use everything I'll just take it back to the botanical garden."

I studied him in disbelief. "A few things? There's a truckload out there. I don't know that I can . . ." I trailed off, suddenly shy.

Edward's face cleared. "Ah, you are worried about the cost! Do not give it a second thought. It is all paid for by my company because I am going to take before and after photos and make it a work expense. In fact, I am thinking of doing a book about the course."

Eloise spoke. "You could do before-and-afters of everyone's garden, as part of the book. It would be interesting to see how learning to garden has changed people's outdoor space."

Edward nodded. "And we can ask Lilian to illustrate it." He smiled at me. "You're illustrating my family's vegetable guide, aren't you? That's the book you talked about the first time?"

I frowned. "Yes . . . how did you know that?"

He shrugged and looked embarrassed suddenly. "I was talking to my sister, who runs the book-publishing business, and she mentioned we were trying a new publisher

170

and that they'd said they were going to send an illustrator . . . I just put two and two together."

I looked at him, not quite sure what to say. He was talking about me with his sister? Or did they often discuss business? There was a pause, which luckily Eloise interrupted with a question about how they might format a book about the course. I let it slide and went back to the kitchen, where apparently Rachel had been watching us through the window.

"You're freaking out. What's the matter?"

I wasn't sure, and said so. "I've been a little bit stressed-out lately, about changing things."

She looked at me thoughtfully. "Is it about planting things in the garden, or crushing on the teacher?"

"I have no idea what you're talking about. You're a hopeless romantic, Rachel. I'm not interested, OK? Quit it." I started to make coffee, pouring what turned out to be a full and hot jug of the stuff down the sink.

"You made coffee already?"

She nodded. "It just finished." I saw a mug in her hand, with cream in it.

"I'm sorry."

"I'll get over it. Make another pot, though, and quick, because I think I saw Bob, and I need coffee to gear up."

"So you did sleep with him."

"Not yet. Maybe later. Make the coffee." She put the mug down by the sink. "And don't throw out my cream, or I'll beat you."

I got the coffeemaker started again. Frances and Mike wandered in.

"Are they ready for us yet?" They peered through the window.

Mike smiled at me. "Your kids are cool."

Frances smiled, too. "They really are, Lilian. They're very smart and interesting. I would have liked to have them in my classroom when I was working."

"Well, that's nice to hear." We heard a shout from the garden, and turned.

"Come on, you lazy ones, come and help." It was Edward, yelling around a bag of soil amendment. He and Gene were unloading, and Eloise was placing the various plants around the small garden. We all piled out.

Bob had backed the truck up to the gate and propped it open. Somehow Frank had jumped up onto the tailgate and was supervising. Showing off for his new friend Gene, I imagine. With everybody helping, it was remarkably quick, but still there was so much stuff.

"I think you're delusional, Edward," I panted, looking around. "There's barely enough room for everything. How are we going to plant it all?"

"Trust me." He made his voice even deeper. "I am an expert."

Clare and Annabel giggled. They and Bash were standing in the kitchen doorway, watching us all sweat.

"Aha!" Edward saw them. "Come and show me where you want your fairy garden to be."

The girls squealed, but Bash made a noise that only five-year-old boys can make. It's the sound they make when something girly is proposed, and it combines a snort, a laugh, and a throwing-up sound all in one.

"Fairy garden? That's no fun."

"You are wrong," Edward informed him. "Boy fairies are very tough fighters, and use all kinds of sticks and stones as weapons. You will see. Defending a fairy kingdom against weasels and rats is no easy matter."

"Great," Angie muttered beside me. "Teach him to throw more stuff, go ahead."

"Don't worry," I reassured her, "he's not going to buy it, anyway. A fairy is a fairy. There's nothing tough about fairies."

But I was wrong, again. Bash got into it. They picked a spot for their fairy garden, whatever the hell that was, and Edward promised to come by during the week to put the finishing touches on it. I don't know what he had up his sleeve. All I heard was that he was coming by later in the week. Sometimes I worry that I'm self-obsessed, and then I worry that I'm thinking about myself too much.

The pizza arrived, and we all sat around to eat it. Gene continued to be chatty.

"So, Frances, how did you and Eloise meet?"

There was a pause as they looked at each other. Eloise had her mouth full and her hands busy dealing with a mountain of melted cheese, so Frances answered. "At school. Where else? Neither of us ever went anywhere else." She smiled. "And in those days, there weren't lesbians all over the media the way there are today, so we weren't as open as we can be now."

"How long have you been together?" Mike was reaching for another slice from his spot on a warm bag of fertilizer.

"Oh, a while. More than twenty years at this point. I had just started teaching and wasn't even sure I could approach another woman." She looked over to where the kids were playing, but they were paying no attention at all. "And then, after a semester of finding my feet, Eloise arrived to teach art and that was that."

"You've been together ever since?"

"On and off. Mostly on." She looked around. "What about you, Rachel? You're single, how come?"

Rachel shrugged her famous shrug. "I've been practicing a lot. When I get it right, maybe I'll get married. I was married once before, but it didn't last long."

"How long?" asked Eloise.

"Thirty-six hours."

"And she's been kind of busy helping me raise my kids." My tone was light, but I wanted to make sure she got her props.

"But luckily," grinned Rachel, giving it right back to me, "I get nights and weekends off for good behavior, and I use the time to indulge in bad behavior, so that's all right." I looked over at Bob, who was looking at her and smiling faintly. Maybe his goose wasn't as cooked as I thought.

"And you, Edward?"

He turned his hands up. "Not very interesting. I am divorced, too, I have a son in Amsterdam, and I am pretty much single."

Eloise was persistent. "No one special?"

Edward blushed. "Not at the moment."

Rachel looked at me and waggled her eyebrows, the idiot.

Eloise looked like she was far from finished, but Edward stood up and wiped his hands on his jeans. "Let's get back to work. We lose Bob at four, and we'll be slower without him."

I wondered where Bob went — parole officer? photo shoot? — but it was true that he was a gardening machine. He dug and refilled beds at the end of the garden, and had them planted with flowers before the rest of us had barely begun. Frances and Eloise entertained the kids indoors, with occasional help from Mike, and the rest of us just did as we were told. Rachel filled containers; I dug a ring around our one tree, piled up some manure and mulch, and gave it a big drink; and Angela planted tall flowers in the bed that ran along the side of the house. Edward had his back to me, but was presumably doing his mystical fairy garden, because he had trays of moss and ferns next to him.

Just before four, Bob stepped back from his work and stretched. We all watched. It was like an art exhibit; you couldn't not look, it would have been rude. He had finished the bottom bed, and it looked like a page from a garden catalog. I was impressed, and said so.

"I'm very grateful. Thank you so much for helping. It's very nice of you."

He smiled easily. "You're welcome. Besides, if I didn't like working in the garden, I wouldn't do it, right?"

"I guess not." I waited a second, but then plunged in. I really wanted to know. "So is gardening what you want to do, or are you in Los Angeles to get famous?"

He laughed. "Good God, no. The more I can stay out of the city, the better. I was raised here, it's not very glamorous to me. I want to be a farmer, and I'm getting my agriculture degree at Pierce." He nodded his head at Edward, who was fiddling with his ferns. "I take his course right now. That's how I got roped into his free class. I don't normally work on the weekends."

"And where are you going now? More school?"

"Nah, I volunteer at an adult literacy class. My mom spoke Spanish at home, so I did, too, and it helps to be bilingual."

I gazed at him, the tinkling sound in my head the shattered pieces of my assumptions hitting the ground.

"Well, OK, then."

He grinned and loped off, pausing to speak to Rachel as he went. I couldn't hear what they were saying, but she looked up at him and smiled an unmistakably flirty smile, and nodded. I hoped she wouldn't eat him for dinner, so to speak.

After that, they all started to trickle off one by one. Eventually it was just me and Edward in the garden, with the distant sounds of the kids starting to fall apart in their bedroom. I knew that any minute now one of them was going to start crying, or yelling, and that this peaceful moment was going to be over, but for the time being I was happy. I found a bottle of wine and two glasses, and sat on the stoop and gazed around. It didn't even look like my garden anymore. There was dark healthy soil in all the flower beds, fresh plants everywhere, leafy glades of moss and ferns. It was magical.

Edward came to sit next to me on the stoop. Often, in Los Angeles, the evenings are surprisingly cool. But at this point, just as the sun was going down, it was warm and he was still in his T-shirt. I could feel his bare arm brush mine from time to time, and went to get a sweater. I wasn't cold; I just needed an extra layer.

"Was your husband a gardener, Lili?" The question surprised me. Normally people avoided talking about Dan, myself included. I shook my head and smiled.

"Not at all. Like me, he was used to being in the city, and probably didn't even think of this space out here as a garden."

His lips twitched. "He probably wasn't alone in that."

I nodded. "It's much nicer now."

"Would he like it, do you think?"

I looked around and nodded again. "He would. Because it's good for the kids, you know, and he loved to watch them play." I swallowed. "He never saw Clare play, though. She was too young when he died."

His hand reached to cover mine. "It must have been awful. I am so sorry for your loss, Lili."

People say that all the time, of course. And like the question "How are you?" it comes in a million different flavors. He meant it. I felt a lump in my throat and willed myself not to cry. Change the subject, change the subject.

"Was your wife a gardener?" OK, not a total change of subject, but still, I was scrabbling. He took his hand away.

"No. She was, and is, a lawyer. We knew each other, vaguely, as children, and then met properly in college. Amsterdam isn't all that big of a city, and our parents knew one another. It was one of those, 'Oh, you should see if you can find Anneke at college. She's there, too.' But we met, and fell in love, and there you have it. She likes flowers, but in vases rather than dirt." He grinned, "Our son, Theo, loves to dig in the mud, so I guess genetics won out a bit."

"How old is your son?"

"He is twelve now." He looked at me, and his face was very close. "I miss him more than I miss my wife, of course, but what can you do?"

His eyes were green, I realized. Well, green and gray. He had enviable eyelashes, and the curve of his upper lip . . . Why was I gazing at him like a teenager? Head in the game, Lili. I looked down and wiped my hands on my pants, not that they were dirty. There was a pause, then he stood suddenly and headed toward the back wall of the garden.

"I see a problem," he said. "One of these asters is taller than the others. It must fall in line." He crouched down to fix the offending plant, and I watched him, feeling a physical attraction I hadn't felt in literally years.

It was horrible.

He turned around and looked at me, and for a moment he could see what I was feeling. I could read it on his face. Both the attraction and the confusion. He stood and walked quickly toward me.

"Are you all right, Lili?"

I nodded. This time I couldn't stop the

tear that trickled down my cheek, and Edward wiped it away with his thumb. He took my hand and squeezed it.

"You are still so sad. How long has it been?"

I shook my head, even though it was true. "Nearly four years. It's not . . ." I didn't know what it wasn't, so my voice trailed off, and I bent my head and let my hair cover a lot more than just my face.

Suddenly he leaned forward and kissed me on the cheek, where the tear had been. One of his hands was in my hair, the other tightened around mine, and for a split second I pulled toward him, wanting to be held, wanting to cede control because it was so very tiring, keeping it all together, all the time.

But instead there was a bloodcurdling scream from inside the house, followed by small voices raised in anger. I pulled away from Edward, made an apologetic face, and went to assist the wounded. Which is, of course, ironic.

When the dust had settled, he was gone.

People had started telling me to move on after about two years, especially my mom and, strangely, Dan's parents.

My mother-in-law had been quite specific.

"Sweetheart, we all miss Dan, but if you'd been the one who died, we would be telling him to move on and remarry, and if Rachel was in your position, you'd be telling her the same."

I shook my head, hard. "I wouldn't. I would respect her need to grieve at her own pace."

She smiled at me. I was lucky. I had a great mother-in-law, who was way more nurturing than my own mother.

"You're never going to stop grieving, Lili, none of us are. We will miss him every day, in a myriad of different ways, but that doesn't mean it's not OK to laugh or meet new people. The kids need a father, and you deserve to not be doing this alone. If Dan were around, he would want you to be happy."

This was something people said all the time, and it really pissed me off. Dan would want you to date, they would say. Bullshit. I knew this because he and I had discussed it. We'd discussed everything, that's why I missed him. If he had been lame, it wouldn't be so fucking painful.

"If I die," he had said, lying in bed years before we had kids, "I want you to do a complete Victorian mourning, got it?" We had "assumed the position," the one where he lay on his back and I curled around him like a vine, my head resting on his shoulder. It was the most comfortable, secure place in the world.

I grinned into his neck. "You mean like seven years in black, three in purple, three in purple with a bit of white, that kind of thing?"

I could hear him smile. "I think you're wrong about the purple, but yeah, veils and everything."

"Weeping and rending of garments?"

"I think the rending of garments is Judaism, but sure, mix it up. Pull from as many sources as you want." He stroked my back, under the sheet.

"I could lament."

"Loudly, I trust."

"And piteously. I will wander sightless."

He squeezed my waist and turned his head, kissing my hair. "Now you're getting crazy. I just want the proper respect."

"You got it, babe."

And, admittedly, I had once said to him, after we had kids, that if I died, he should feel free to go Mormon and remarry several women at once, but mostly I was saying it because I was annoyed he hadn't emptied the dishwasher. He'd said he would remarry the entire October issue of *Playboy,* and I said that was a plan, because I knew those nineteen-year-old hotties would go nuts for a middle-aged guy with ten extra pounds. Then he'd thrown a pair of (dirty) boxer shorts at me. One has these conversations lightly, or even angrily, and then they're set in stone.

And it's not as if you can prepare for sudden death. That would be the kicker of that whole *sudden* part. You think you can imagine it, but it's like when you're about to have your first baby — people tell you what it's like, you've seen other people do it. How hard can it be? And then it happens, and the first three months are like Vietnam without the drugs. Grief is like that, but really an enormous amount worse. Vietnam without drugs, weapons, or the outer layers of your skin. I'm not going to sugarcoat it: Every breath I took was an insult, every smile I automatically returned in the drugstore was an affront, every morning I woke up alone was a vicious punch in the throat. I missed listening to him brush his teeth, the pause before he spat. I missed that when he came out of the shower, he always had an idea he wanted to tell me. I missed hearing him in the other room talking to the baby, or to the dog. I missed the sound of his key in the door. I missed the sight of him sleeping like a log when I climbed back into bed after going to the baby, the bastard. I missed the smell of his neck. I even missed the irritating things he did, like the fact that he always left his wet towel on the end of the bed. If I close my eyes right now I can see him throwing it down and turning slowly around in circles, looking for the boxer shorts he'd left lying on the floor.

So I closed my eyes and fell asleep watching him turn.

HOW TO GROW A GREEN BEAN

Seeds can be sown outdoors any time after the last spring frost. The ground should be warm enough to work easily.

- Bush beans: Plant 2 inches apart.
- Pole beans: Set up trellises, or "cattle panels," and plant 3 inches apart.
- Beans need supports to grow on, but you can use a lot of different things: Fence panels, bamboo stakes, strings, wool you tie across the garden area, your ex-husband's golf clubs. Whatever works.
- For a harvest that lasts all summer, sow beans every 2 weeks. If you're going to be away, skip a planting. Beans do not wait for anyone. Seriously.

CHAPTER 9

That Tuesday at work something unexpected happened. As is often the case, it started with the telephone, which rang.

Rose. "There's someone here to see you in reception."

"Really?"

"No, I'm making a prank call. Yes, really. She says she knows you but refuses to give her name." I could hear her glaring at the poor woman in question. I frowned.

"OK, that's weird. I'll be right out."

As I rounded the corner, I realized that thinking about my mother-in-law must have been a premonition.

"Maggie!" I literally squeaked with excitement, and more or less ran across reception.

My sister-in-law, Maggie, was not only Dan's sister but also one of my oldest friends. I had known her first, in fact, because she and I had been in homeroom together during our freshman year of high school. From the first minute we saw each other, we knew we were going to be friends, and it wasn't just because we both had Flock of Seagulls haircuts. We were kindred spirits, and even though the teachers quickly realized their lives would be easier if we were kept apart, we were mostly inseparable. And, of course, then she introduced me to Dan. I had only seen her twice since he'd died, because she lived in Italy with her husband.

"I cannot believe you're here! Why didn't you tell me you were coming?" I kept hugging her and laughing. "Rose, this is Maggie, my sister-in-law."

Maggie smiled. "Hi, Rose. Sorry to be weird about giving you my name, but I wanted to surprise her."

"You succeeded."

"Why are you here? Where's Berto?"

Maggie paused and looked at her watch. "Can you come out for lunch?"

"Of course, wait here." I went to grab my bag and tell Sasha to cover for me in case it turned into one of those three-hour lunches. We headed out of the office, and once we reached the street, I hugged her again.

"My God, the kids are going to freak!"

"If they remember me."

"They probably will. Or at least they'll say they do. They were pretty small last time you met. Rachel will be stoked, too. Shall I call her?" Obviously Rachel and Maggie were friends, too, although Rachel had been two years behind us at school. "What kind of food do you fancy? Not Italian, I guess."

She smiled faintly. "Anything but. How about sushi?"

"Great." I directed us down the street, and once we were seated, I just sat and looked at her. She was a female version of Dan, tall and thin like him, but with dark red hair instead of brown. Something was obviously bothering her, because she seemed tired, an adjective that had never applied to her before. Like her brother, she had always been full of life and good humor.

"So, what's up?" I waited, but she said nothing. "Where's Berto? Did he come with you?"

She straightened her chopsticks and fiddled with the soy sauce. "Berto is currently having sex with one of his students, I expect, who he left me for a month ago. For whom he left me, I should say." Maggie was a professor of English Literature. I think it physically hurt her to split an infinitive.

"Get out."

She shook her hand. "Can't."

"You're joking."

"Is it funny?"

"But Berto loves you."

"And says he still does. But strangely that love allows him to stick his penis in someone else. He says he cannot help himself, it is passion, it is *amore,* it is total and complete bullshit." She looked at me with eyes that had clearly run out of tears. "I have no idea what to do with myself, and the semester ended, so I just flew home. My parents don't even know I'm here yet."

The waiter came over, and we did that thing where you pretend everything is fine for the two minutes it takes to have a social exchange of information, and then dove back into the conversation.

Maggie looked a little green. Maybe sushi wasn't such a good idea.

"Are you OK? You look like you're going to throw up."

"I think I'm OK. It's like a dream or something, and not the one where Johnny Depp gets a flat tire in front of my house. I thought I knew Berto, inside and out."

I nodded. "So did I. I'm totally thrown for a loop here. It's not like him at all."

She made a face. "And yet that's how it was between us when we first met."

I remembered. Maggie had gone to Italy

for her second year of college, to learn Italian and study Dante, like you do, and came back a different woman. Not only was she speaking Italian, she was passionately in love with Berto, who'd also been on the Dante trail, and the two of them spent every possible vacation with each other until they graduated. I remembered, too, when Berto had first come to America to visit, how wonderful he was, how funny. We all fell in love with him a bit, even the guys, because he was just charming and unusual and gorgeous and completely Italian. They got married right after graduation, and Dan and I had gone to stay with them at least once a year from then on. They worked as teachers, living in tiny, ancient apartments, then gradually worked their way up until they were professors and lived in slightly larger ancient apartments in Florence. Idyllic. And now, apparently over.

Maggie was getting more pissed off. "Why is it that men get a second chance at being dickheads, and we're supposed to keep aging gracefully?"

I shrugged. "There's nothing stopping you from chasing younger men if you want to."

She sighed. "And we were trying so hard for kids for so long. I guess it's just as well we don't have any." Her eyes got shiny. "But maybe if we did, he wouldn't have fallen in love with someone else."

The sushi came. We paused to eat. She was obviously hungry, because her color got better with every eel roll.

"You know what sucks the most?" She pointed at me with her chopsticks.

I shook my head. It all seemed pretty bad.

"I can't really blame him. I mean, I can blame him, and I do blame him, for being such a selfish bastard, but when he came to tell me about it, I could see that he was having the most wonderful time. This lovely young woman is interested in him, and they're going to museums together and spending all day in bed having sex, and staying up late talking, and it's all like being twenty again. I mean, I get it, I get why that's appealing. I'm just furious that it's more appealing than protecting the feelings of the woman you've been married to for so long."

I tried to think of something to say. "Hey, maybe it will blow over, and he'll come crawling back."

She shook her head, mixing more wasabi into her little soy-sauce dish. "I don't care if he does. I'm done."

"You're just mad."

"You're right. But I plan to stay mad for a

bit and then move elegantly into disinterest. When she throws him over for someone whose stomach doesn't hang in front of his dick, he'll probably come back, but I've lost respect for him." She leaned in closer. "He dyed his hair."

"No."

"Yes. And bought a yellow Vespa."

I laughed, I couldn't help it. "No way."

"Way. He's knotting his sweater around his neck and leaping on and off the blasted thing like he's in a Fellini movie."

"Maybe he'll have a stroke and die."

"There is hope. Although, of course, then I would be heartbroken, which is the real kicker. I still love him right now, as well as hating him, and being embarrassed by him, and ashamed of him, and happy for him, and jealous of him."

I finished the last roll and signaled for another Coke. "I find it hard to believe you're happy for him at all. He's an ass-hole."

Her mouth twisted. "For sure. But I've loved him and been his best friend for so long, you know? If I put my own rage and disappointment aside for a minute, which is pretty hard, then I can see that he's happy, and I want him to be happy. While at the same time wanting him to lose control of his bowels in public." She fell silent. "It's all very hard."

And then, finally, she started to cry.

After lunch, Maggie went to her parents' house to break the news, and I headed back to the office. I was pretty upset. I've reached the age where couples whose weddings I went to are starting to get divorced. It seems to happen when the kids are in third and fourth grade, for some reason.

Here's the pattern I see, with the caveat that I won't experience it myself, seeing as my husband croaked: You get married, you love each other, you have a lot of sex, you argue occasionally, but all is well. You have babies, which we've already agreed is hard work. You pull together or apart, under the stress, and if you're lucky, it's the former. Years go by, and at first you argue about the sex you no longer have and the time you don't spend together, but then you stop missing both and start feeling relieved you don't even want it anymore. You stop telling each other what you did all day, because who gives a shit? If you hear a good joke, you don't bother retelling it. If you read a good book, you loan it to a girlfriend, because he doesn't like the same books you do anyway. And then bing, bang, bong, it's all over. Thirty-one . . . thirty-two . . . forty, fifty, sixty, dead.

When I got off the elevator, Rose was standing on her desk. Literally standing on it. I realized that in more than a decade of working at Poplar Press, I had never seen her ankles. This whole day was starting to get a little tiring.

"Rose? Is there a mouse or something?"

She shook her head. "No, Lilian. I am protesting."

"OK. Do you need support?"

"No, although you are welcome to join me."

I put down my bag. "What are we protesting?"

"They're closing the department."

I looked at her and frowned. "Which department?"

"Our department. The creative department."

"I'm sorry?"

A trace of the old Rose flashed across her face. "Lilian, please try and keep up. Miss Roberta King came down during lunch."

I felt sorry for Miss King, suddenly.

"She asked me to sit down, and then she thanked me for my decades of service and fired me. Or rather, she attempted to fire me."

"She didn't fire you?" Jesus, I'd only been gone two hours.

"Well, she did, but I didn't accept it, and still don't. I've been here longer than anyone. They can't fire me." She raised her voice at the end, and stamped her foot in its sensible shoe.

"And then what happened?"

"Then she went to the main conference room, where everyone was invited to join her." She frowned at me. "You're welcome to climb up here on the desk, but I think she'll want you with the others."

Crap. I picked up my bag. "How long ago did this all happen?"

She shrugged. "A matter of moments."

I turned and headed toward the main conference room. I half expected to see a melting giraffe or giant baby head on the way, seeing as all rules of reality appeared to be broken.

The conference room was pretty full. There aren't that many of us, but it isn't a very big conference room. Roberta had been talking when I opened the door, but she stopped and gave me a reflexive smile. I smiled back, similarly bound by centuries of social conditioning. Inwardly, I was freaking out.

I sat down next to Sasha, who was crying.

I squeezed her hand.

Roberta cleared her throat. "Glad you're here, Lilian, although it's really a very sad day. As I was just explaining to the rest of the group, management has decided to outsource all new jobs overseas. We already make extensive use of freelance writers, as you know."

Everyone turned to look at Elliot, the only person in the room with the title of writer. He blushed. "I'm more of an editor, really."

Roberta continued, "And while the fact-checking department will stay in-house, for quality-control reasons, the illustration, layout, and design departments will finish up the projects they already have and then be free to leave."

There was a long silence, then a woman who worked in layout raised her hand. "Are we free to leave before then?"

Roberta looked surprised. "Well, of course. But if you leave before you're officially laid off, you won't qualify for COBRA or unemployment benefits or . . ."

She stopped, because the woman had risen to her feet. "I don't care about that. I'm out of here," she said. "I've been saving for years, squirreling away every meager bonus, every extra hour, and now I have enough to live my dream." She gathered her stuff, her face glowing. "I am moving to Canada to raise miniature ponies. Losing my job is just the push I was waiting for."

Elliot the editor had a question. "Can you just move to Canada? Don't you need to get a visa or something?"

The layout lady looked surprised. "No. I'm Canadian." She looked at Elliot and frowned. "We slept together for six months in 2009, you didn't know that?"

He shook his head. "I knew about the ponies . . ."

The layout lady shrugged and left, and we heard her whooping as she skipped down the hall.

The children received my news with their usual brand of aplomb. Clare said yay, because she thinks work is something boring one has to do, and Annabel asked how long it would be until we ran out of money.

"A long time. I'm not going to be out of work forever, and we have some money in the bank. We're fine, don't worry." I was leaning against the kitchen counter, watching them eat PB&J as their post-school snack. Leah was picking up in their room, but I could feel her listening.

Annabel frowned. "Well, are we going to have to sell the house?"

Since when did seven-year-olds worry about this shit? When I saw little girls playing with dolls, their braided heads close together, were they actually debating the decline of the real estate market? Was Barbie about to lose the Malibu Beach House? Were bailiffs repossessing the Jeep? I felt momentarily grateful that the house was paid for, thanks to Dan's life insurance. The one good thing that came out of his death was that we weren't going to be homeless. However, heating and lighting the place was a totally different matter.

"No, we're not going to have to sell the house. Nothing is really going to change that much, to be honest, except I'm going to be around more. And I'm going to be at work for another month anyway, finishing up stuff." I hadn't had a chance to ask Roberta King about the vegetable encyclopedia, and wasn't sure if it was officially in-house or not yet. I made a note to ask her the next day.

Leah came into the kitchen but didn't meet my eye. Annabel observed this, being the tiny anthropologist she is, but for once she kept silent. She turned her attention back to me.

"Well, you can always get a job at McDonald's."

Clare perked up. "Yes! Get a job at Mc-Donald's! Then we can have free fries!"

Clare loves a McDonald's fry. It's the crack they sprinkle all over them.

"I'm not going to get a job at McDonald's. I might not even look for a job. I might just do freelance illustration."

"What's freelance? Do you work for free?" Annabel looked skeptical.

"Have you finished your snack?" She nodded. "Do you want something else?" She shook her head. "Freelance doesn't mean you work for free. It means you work for yourself."

"Where?"

I shrugged. "From here."

There was a pause. Then Clare pushed her chair back and carried her plate to the sink. "I think that sounds like a good idea. Then you will be here all the time. We can clear out the garage to make an office for you." And with this piece of inspiration, she wandered off, calling Frank to come and play. Frank often lay next to her while she played her complicated imaginary games with tiny plastic animals, and she would ask his opinion and advice now and then. I had never heard him respond, obviously, but apparently he added a lot.

Leah looked at Annabel. "Do you have

homework?"

"Just reading."

"Do you want to go and do it?"

"Sure." She got up and wandered off to her room, then came back. "Clare and Frank are being noisy. Can I read in your room?" I nodded.

Leah looked at me.

"So . . . am I out of a job?" She comes to the point, that girl.

I shook my head. "No, not now at least, and hopefully not at all. If a month or two goes by and I can't find any work, then we might need to rethink the situation, but we should be OK. I've no idea how much freelance work there is out there, and I kind of want to do a book . . ."

She raised her eyebrows at me. "What kind of book?"

"A kids' book, I guess. I don't really know." Which was true. At that moment, I really didn't know what the hell was going to happen. So I did the obvious thing: made myself a huge ice-cream sundae and called my sister.

How to Grow Garlic

Garlic is easy to grow and produces numerous bulbs after a long growing season. Not only does it taste great in butter, it's a natural insect repellent.

- Do not plant cloves from the grocery store. Firstly, they might not be the right variety for your area, and secondly they've been treated with something that makes them last longer on the shelf. This makes them surly and resistant to growing. And, frankly, who can blame them?
- Place cloves 4 inches apart and 2 inches deep, in their upright position (wide side down).
- In spring, as the weather warms up, shoots will appear and neighborhood vampires will retreat.
- To harvest, lift them carefully with a garden fork, dust them off, and let them cure in an airy, shady spot for two weeks. You can tie them on a string and hang them upside down to be sure all sides get plenty of air.
- Some people eat garlic raw, claiming it gives them eternal life or something. I think it's more likely that no one will come near them afterward, making life

just extremely peaceful rather than eternal. Totally your call.

CHAPTER 10

Rachel showed up in time for dinner, and brought Maggie. Her parents had been happy to see her, she said, sad to hear about her marriage, and ready to take out a contract on Berto.

"How hard could it be to have the Mafia bump him off? It's Italy, for crying out loud." Her dad, my father-in-law, was a practical man. (You know, it's weird. When you divorce someone, you basically cut off their whole family. You no longer have in-law status, so you no longer have in-laws. But when your husband dies, you still have your in-laws, and there isn't a revised term for them. Late sister-in-law? No, because she's not dead. Ex-mother-in-law? No, because she's still your mother-in-law, even if her son is gone. It's tricky, and a good example of an epic fail on English's part.)

The topic at hand was, "What the hell does Lilian do now?" Leah and the kids were adding their two cents.

"Maybe you should go back to school for something totally different." Rachel had brought two bottles of wine as well as Maggie, and things had gotten a little giggly.

"Such as?"

Maggie raised her hand. "How about nuclear physics?"

I shook my head. "Too much math."

"Vet?" Rachel's suggestion.

I shook my head again. "I barely keep the animals I have alive."

Clare got into it. "You could be an ice cream maker. I like ice cream."

I smiled. "I do, too, but I doubt there's much money in it."

Rachel frowned. "Tell that to Ben and Jerry."

"What about being a doctor? You're good at taking care of people." Annabel was under the table, playing with Frank.

I was surprised. "You think? No, see earlier comment about math. And besides, I'm too old to do that much school again." I stood up. "Now, ladies, it's time for your bath."

"No!" Clare tried to be fierce, but it didn't work. I went to run the bath, herding her in front of me. Maybe I should be a sheepdog. I've had plenty of practice.

Once the bath was run, with both girls in it, I wandered back to the kitchen for a fresh glass of wine. They had been plotting in my absence.

"Maggie needs to get out," announced Rachel, "and I have deemed that it shall be so."

"You've had too much to drink," I responded. "You always start talking like that when you're buzzed."

"Like what?"

"Like an English lord or something."

"Gadzooks, Lilian, you couldn't be more in error."

I raised my eyebrows. She ignored me.

"So, we are going out on the town, and Leah has graciously agreed to babysit."

I looked at Leah, who grinned at me. "Are you sure you wouldn't rather go out with them and leave me with the kids?" I said.

She grinned harder. "I don't know how to break this to you, and don't take it the wrong way, but spending an evening with three drunken middle-aged single women isn't all that appealing."

Maggie and Rachel protested. "That's just harsh!"

"Wow, that's vicious."

I laughed. "They're upset at the middle-aged part, not the drunken part." Then I shrugged. "OK, why not? But nowhere crazy, Rachel. Let's just go get a drink, or maybe coffee and pie somewhere."

Rachel put her fingertips together. "I'm way ahead of you. I have the perfect place in mind. Think of it as dessert."

It turns out they don't serve food at strip clubs. I guess they worry about slippery floors. After all, when a guy's leaping around your table dressed as a Native American, or at least a muscular person wearing a feather headdress and a small quiver for his arrow, the last thing you want is for him to slip on a potato skin. It would ruin the mood, for starters. And just think of the liability.

It had taken Rachel and Maggie twenty minutes to persuade me to go into the club, which Rachel persistently referred to as a bar. She said I had to do it, for Maggie's sake.

"She needs distraction. She needs to see other men."

"Does she need to see them naked?" We both looked at Maggie.

She shrugged. "I've never been betrayed by my husband before. I don't really know what will help. But if a young, naked man sitting on my lap might lift my spirits, then I'm willing to try it."

Rachel pointed at her, carefully. "You, madam, are a scientist."

Maggie nodded. "True story."

The clientele was female, unsurprisingly, and those videos of young girls going wild on vacation have nothing on the mostly middle-aged women yelling "Show us your cock" while falling out of their push-up bras. I stepped between a woman and a carpenter (tool belt) who was apparently fixing the leg of her chair (well, he was kneeling down) and nearly got knocked to the ground.

But I was here for Maggie, for moral support, so I found us a table next to the runway thingy, and let Rachel order us all more drinks while I surveyed the scene.

There was a lot of creativity going on. Apart from the carpenter and the Native American, there was a pilot (peaked hat and a gold-braid thong supporting a passport for coverage), a doctor (stethoscope and some carefully wound ACE bandages), and, my personal favorite, a pirate (large hat, small skull-and-crossbones flag). There were also waiters, who were wearing bow ties and boxer shorts, which actually looked sexier to me because I've never had sex with a pirate, but have frequently had sex with someone wearing boxer shorts — at least up until the last minute. They were all young and handsome, too, which didn't hurt, but again I must be missing something because several of them looked young enough to be high school students, and all I could think of was, Shouldn't they be home on a school night? And was it even legal for them to be in here?

Maggie looked a little nervous, too, but we applied ourselves to the tequila shots and eventually the place took on a homey air.

I leaned on my elbows, somewhat carefully, and shouted at Maggie.

"Tell me, are you still missing Berto, or is this helping?"

She looked thoughtful.

"I'm mostly distracted," she yelled back. "But sometimes I think of him and forget that he's a cheating sack of shit, and just wish he was here." She sighed. "It's pathetic."

A dancer appeared at the table, literally flinging his thing about, side to side. If the music hadn't been so loud, I imagine there would have been a gentle thwapping sound.

"You're going to get a bruise if you keep doing that, you know?" Rachel yelled conversationally.

"Two bruises," added Maggie. "One on

each side of your head."

He went away.

"I never found penises all that attractive per se," I shouted. "It's what's inside that counts."

"Inside the penis?" Maggie was confused.

"No, well, that counts, too, but I meant inside the person. Honestly, the handsomest penis in the world can't disguise a horrible person."

"Nope," said Rachel seriously. "Not unless it's really big."

"Right," I said, pointing my finger at her.

"And," she went on, warming to the theme, "some of the least impressive penises have turned out to be the most impressive, once they've gotten going."

"Amen, sister. I believe the phrase is 'grower, not shower.' "

"Right! It's all about hidden potential."

"Yes." I pointed the other finger. "And all this waving about can't be good for them, although at least they're getting some air."

"I'm going to be sick," Rachel said, then got up and did one of those fast but erratic walks to the bathroom, where you can see the floor going by as if there was a hole in the car floor, and suddenly you're in the bathroom and the tile comes up at you a little fast, but you're so glad to feel it.

Maggie and I waited at the table for a while, but she didn't return. It was a prime spot, and there were several clumps of women eyeing it, but we weren't moving. I got up, making Maggie promise not to pay for a lap dance, and went to find Rachel.

It wasn't hard to find her. Her long hair was streaming out from under one of the stall doors.

"Are you OK, Rach?" I asked.

The hair moved.

"I'm dead," she replied.

"I hope not, you have work tomorrow. Can you stand up, or do you need to puke some more?"

There was a pause, and the hair disappeared. "Hang on, let me do a systems check." Another pause. "I'm good. I think." I heard the lock slide back, and she appeared, looking totally fine.

"I had a little nap, I feel much better."

I raised my eyebrows at her. "On the floor?"

"Yes. It wasn't too bad. I was very tired."

"Let's go home."

She shook her head. "No, let's go eat something. I'm starving now. Let's go to Pink's and get hot dogs."

Pink's is an L.A. institution. People line up for hours for hot dogs, which, unless they're made of filet mignon, could not possibly be worth it. It's the slowest line in history. People starve to death, and their bodies are kicked aside. But at that moment, it sounded awesome.

"You're a genius, Rach."

"You are, too, but I've forgotten your name. I knew it, but then I opened my mouth and it went away."

"I'm Lilian. I'm your sister."

"That's right."

With that clarified, we gathered Maggie, headed out of the club, and went off to eat hot dogs, which at least maintained the phallic theme.

The cool night air helped a little, and we managed to wander over to Pink's without any major incidents. Maggie had reached the silent, owlish portion of her drinking, and I was feeling a little cranky. Rachel, having significantly decreased the amount of alcohol she had on board, was feeling full of beans and chatty as a jaybird.

"You could always teach art at a school. Maybe you could get a job at the girls' school, and then they could be the teacher's kids, like that girl Jessica was at our old school. I always wanted to be a teacher's kid."

"You're babbling." Her voice was starting to annoy me. "Besides, being a teacher would be fine, except there are all those kids around."

"True. How about just going all bohemian and painting wonderful pictures?"

I snorted. "Fine, but who would pay all the wonderful bills?"

"Edward! You could go out with Edward. He's rich."

"Great, so now I'm a prostitute?"

She laughed. "No! A bohemian artist with a rich boyfriend. Totally different."

I frowned at her. "And what about my daughters? Should I farm them out, too?"

We stood in line for five minutes and moved forward three places. I sulked.

Rachel spoke again. "Something will turn up. It always does. You're lucky like that."

I was feeling sick, which is probably why I lost my temper. "Lucky? In what way am I lucky? In the widowed-at-thirty-four sense? In the single-parent sense? In the unemployed sense?"

She flared up, too. "Or maybe in the no-sense sense. Why are you getting mad at me? I didn't do anything wrong. In fact, I've done everything I can to help you, and all you do is complain."

There was a pause. If, at that moment, I

had just apologized, it would probably all have been fine, but I was too far gone to save myself.

"Complain? I never fucking complain! I am so pathetically grateful to you. Everyone knows you saved my ass. Saint Rachel, she gave up her life to help her crazy sister. She took care of her crazy sister's kids for her. Poor Rachel sacrificed so much, blah, blah, blah." I may have tossed my head. I was certainly feeling like a thirteen-year-old having the third period of her life and completely losing her mind.

Rachel had gone totally white. Everyone else in the line had turned to look, with that openly interested and enthusiastic air that people in L.A. have. Either they're actors and this is raw emotion they can feed off, or they're writers and it's material. Maggie just looked glazed.

My sister was spitting mad. "You are so full of shit. I have never once, not once, asked you for thanks, or even expected it. I did for you exactly what you would have done for me. You're just pissed off because your libido woke up and you're too chickenshit to deal with it." She started to walk away, furiously, the line pivoting to watch her exit, and then turned back. "And as for the Saint Rachel thing, what about your martyr complex, you selfish bitch? Poor Lilian, lost her husband, love of her life. Well, what about me? I lost one of my best friends. What about the kids? They lost their dad. What about Maggie, eh? She's standing right there and she lost her only brother. It is not all about you, and it's about time you realized that." And with that final salvo, she really did walk away, and I stood there and realized that (a) she was totally right, (b) I was a total dickhead, and (c) Maggie had just thrown up on my shoes.

I managed to call a car and get Maggie home, and Leah and I cleaned her up with a whole packet of baby wipes and put her in the guest room. She had essentially been unconscious through the whole thing, but as I backed out of the bedroom, she called my name.

"Yeah, Mags?"

"Don't tell Berto we went to a strip joint."

I nodded. "I promise."

"Or that I puked on you."

I smiled. "OK."

She let out a little sob. "The room is going round and round, and I miss my husband."

My throat felt tight. "I know, sweetie. It'll be better tomorrow." Which was, of course, a big fat lie.

I started the next day the right way, by throwing up. I'm not a big drinker, largely because I'm not very good at it. Dan used to describe me as Fratboy's Remorse: "You're supercute, which is great, and you get drunk on two drinks, which is better, but then you get bitchy, which is not so great, and then you puke, which is a total downer. You're every guy's best dream turned worst nightmare." Then he would smile fondly, and I would give him the finger. Good times.

I tried to call Rachel as soon as I woke up, but she didn't answer. I felt awful in every way possible.

Needless to say, the kids couldn't have cared less that I was hungover. When you're rosy with the glow of new pregnancy you don't fully appreciate that the job you just signed up for involves working for socio-paths, 24-7, for the rest of your life, with no vacation days and the opposite of health benefits. I dug deep and found the super-human strength required to dress and feed the little swines.

Then I tried Rachel again. Still no answer.

Maggie stumbled out of the guest room while I was hopping around trying to get

216

my legs into my jeans, which turned out to be more physically challenging than usual. She didn't look much better than I felt, and she leaned against my bedroom door to watch me.

"Do you need help?"

I shook my head, and regretted it.

"Did I do anything really bad last night?" Her voice was hoarse.

"You don't remember?"

She shook her head, stopping just as quickly as I had. "Ow. Fuck. No. I remember the club, but that's about it. Did we eat?"

"No. We went to get a hot dog, but Rachel and I had a fight and you threw up on me, so we came home."

She shut her eyes. "Sorry."

"No big. We went to college together, remember? I believe I've thrown up on you more times than either of us can count, so one in the other direction is probably well deserved. Can I get you some coffee?"

"No, I'm not ready yet. I may never be ready. What did you and Rachel fight about? You always fight with someone when you drink, what's up with that?"

I shrugged, which wasn't much better than the head shaking. "No clue. Suppressed inner rage? Social anxiety? We fought about her being so supportive and wonderful."

"Yeah, I can see how that would rile you up." She kept swaying slowly back and forth, apparently without realizing it.

I finally got my pants on.

"I have to take the kids to school and go to work. Are you going to be OK?"

"Sure. I'm going to surgically remove my head and rinse it under the faucet, then go back to sleep."

"Good plan. I'll call you later."

We hugged, carefully trying not to wobble each other, and I bravely headed out the door, into the achingly bright and aggressive Los Angeles sunshine.

I called Rachel every hour, all day. Voice mail. In the beginning I left messages in which I babbled my apologies, but as time passed I started singing songs or making up poems. But she didn't pick up at all, and by the end of the day we still hadn't spoken. It was awful. When you're used to speaking to someone three times a day, silence can be very pointy.

When I got home, Maggie was just leaving, having finally regained control of her central nervous system. She headed off to her parents' house, and I tried Rachel's number again. Bubkes. Maybe she'd gotten hurt, or ended up somewhere unexpected. I absentmindedly made the kids their dinner and poked at mine. When someone knocked on the door, I jumped up, thinking it was her, but it was Edward. He was carrying a huge box and grinning. The girls were beside themselves, screaming and clutching at him, because they remembered what he'd promised to bring. He looked at me over their heads and smiled, and I was surprised by how glad I was to see him. He saw the dinners still uneaten on the table and spoke to the girls. "We're not opening it until you complete your dinners. Otherwise, your mother will be mad at me."

They started to whine, but he started to pick up the box again and they stopped. Besides, they liked lamb chops, so it was a win-win for them. Thirty-two seconds later, they were done. Forty-five seconds later, they had also finished their peas, and Edward was happy.

Once they had bussed their plates and pushed all the other crap on the table to one side, Edward was ready.

"Drumroll, please, Clare." He had somehow discovered Clare's secret beatboxing skills, maybe during My Little Ponies. She did an excellent drumroll.

He pulled out a stone house, about three feet high and very detailed. It was shaped like a mushroom, with little rooms and stairways inside and an attic in the spotty cap part. It was ridiculously cute. Then he pulled out a smaller box, filled with a dozen tiny fairy figures, all made of weather-resistant resin, presumably, but still remarkably detailed and colorful and, well, magical.

There was silence as the girls took it in. Clare leaned across the table and moved one of the little fairies inside the house. Then she reached over and took Edward's hand. I looked at him, but he was looking at her.

"Edward," she piped in her little voice, "this is the most awesomest, awesomest, *awesomest* thing ever. You are the nicest boy I have ever met, and next time you can play Sparkleworks." Then she dropped his hand and waited. She knew a moment when she saw one.

"Truly?" asked Edward, still looking at her and smiling.

She nodded solemnly. I literally felt a lump in my throat. Sparkleworks was Clare's favorite Little Pony. Nobody got to touch Sparkleworks.

"Thank you," said Edward. "Do you like

it, Annabel?"

Annabel nodded, utterly overcome. She had taken one of the little figurines and was turning it over in her hands. There were several boy fairies, too, which would be nice for Bash, although they looked a little like Broadway chorus dancers, rather than gnome-stomping terror machines.

All three headed to the garden, and I watched as they placed the house in the perfect spot. After a few minutes, Edward came back in. He looked ridiculously gorgeous and flushed with success.

"A triumph, I think. Do you think so?" He peered out of the kitchen window and tried not to preen.

We stood and watched. "Just promise me you'll stay until I have to send them to bed. Otherwise, I will be shit out of luck and they will try to sleep in the garden. It's a wonderful gift. You're very nice."

He turned and leaned against the sink. We were very close. I couldn't help it, I blurted, "I had a big fight with Rachel last night, and now I can't reach her and I'm worried about her." I don't know why it came out, it just did, and then I made it worse by starting to cry. He was going to think I was a complete nutcase.

He handed me a paper towel. "Why did

you fight?"

I shrugged. "Because we had too much to drink and I am an asshole."

He smiled. "Everyone is an asshole when they drink too much. Do you think she is fine and just angry with you, or do you actually think she's in trouble?"

"I don't know. She stalked off into the night, and I haven't spoken to her since."

"You fought outside?" He was confused.

I nodded, ashamed. "Yes, in the street, like teenagers, or hookers."

He made a mock shocked face at me. "I am shocked. Except not at all. Everyone does it once or twice."

"They do?"

He shook his head. "No, just teenagers and hookers, but I am trying to make you feel better." He pulled out his phone. "Why don't I try calling her, and then if she's avoiding your call, she'll answer and we'll know she's fine. And if she doesn't answer, then we can alert Interpol."

He was so calm and capable. I gave him the number. He dialed and waited.

"Hello, Rachel? This is Edward Bloem, your gardening teacher."

She was alive, that was good. However, I was clearly on her shit list, and that was bad.

"I am visiting your sister, and Lilian was

worried about you." He listened for a moment, and his mouth twitched. "I don't know if I can pass on that message verbatim. Are you sure you don't want to just speak to her?" He paused. "I'll tell her." He hung up and looked at me. "She doesn't want to talk to you, but says to tell you that she's fine."

I looked at him. "What was hard about delivering that?"

"I had to edit in English. It's not my first language, you know." He looked at me thoughtfully, and smiled slowly, his green eyes warm. He smelled of the outdoors, he was so tall and broad shouldered and so . . . male . . . in this house of women he was shockingly different. All I could think of was how much I wanted to kiss him. I was clearly losing my mind.

Needing a minute to think, I stepped closer to the sink and peered out the window to see if the children had started fighting yet, but so far peace reigned in the fairy kingdom.

"Do you know," continued Edward in a conversational tone, "that the side of your neck has a curve like the inside of a shell, and that the place where you hair touches it is where I would most like to kiss you?"

I flushed. And someone's voice said, "Go

ahead," and it was my voice, amazingly, as apparently my mouth had seized control of my brain.

Edward leaned forward and kissed the side of my neck. It was the most romantic moment of my life for years, and I literally felt my knees buckle. He put his hands on my shoulders and turned me to face him, but it was me who leaned harder into the kiss, me who put my hands on his hips and pulled him closer. And it was definitely me who forgot in this sudden swoony blast of lust that I had kids, a dead husband, a lost job, and a furious sibling. All I could think about was the taste of him, the strength of his hands on my back, and the shocking awareness that I wasn't dead from the waist down.

Edward pulled back and looked at me, his pupils as dilated as mine were. This wasn't just a kiss, and we both knew it: We were going to be lovers, we were going to undress each other and taste every inch of skin, we were going to please each other over and over again. It had been so long since my body had felt this aroused; I was drunk with anticipation. He could see it in my face, and his skin flushed, his mouth was hot on mine again, his hands tightening in my hair. This is one advantage experience has over youth:

You know that it's real, you know you want this man inside you, you know it's going to happen, and it's as certain a knowledge as any in human experience. There is nothing, *nothing,* as powerful as the first hour of a sexual relationship. It's like rocket fuel. Edward started to move away, tugging my hand, pulling me toward the kitchen table, starting to push things aside.

Which is exactly when I heard Clare calling from outside. "Mom! Annabel told me my fairy was badly painted!"

We had about fifteen seconds before the kids came roiling into the room. We looked at each other, and Edward said something in Dutch that sounded deeply, deeply frustrated.

I laughed, shakily. "Shit, I have kids."

The color was still receding from his face, but he gathered himself enough to reply, "I am ashamed to say I had completely forgotten them." He was still holding my hand, and he quickly pulled me to him, kissing me hard one more time and whispering against my mouth, "We are not done, this is a promise." He bit my lip, gently, and released me. I was aching, literally aching with desire, but as the kids crashed in, it just . . . evaporated. It was shocking, but it had to be that way, and I knew it.

Clare was still pissed at her sister and didn't see anything strange about two adults standing in the middle of the room with red faces. "Annabel said this fairy doesn't have a nice dress on, which is totally untrue."

Annabel was behind her and stopped inside the door to take in the scene. She knew she'd walked in on something, but she didn't know what. Her eyes narrowed, but she was also overtired and not willing to parse the social indicators at that moment.

"I didn't say that, exactly."

Clare changed tack. "I'm taking the fairy house to bed."

I shook my head. "No, you're not. However, it is time for you guys to get ready for bed. Edward was just leaving."

He smoothly took my suggestion, reaching for his jacket. "I will see you girls in class on Saturday, and you can tell me if you still like the fairy house." He turned to me. "Good-bye, Lilian. We will speak soon." He didn't need to say anything else. We were still both trembling. Besides, Clare chose that moment to throw herself at him and thank him about a million times, hugging his legs and gazing up at him. She's effusive, I'll give her that.

I switched on my autopilot and started bedtime. The sudden downshift from desire to domestic felt painfully familiar. There are so many times when what I want to do conflicts exactly with what I have to do. I want to sleep, but I must get up and help a child with a nightmare. I want to go lie in the park and read a book, but I must push a swing instead, must adjudicate little fights, must stay focused when all I want to do is daydream and drift.

After Dan's death, I would have happily starved myself to death but there were *these children in the house* . . . they needed feeding, they needed clothing, they couldn't have cared less that I was grief-stricken. They just peed and pooped and cried and ate and slept as if nothing at all had happened. Often, in the hospital, I would forget they were alive. I was living shallowly, refusing to eat, refusing to drink, aching to just let go and spiral slowly off the cliff like a scrap of vellum, transparent. Some days I remembered they were out in the world somewhere, and part of my heart would ache for them, shame slowly chilling me, a colder breeze on an already cold day. And frequently I would wish them dead, too, because then I could just shut my life down and stop breathing. I never told anyone that

I wished for that, not even Dr. Graver, and sometimes now my heart clenches in case God heard my wish and wrote it down somewhere.

Once I was out of the hospital, and mostly accepting the fact that I had to keep going, I found the mundane repetition actually helped. I knew how to do this stuff, the stuff I had always done without Dan. I mean, he helped, but I was used to flying solo as a parent and could handle it. It was harder to do the many things we had done together, or that he had always done. I have a friend in AA who calls it "sober reference," the concept that you need to do things sober that you used to do drunk. I don't have a snappy name for it, but I had to do things sadly that I used to do happily, and that slowly became acceptable. Somehow, I continued breathing, and here I was years later, still alive.

The kids talked about the fairy house all through their bath. Apparently, I hadn't been sufficiently appreciative, because I heard all about its wonders and secret rooms through the drying off, the pajama choosing, the stories, and on until it was time to turn out the light.

"And if you look at the back of the bedroom, there's a little closet door, and inside there is an actual closet with teeny-tiny hangers painted in there, with very small clothes on them."

"They're really small."

"But you can put a fairy in there."

"Why would you do that?" I stroked Clare's hair from her forehead, wondering how she'd gotten chocolate pudding into her hairline and how I'd missed it in the bath. I scratched at it until she batted my hand away.

"Well, I did it so my fairy could jump out at Annabel's fairy, but I guess you could do it for other reasons."

I shut the door, then opened it the obligatory three inches, and wandered into the living room. Frank had poured me a glass of cabernet and was readying the massage table . . . kidding. Without the distraction of the kids, my body was starting to complain about its recent disappointment. What the hell? it was saying. Why did you start that and then not finish it? Jeez. Strangely, I wished Dan was there to talk to, but he wasn't. He was dead, dead, deadedy dead. And Rachel wasn't even talking to me.

I tried her again. This time she answered.

"OK," she said, "it's been twenty-four hours since you were an asshole. I am ready to accept your apology."

"I'm very, very sorry."

"I expect you are. Tell me some more."

I smiled. "I really, really am the biggest dickhead. I am totally grateful for all you've done for me and don't for a minute think you are a saint or anything. I have no idea where any of that came from."

She sighed. "Fine, it's over. But I think it's healthy for us to occasionally air our inner grievances, however weird and unprovoked they might be. Next time, let's do it indoors, though, agreed?"

I nodded, not that she could see me. "Did you get home OK?"

"I did. I realized once I had stomped off that I had left you in the middle of the city with a very drunken Maggie, but I could hardly go back after my grand exit. Did she throw up on you?"

"Yes."

"Good. So, what's happened since then? Why was Edward with you? What happened?"

"He came over to drop off a fairy house."

She snorted. "If I had a dime for every time a guy used that excuse . . ."

"And we nearly had sex on the kitchen table."

There was a pleasingly lengthy pause. I'd actually surprised her.

"Wow. Way to bury the lede."

I shrugged. "You were the one who encouraged me to broaden my horizons."

"True," she replied. "But I didn't think you'd go all the way on the first date."

"Why not? You always do."

She laughed. "Well, how else would I know if I wanted a second date?" She sighed. "But presumably you remembered you had children just in time, and didn't actually do it?"

"Exactly." I sighed, too. "Now I'm just all confused and stressed-out. This is exactly why I don't want to start dating again." I plucked irritably at a loose thread on the sofa. "I don't want to do this."

"You were honestly planning on spending the remainder of your life celibate and unattached? You're only in your thirties. You could live another sixty years."

I leaned back on the sofa and looked around my living room. Everything was as it always was. I had invested a lot in creating routine and predictability in my life since Dan died. I tried to explain it to Rachel. "It's not that I don't find Edward attractive. I assure you, I really do. I honestly forgot the details of my life for about five very hot minutes this evening, and that's really compelling because, let's face it, those details aren't exactly the stuff of legend. If it were just me, then sure, I'd already have broken the kitchen table, but it's not just me, and by the time it is, it will be too late anyway." I felt my throat starting to close up, and got irritated. "And now I feel like crying, and I don't even know if I'm sad because I didn't get to sleep with Edward or because I don't get to sleep with anyone, or if I'm just still sad because I miss Dan so much that it's like another person in the room the entire time. I don't need that kind of confusion, Rachel. I want to know what I'm crying about, get it?"

She sounded sympathetic. "Hashtag life goals: To know what I'm crying about."

"Yes. Exactly."

"Shall I change the subject so we can talk about something else until you feel OK enough to hang up?"

I loved her so much. "Yes, please." I sniffled a bit, and wiped my nose on my sleeve.

She took a breath. "I was thinking about adopting a cat. What do you think?"

HOW TO GROW A PUMPKIN

You need a spot with lots of room and plenty of sun. And so do pumpkins.

- The soil will warm more quickly and the seeds will germinate faster if you plant them in little hills. You have to make the little hills, they don't sell them at the garden store.
- Plant the seeds inch deep into the hills (4 to 5 seeds per hill). Space hills 4 to 8 feet apart.
- When the plants are 2 to 3 inches tall, thin to 2 to 3 plants per hill by snipping off unwanted plants without disturbing the roots of the remaining ones.
- If your first flowers aren't forming fruits, that's normal. Both male and female blossoms need to open, get to know one another, maybe hang out and watch a movie and, just, you know, chill.

CHAPTER 11

In the morning, after a night of dirty dreams, I felt cranky. Annabel also woke up on the wrong side of the bed, and the two of us growled at each other all morning as we got ready for school.

She needed the pink T-shirt.

Not that pink T-shirt.

Not that one, either.

Not that one, either. God, Mommy, the one with the horse.

Yes, that one.

It was dirty.

Tears.

Why was nothing ever clean in the house? Why did no one care about her? Why was I so busy with other things (said with deadly emphasis) that I didn't do the laundry?

How about this other T-shirt with a horse?

No.

Or this other pink one? No horse, but pink.

No.

Firm voice: Choose the shirt you want. I'm going to make breakfast. What would you like?

Nothing.

Toast?

Nothing.

Eggs?

Nothing. I'm going to starve because no one cares.

I care. I want to make you breakfast. Clare, what would you like?

Pancakes.

Pancakes it is.

I don't like pancakes. I want eggs.

No, I'm making pancakes.

Tears.

Stomping to the kitchen. (Me)

Wailing in the hall. (Her)

Clanging on pans. (Me)

Wailing outside the kitchen door. (Her)

Throwing up from stress. (Frank)

Then I had to get them ready to leave the house, which involved shoes.

If they repealed the wearing of shoes, I would run into the streets and set off fireworks. I own three pairs of shoes, my children own about a dozen between them but will only wear one favored pair at a time, and those they like to hide each afternoon when they come home from school. Sometimes they only hide one of them, so I can be filled with hope when I see it, only to be dashed against the rocks of despair when I realize the other one is nowhere to be found.

It's these small periods of intense aggravation with my kids that make me wish I had died and not Dan. Ten minutes later, the feeling has gone away, but in the heat of an argument with my seven-year-old about which socks she will consent to put on, I am possessed by a depression so pure and all-consuming that life seems unbearable. When I hear about a woman beating her children, I often think the sentence "But those aren't the *Dora* ones" must have been the last thing she heard before the red mist took away her sanity.

Eventually I dropped them off at school, and on the way to work I decided I was going to put the whole Edward kiss thing out of my mind. I was not interested in Edward, or any romance of any kind. I would work like a fiend all day, tidying up my projects, clearing out my desk, and looking for another job. I would eat a salad for lunch. I would lose ten pounds. I would use the electric toothbrush for the *whole two minutes.* I would immerse myself in self-care.

■ ■ ■ ■

When I got to work, however, Edward had sent me flowers.

I actually smelled them before I saw them. I'd mentioned to Edward how sad I thought it was that roses didn't have much scent anymore, and he had talked about heirloom roses and some other things I didn't understand.

Normally men don't really listen all that well. You can mention that you like apricots, or The Cure, or kittens, and it just goes out of their heads the minute it's out of your mouth. I personally seize on these clues about people. For example, I know that Sasha loves the smell of violets, and that Rose enjoys novels of a bodice-ripping nature and walks for exercise and has a Siamese cat called Dr. Oodles, but if I'd asked Dan what his best friend had studied at college — where they were roommates — he would have had no idea.

Anyway, Edward was apparently different, because he'd sent me a gorgeous bouquet of roses that filled the room with an intense, sweetly lemony, rosy smell that was mind-blowing. The roses themselves were a rich cream and stuffed with petals that made them look like roses in paintings.

Sasha was looking at me.

"Well, you must have done something pretty amazing last night. I've been sketching these since I got in. They're the most gorgeous Madame Hardys I've seen in a long time." I could see she had also been getting her shit together; there were open cartons on her desk, and she'd brought her portfolio to the office.

"Aren't they roses?" I was bending down, sniffing deeply. I looked for a card.

Sasha laughed. "The name of the rose is Madame Hardy. It's a damask rose, and one of the most famous old roses available these days. Someone knows their flowers."

There didn't appear to be a card. Hmm. That was a little presumptuous.

I turned to Sasha. "Since when do you know anything about roses?"

"Since you and I did rock, paper, scissors last year for who got to do the third edition of *Kittens and Puppies,* and I lost. I got *Roses of the World, Second Edition.*"

"Oh, yeah."

I looked at the roses. "Well, whoever sent them didn't include a card, so who knows."

"Right, because you're interested in several hot horticulturalists right now, and it could be any of them."

"I have no idea what you're talking about." I closed my eyes and sniffed.

"Lilian, when someone uses the word *interesting* about a guy more than four times in one conversation, nobody thinks she actually means interesting. You might as well wear a T-shirt saying, I'M HOT FOR TEACHER."

I didn't want to dignify that with a response, and, luckily, the phone rang.

"Hello?"

"Did you get my flowers?" Edward's voice was deep, and his accent seemed heavier on the phone. I flushed.

"Oh, they're from you?"

He laughed. "Let me clarify. I sent old roses. Any other flowers you have must be from one of your other admirers."

God, he was annoyingly together. Another man might have sputtered a bit, but Mr. Confident just rolled right over my rudeness.

He cleared his throat. "You did get them, though?" His voice wobbled a bit, and suddenly I felt OK. Romance in the abstract was not interesting, but Edward himself was.

I smiled. "Yes, they're right in front of me, and they smell wonderful. Thank you very much."

I could hear him smiling, too. "You're

welcome. How was the rest of your evening?" His voice dropped a little. "I had trouble getting to sleep, I will admit."

And then, just as suddenly, I was anxious again. I was such a mess. I was giving myself emotional whiplash.

"It was fine. I talked to Rachel for a long time."

"You made peace?"

"Yes, totally."

"Can you have lunch today?"

Aargh. "Um . . . I don't know. We actually all got laid off a couple of days ago, and I'm trying to . . ." I paused, and smelled the roses again. "I don't know . . ."

His voice was calm. "How about just coffee? Not like last night . . . just coffee, OK?"

"OK." I told him where the office was. I could always just tell him we couldn't see each other anymore. I turned to my desk and ignored the scent of roses as I cleaned out drawer after drawer.

I was actually crouched under the desk, looking for a quarter, when Edward walked into my cubicle. What's worse, rather than getting down on my knees and being sensible about it, I had stayed in my chair and bent down under the desk to reach the coin, which, of course, hadn't worked, so I was actually semi-stuck and refusing to admit it. Let's just say it wasn't my best angle.

"Lilian?" His voice was unmistakable, so of course I backed up too fast and clonked my head.

At least he looked amused.

"I thought I recognized your . . . uh . . . shoes." He grinned. Was there nothing that could throw this guy?

"Are you the one who sent the roses?"

Edward swung around and smiled at Sasha. "That was me," he said, stepping forward. "I am Edward Bloem, and you are . . . ?"

"Sasha." They shook hands, and then he turned back to me, holding out his hand. I took it.

"Shall we?" He tugged me closer and turned back to my friend. "It was a pleasure meeting you, Sasha." She pulled a "he's hot" face behind his back, and I pretended not to notice.

He kept holding my hand as we walked to the elevator. He held it in the elevator, he held it on the street, and he was still holding it when I stopped walking.

"I'm freaking out," I said. It just came out. It was either stop walking and tell the truth or kick him in the backs of the knees and run for it.

He stepped closer to me and looked serious. "You are? Shall I stop holding your hand?" Because he still hadn't let it go.

I shook my head, then nodded, then shook it again. "I don't know. I don't know what's going on. I'm freaking out. I can't really express it any better than that. I wasn't looking for anything. I was doing fine. And now you're here and last night happened, and now I don't know if I'm fine anymore."

He didn't say anything, but he let go of my hand and looked around. There was a diner across the street. "Let's go in there and talk, OK? We can have milkshakes."

I wasn't sure how he knew about my milkshake thing, but, honestly, I could be on the verge of death and someone could suggest a milkshake and I'd rally just long enough to suck it down.

We crossed the street, and, of course, I wished I were still holding his hand.

We sat across from each other in the booth and waited silently until the milkshakes came. Then we both blew the straw wrappers at each other, which eased the tension a little.

"Can I talk first?" he asked, and then went ahead. "I was also not looking for anything. I was also fine. But from the first time I saw you, I knew I wanted to get to know you, to learn about you. You are very beautiful, which you know, but you also have a . . . something." He blushed. "Something that is apparently making me incapable of speech." He took a breath. "But I know your situation makes it difficult. You have children. You are a widow. Last night was . . . deeply distracting, but I'm a grown man, not a teenager. I can wait until you are ready." He sat back and took a long sip of milkshake.

I looked at him and fought with myself.

He smiled. "Why don't you just tell me what you're thinking, Lilian?"

"It's very muddled."

He shrugged. "Tell me anyway."

"I want to go to bed with you."

He burst out laughing.

I continued, "But I also want to run away and never set eyes on you again. I want you so much, I really do. I'm not a teenager, either, and I know how it would be." We were both blushing now, and he reached across the table and took my hand again, his thumb rubbing across my palm. "But just when I think it's really as simple as that, I start to panic at the thought of what it would mean, to be with someone." A sudden thought struck me, and my blush deepened. "Unless you're not looking for . . . maybe you just want to . . ." Scratch

243

that earlier comment about not being a teenager.

He grinned at me. "You are funny. No, I'm not looking to just 'hook up' — I think is the phrase? We could, of course, if that's what you want . . ." His eyes gleamed at me. "But I don't think I would be satisfied with that." He leaned across the table and lowered his voice. "I want to take you to bed and drive every last bit of sadness out of you. I want to make you happy, Lilian." He took his hand away and turned up his palms. "This is not normal for me, either. Normally, I would ask you out to dinner, politely, and maybe we would have a meal or two before I would see if you would let me kiss you, and then maybe we would be lovers, or maybe not. This isn't like that, I'm sorry."

I looked down at the table and tried to work out what I was feeling. Then I realized what it was.

"I'm hungry," I said. "Can we order?"

Unsurprisingly, I felt better once I was eating. We'd both ordered burgers, and they were really hitting the spot. There had been some mutual but unspoken agreement to talk about something else, and he was telling me about his family.

"It is hard. My family all basically work in the same business, and my eldest sister runs the Bloem Company now, so one of the reasons I took this job for a year was to get some space. Amsterdam is a small city, and we saw each other a great deal. They were very critical when my marriage broke up."

I thought about this. "Was it a messy divorce?"

He made a face. "Is there another kind? It was civilized. I feel bad for my son, of course. I've missed a lot of his life after his mother and I separated."

"How old was he when you guys split up?"

"Six. But we had been living apart for a year before we actually split up, and I was working out of the country a lot before that." He looked sad. "I doubt my divorcing his mother made much of an impact on him." He sat back, ready to change the subject. "What will happen with your work now?" He smiled a small smile. "Who will be drawing our vegetables?"

"I'm not sure about the vegetable book, to be honest. We only found out about being laid off a couple of days ago, and nothing's very clear yet." I sipped my milkshake and pondered. "Maybe part of the reason I'm so stressed-out about, you know, you and me, is that everything seems to be happening all at once."

He nodded. "I understand that. But sometimes that's just what happens, right? Like one day it's winter and everything is brown, and two days later it's spring and everything is bursting into bud and flower all at once. Once nature gets an idea in her head, she tends to run with it, no?"

I smiled at him. "Are you saying we're like spring? Just a natural phenomenon?"

He called for the check and smiled back at me. "No, just saying that maybe it's OK to let nature call the shots once in a while."

In honor of that thought, I let him hold my hand all the way back to the office. I still wasn't sure what the fuck was going on, but I decided to just sit with it for a while and see what happened. Something was bound to. It always did.

MAKING PEACE WITH INSECTS

Try to peacefully coexist with ants in the garden as (a) they are beneficial insects and (b) they outnumber you by a factor of about a billion. Use old melon rinds to attract them away from your vegetable beds.

- Aphids on your garden plants can be knocked off with frequent, strong streams of water from the garden hose. Try it, it's fun.
- If you notice yellow-and-black striped Colorado potato beetles or the metallic blue green Japanese beetles crawling on your plants, put down a drop cloth and, in the early morning, when they're most active, shake them off and dump them into a bucket of soapy water.
- Herbs can be used for pest control. Wormwood, yarrow, santolina, tansy, mint, and lavender are traditional moth repellents. Oil of rosemary can also be effective.

CHAPTER 12

That night, several hours after the kids were supposedly asleep, I heard Annabel crying and went to investigate. She was sitting up in bed, looking at something on her lap. By the night-light I could see she was really distressed, so I picked her up and carried her into my room. She brought the thing she'd been looking at, and it turned out to be a photo album I hadn't seen before. I smoothed the tear-damp hair from her cheeks and tucked it behind her ears.

"What's that, honey? What's the matter?"

She didn't say anything, just buried her head in my shoulder and handed me the album. I opened it, and frowned.

"Who helped you put this together?"

"Leah. Ages ago. We went through the baby box, and I picked out the pictures I wanted, and she helped me stick them in. Clare has one, too, but it's all Frank."

I looked at her. "You mean, like a wedding album?" She smiled, briefly, but her face was still drawn.

I turned the pages of her album, a little confused. Mostly it was pictures of her. As a younger kid, swinging on a swing, walking away down the street, being thrown in the air, laughing, on a pony, that kind of thing. There were one or two of Clare, very small, being cuddled, with Annabel peering at her. She was in every one, though.

I clutched at straws. "Does this make you sad because you miss being smaller?"

She looked at me, and, as usual, I got the sense she was suppressing a sigh. She shook her head, and the tears started again. "No, you're not looking at it properly."

I looked again, but I was missing it. I shook my head and looked at her. "Can you tell me about it? Why does it make you sad?"

"It makes me happy and sad."

She lay back on the pillow, her soft hair curving under her cheek, so lovely and small and pulled into herself that I nearly started crying, too. She had always been so close to Dan, and it sucked that he wasn't here to help her with this sadness, although, of course, if he were here, maybe she wouldn't be so sad.

She sat up, suddenly, and in an angry voice pointed to the pictures.

"These are pictures of me and Daddy. Can't you see him? They're all pictures of me and Daddy." Then she threw herself down again and really did start crying in earnest. I looked again.

And this time I saw him. In every picture he was holding her hand, or pushing the swing, or guiding the pony. Just his hands. Or part of his arm. His shoulder she was peering over, his neck she was snuggled into. His hands that had just released her into the sky. I had taken the pictures, of course, and had been focusing on her, not him. But he had been there, in all of them. Little pieces of Daddy.

"That's all there is. He's all gone." A whisper.

I stroked her hair and let her cry.

"Why aren't there any pictures of him around? Don't you miss him?" She was upset with me, but it was difficult. She knew I wasn't to blame for him being gone, but she wanted someone to be responsible, someone that wasn't her. She turned her head to look at me. "I can't remember his face! I was too small and my brain didn't work so well, and I didn't keep track of him." She sobbed.

Oh, crap. She was right, there weren't any pictures. Actually, there were a few family shots, but they were higher on bookcases, at my eye level. I didn't want to turn the house into a shrine, hadn't wanted to be reminded, at every turn, of what I'd lost, but I realized I had accidentally stolen something from Annabel, let her memories of her dad's face fade in a way that made her feel guilty. Rachel had been completely right, after all. I was a totally selfish cow.

I looked at the clock: 11:00 P.M. And a school night, too. I got up.

"Wait there, honey."

I fetched my computer, and some hot chocolate for her. For an hour we sat there together and went through every photo I had of Dan, and there were hundreds, thanks to digital photography. I showed her pictures of us together while I was pregnant, photos of his face pressed against my ridiculous belly, full of her, pictures of him holding her as a baby where you could see the love and amazement on his face. She picked out the ones she wanted, dozens of them, and I made them into a photo book. And we talked about Dan. About how much I'd loved him, and how much he'd loved her, and how much we both missed him.

"Clare doesn't remember him." She was calmer now, better.

I shrugged. "How could she? She was only

really, really tiny when he died, so she never knew him. It's not her fault."

She smiled at me. "I know. I love Clare. I'm just sorry she didn't know him."

I smiled back at her. "But we did, and that's good."

She nodded, and her eyelids finally started to droop. "Can I just sleep here?"

I closed the computer and settled her down, pulling the sheet over her and stroking her back. I watched her face smooth out in sleep, her eyebrows just like Dan's, her cheeks like Rachel's, her mouth totally her own, having no precedent any of us could remember. And for a while after she was asleep, snoring softly, her face totally relaxed, I sat and watched her, trying to atone for being so dense.

Then I carefully got up, pausing to get a glass of wine from the kitchen as I carried the computer to the front room. Then I sat there and went through the photos myself, this time the ones of us together, before Annabel. He had been so handsome, my husband. I had forgotten. Twenty-four when we met, only thirty-nine when he died, and so healthy and full of life. After I'd recovered from the shock of his death, I'd focused on moving forward, trying to show everyone that I had it together, that they could stop worrying now. Nothing to see here, I got it, move along please. My primary feeling, after coming off the psych ward, was embarrassment.

I had always been the practical one, the one who could be relied upon in a crisis. But on the day of the accident, I had completely lost my mind. Stark raving mad. Screaming in the street, running to the car, climbing onto his broken lap, slapping his bloody face, begging him to wake up. The EMTs gently tried to pull me away, but I wouldn't be budged. It was clear he was dead, some piece of car had pinned him to the seat, a slight but deadly shard of metal instantly killing him. He didn't suffer, didn't suffer, so quick they said, so quick. Never knew what hit him, they said. She hit him, I yelled, running after the crying teenager in the other car, she hit him, dragging her to the ground, she hit him, kicking her.

Then they took me away and medicated the shit out of me. I made it through the funeral, more or less, but after that I collapsed and they folded me up and put me away for a couple of months. I don't remember any of it, which is probably good. The kid driving the other car is going to be seeing my blood-streaked face forever, and for that I give zero fucks.

And now, as I looked at Dan's lovely face, intact, alive, but trapped in the photograph, I missed him so much I could barely breathe. I had let Annabel down so badly by falling apart. One minute you're finger painting and eating goldfish, and then you come home from preschool and Daddy's dead and Mommy can't see you right now, sweetie . . . and can't see you for *nearly three months,* and the baby's crying, weaned overnight because Mommy's too medicated to nurse, and there's Grandma and Aunty Rachel, and they're crying, too, and what the hell had she done? What did that feel like to her, just three, old enough to know what blame was? We were teaching her to share. To take some little responsibility for her toys, her dog, to know that things she did had *consequences.* I cried and looked at photos and drank wine in a great sodden lump of self-pity and shame and felt like I'd been planning to cheat on my husband and children simply by being attracted to Edward. In the space of an hour, that attraction had been scorched under the hot lights of remorse and responsibility, and it was going to take more than spring to revive it.

Eventually, I fell asleep, and when I woke up in the morning, I felt like flash-fried shit. It was awesome.

■ ■ ■ ■

Once I was at work, I called Rachel and told her about Annabel. I heard her voice break, but, as always, she surprised me by being more concerned about me than she was about anything else.

"Does this mean you won't keep seeing Edward?" She answered her own question, "You won't, will you? You're going to just pull back into your shell."

I doodled on a piece of paper. Boxes in boxes. "The kids come first, Rachel, they always will. I need to focus on Annabel, on getting a new job, on getting things stabilized, OK? Edward will understand."

"And what about you? What about letting yourself be happy?"

I frowned. "I am happy. Things are fine. I can always date later on."

"Are you going to tell him?"

I nodded. "I sent him an e-mail this morning. It's already done."

"You sound like Clare."

"There are worse things to be."

"True," she said, and sighed. "OK, I'll see you at class tomorrow. I'm sorry, Lili."

I was brisk. "Nothing to be sorry for, Rach. It's just the way it is."

255

And then I hung up and got on with my day. Nothing to see here. Move along.

HOW TO GROW LETTUCE

Before you even *think* about planting lettuce seeds, make sure your soil is prepared. It needs to be loose and well drained, and you should treat it to a little organic matter a week or so before planting.

- Lettuce seeds are very, very small, so make sure your bed is well tilled, as clumps will frustrate the lettuce's best efforts. If you're nearsighted, make sure you have your glasses on. I mean, really, these seeds are *small.*
- Once they start popping up, thin them out to the proper spacing:
  Leaf lettuce: Plant 4 inches apart
  Cos and loose-headed types: Plant 8 inches apart
  Firm-headed types: Plant 16 inches apart
- You can sow additional seeds every two weeks for continuous harvest. Assuming you can remember where you put the seed packet, in which case you're a more organized person than I am.
- You can tell when your lettuce needs water just by looking at it. If it's droopy and exhausted give it a little drink, it'll perk right up. Unless it's

truly depressed, in which case just hang out close by until it feels better.

- Harvest leaf lettuces by simply removing the outer leaves first so the inner leaves can keep growing.

CHAPTER 13
THE THIRD CLASS

Surprisingly enough, and despite my dark mood, the next gardening class was a roaring success. We were all happy to see our little plots, and delighted to see tiny shoots popping up all over the place. I've taken my kids to Disneyland, and the screams of delight at the botanical garden when they saw that actual plants were growing beat the happiest place on earth, hands down. To be fair, it wasn't as outrageous as when Clare saw Ariel across Main Street in Disneyland and screamed so hard they alerted security, but that was an extreme case. (Side note: If you want to see something impressive, watch Disneyland turn into a Jerry Bruckheimer movie when they think a kid is being snatched. Guys with guns drop out of the trees, dwarves pull Kalashnikovs, and Cinderella assumes a Jedi fighting stance. OK, I'm exaggerating, but they do take it very seriously.)

My tomato plants were growing, my corn had put out new leaves, and Rachel's lavender was growing nicely. Gene and Mike were preening themselves over their lettuces, and Eloise and Frances were nonchalant about the fact that each and every seed they'd planted had come up.

Edward had gathered us into a circle. I looked at my feet, realized I'd had those particular boots since Dan was alive, and started looking at the trees instead. Edward had sent me an e-mail in response to mine, and it said simply, "I will wait for you. I am a patient man, and you are very special." What an asshole. I listened to his voice and tried not to feel sorry for myself.

"Today is a very exciting day, because we are going to enlist the help of Mother Nature's wonder workers."

Clare turned to me and hissed in the worst and loudest stage whisper in the world, "Worms, Mom, he's talking about worms!"

Edward laughed. "Clare is right. I am talking about worms. Earthworms are one of the most important allies of the gardener. Not only do they aerate the soil simply by moving about, but as they digest organic matter, such as old plant material, or kitchen scraps, they produce worm tea, which is one of the most potent fertilizers available to us."

Gene, the retired banker, clearly had a mental disconnect. "Worm tea? How do they manage that with no hands?"

We all got the same image, of worms trying to manipulate a teapot, not to mention the hot kettle. It was a disturbing moment for all of us, I think.

Thank goodness Clare was going to public school. "It's worm *pee.* I don't know why they call it *tea.* It's just *pee.*"

Edward grinned and nodded. "Worms exude liquid waste, essentially their pee, and it's very rich in nutrients. It's so strong, you have to water it down a lot. Otherwise, it would burn the roots of your plants."

"And how do we get this pee?" Angie was as practical as ever, keeping one eye on Bash as he did speed laps around the garden. It was like taking a small greyhound, in a Transformers T-shirt, out for a run. "I assume we don't catheterize them."

"Too fiddly," chimed in Rachel.

"They wouldn't like it," added Eloise. "They're very private creatures."

Edward remained calm. "We don't. They give it to us. All we do is build them homes and give them food."

And with that, he pointed to the stack of

boxes over on one side of the garden. "So let's build."

While I dream of a cottage in the country, or an apartment overlooking Central Park, apparently worms dream of black plastic bins on stilts. They were pretty heavy, so Impossibly Handsome Bob was enlisted. He threw them about like egg boxes.

Gene and Mike were already unpacking their worm farms and continuing to develop their strange father-son/banker-surfer relationship. You would never have put them together, and if it weren't for this class, they probably never would have met, but somehow they meshed perfectly. Also, Gene had brought us both news of his new grandchild *and* cupcakes.

"The frosting is pink, in honor of little Emily, who really is the most perfect baby in the world."

He showed us pictures of the usual Winston Churchill look-alike, and we all oohed appropriately. He even gave us gory details of the labor and knew the right weight and length, for which I had to give him props. Even my late husband, who was actually there in the room both times, could never remember what the girls weighed, or anything like that. He complained it was like asking a soldier to remember what caliber weapon he got shot with, as the trauma of childbirth had wiped his brain clean, but I reminded him I was the one who'd gotten shot. Whatever, he was not a numbers guy. But Gene got it all on the nose, and handed out cupcakes with abandon.

He also asked us for a favor.

"I want to put together a scented garden for my wife, to . . . uh . . . for my wife." He was blushing. "While she's away . . . as a surprise. I got all the plants and stuff. Edward helped me. I was wondering if any of you would like to come to my house and help me put it in. I'll get pizza, and there's a play set for the kids."

"I'm in," said Mike, somewhat unnecessarily.

"Me, too, and Bash," Angie added. I nodded, and in the end, we were all on board. What an amazing gardening class/activity team we'd turned out to be. Then we got back to the job at hand — worm housing.

Putting the worm bins together turned out to be fun. They slotted together very easily, basically two deep trays on legs, one that nestled inside the other. Meanwhile, the kids helped Lisa to soak blocks of some kind of fiber stuff to make bedding for the worms, and we all looked curiously at the little linen sacks that presumably held our tiny helpers.

Once they were all set up, with their moist bedding in place, we opened the little bags and tipped in a wriggling mass of tiny red worms. I was a little disappointed, as I had been expecting the standard earthworm, long and fat with those weird little bands of whatever it is.

"Red wigglers," Lisa informed us, "are the most popular worm for this job."

"Did you know," chimed in Annabel, eager to share her worm expertise, "that you can't really cut them in two and make two worms?"

"Nope," agreed Clare, "that is an old woman's big fat lie."

I started to correct her but lost motivation halfway.

Lisa obviously had more patience for my kids than I do. "You are right, although a worm can survive being sliced in two, under the correct circumstances. Basically, a worm has a brain and two hearts, a major one and a minor one. If you cut it in half and one half has the major heart and the brain, then that half will survive. If you cut it in half and one half has the brain and the minor heart and the other has the major heart, then both will die."

To which there was nothing to be said,

but it was good to know if I needed to do an emergency worm bisection a very small X-ray machine would be a must-have.

Once the bins were set up side by side under a canopy that Bob had built, we all retired to our little areas to weed and examine and tidy and, basically, chat.

Edward came over to talk to me about my Three Sisters garden. It was a pity, but clearly my body hadn't received the memo from my brain about not being interested in Edward anymore, because as soon as he drew near, I could smell the scent of his skin and found myself watching his mouth, his hands. I chastised myself and told myself to pull it together. It didn't work, but it made me feel worse about myself, so, you know, score.

"So, last week you planted the first sister, the one that takes the longest to grow and provides shade for the other two — the corn."

I nodded. I was very proud of my little corn sprouts, although I couldn't yet imagine that they were going to turn into those giant swaying stalks I saw on the Green Giant cans.

"We're going to plant the beans now, and as they grow they'll use the cornstalks as supports. It's very elegant."

He showed me how to make a little hole in the earth and drop in a bean seed. Pretty easy, really, and somehow it felt natural. What didn't feel natural was having him so close to me without reaching out and touching him. He didn't like it, either; when we both stood up, he looked at me and smiled a small, sad smile. Then he walked off toward Gene, and if I wanted to run after him that was my tough luck.

I turned my attention to my tomato plants, looking for weeds. I hurt, and someone was going to pay.

"Feeling the need to pull weeds?" I jumped and turned around. Eloise was smiling down at me, the sun behind her throwing her face into shadow. "It's very satisfying sometimes to pull things up by their roots and throw them over your shoulder. Clears the mind."

I grinned. "Until you turn around, presumably."

"Did you look for caterpillars?" She started peering at my tomatoes. "Oh, there's one." She pulled a little green caterpillar, very small, from a leaf and tossed it over the fence. "Off you go, you little creeper." She kept hunting. "They eat through the leaves and hurt the plant. Once the tomatoes come in, they go through them, too."

I frowned. "Well, that's not acceptable." I found one, too, and pried it off the leaf. "Let go, you swine." The caterpillar held on with its grippy little feet, and for a moment I felt sorry for it. Then I saw the hole it had been chewing in one of my precious leaves and hardened my heart. "Scat, you little swine." I think I heard a tiny *"aiyeee"* as it flew away over the fence, but maybe I just have very sensitive hearing.

Eloise sat down on the other side of the tomato bed and made herself comfortable. She was a rounded woman, built along comfortable lines, and she moved confidently. There was none of that hesitancy I saw in women who used to be thin and had gained weight and now moved about the planet in a darting fashion, trying to stay hidden. There was an ineffable air of *fuck you* about Eloise that I liked.

"You're clearly the teacher's pet." She peered at me between some leaves, somewhat like a giant caterpillar herself.

"I'm sorry?" I felt myself blushing a bit, and busied myself with some intense leaf study.

"Well, first he brings plants to your house in a semi, and then he lets you mind the tomatoes. They used to call them love apples, you know."

I made a face at her. "You're nuts. In the nicest way, but nuts."

She shrugged. "I'm just saying he likes you. We can all see it."

I just smiled a tight little smile, and suddenly she frowned. She opened her mouth to ask a question, but Frances appeared, her shadow falling across both of us.

"I thought I heard your leaden footfall, my dear." Eloise finished decapitating some poor defenseless bug, and got to her feet. "I was just encouraging Lilian to pursue the gardening teacher." I looked up, shading my eyes against the sun. Frances was smiling at me.

"I expect she can handle herself, El. You should stop meddling."

"Oh, fuck off, Frances. You're just as incorrigible a romantic as I am. Which one of us has a tattoo of the other one's name, eh? That would be you."

I grinned. "Where's the tattoo?"

"I'll never tell," Frances replied airily, turning away. Eloise silently pointed to her partner's butt, and followed her. I smiled to myself, and then relaunched my battle against the insect army. I could hear tiny little horses stamping in the potting soil and wanted to set up battlements in the compost area. They wouldn't know what hit them. A little bit like me.

Once the class was over, we got ready to head over to Gene's house, which was in Beverly Hills. Gene had already gone on ahead to get things ready. Rachel looked at the address and raised her eyebrows. "Huh, I guess banking's more lucrative than I thought."

Eloise and Francis snorted, both lifelong trade union members. "You're joking," Eloise said. "You thought banking was charity work? It's about making money, for crying out loud."

"True," Rachel conceded. "But I guess I had retired bank-branch manager in my head."

Mike had wandered over. "Nah, Gene used to run the West Coast for a big investment bank. You know, trading stocks on the Asian markets and things like that." He laughed. "We bonded over bonds, actually, because I maintain a pretty diverse portfolio, especially in the current climate, and he thought I'd made some smart choices."

There was a pause as we all struggled to reconcile this piece of information with the assumptions we'd had about Mike. Angela eventually said what we were all thinking. "I'm sorry, you have a portfolio? I thought you were a surfer? I thought surfers lived for the water, man, hanging ten and living for the moment?"

Mike was a serious guy, despite the haircut. Like his BFF, Gene.

"Look, Angela, if you don't plan for the future, you can't afford to live in the moment, that's what my old man taught me. He was an economics professor, but he was careful when he was young, and retired at sixty with money to spare. I think that's cool."

"It is cool. My old man is still working like a dog, and he's nearly seventy, but he never made enough to put anything aside. It's easy to save when everyone is fed, but if you don't make enough to do even that, then saving is just impossible."

There was an uncomfortable pause, but Angela didn't seem upset. She was stating the truth. Mike didn't look bothered, either. He nodded. "Luck has a lot to do with it, I guess. We're about the same age, so our parents are probably about the same age, and they got different breaks, is all." The two of them looked at each other and smiled, shrugging. "And yet here we are, meeting up at a gardening class." Mike seemed amused.

"And our parents will probably never meet," Angela said.

"Except maybe at your wedding." Rachel laughed.

There was a pause, and then, surprisingly, both Angela and Mike blushed. I looked at Rachel, then at Eloise. Both of them raised their eyebrows at me.

Mike mumbled something and wandered off. Bash called to Angela, giving her an escape route, too.

"Hmm," said Rachel, "that was interesting."

The kids came running over, with Angela trailing after them.

"Bash ate a worm," Clare informed us. "But he says he can't feel it wriggling anymore."

Angela opened Bash's mouth and peered inside. "Did you swallow it, really?"

Bash nodded.

"Are you worried about Bash, or the worm?" I asked.

"Both," said Annabel. "Although the worm is probably dead. He chewed."

We all looked at Bash with renewed respect.

Lisa was right behind them.

"OK, is anyone else ready for lunch?"

It turned out she was referring to the pizza Gene had promised, but for a minute it wasn't clear.

■ ■ ■ ■

I was worried, driving over to Gene's, that we were all going to get parking tickets, but it turned out that Gene's driveway was bigger than my street, and therefore we had plenty of room. It was the kind of house you normally see on travel shows about the French countryside. Yellow stone, terracotta roof, the whole thing looked as if it had been there for centuries.

"Nineteen seventy-two," Gene told me, in response to my question. "Built by a set designer, for he and his partner to live in for the rest of their lives, which sadly turned out to be much shorter than they hoped, AIDS being what it was. And is, I suppose. I've lived here since the mid-nineties, and I hope I die here, too."

Inside the house it was lightly and simply furnished, with a great deal of space. Big bouquets of flowers stood everywhere, and as you walked through the house, it was as if you were moving through clouds of perfume.

Clare and Annabel were running ahead, following Gene. The rest of us formed a sort of tour group. I looked out for a gift shop.

Angela kept Bash close, maybe scared that

he would break something, but to be honest there was nothing to break. It was a remarkably uncluttered home. Actually, it was the polar opposite of my mother's house, where every surface is cluttered with photos, books, magazines, and children's artwork. Only my mother knows where everything is, and she isn't telling.

At the back of the house, through an enormous living room, three sets of French doors opened into the garden. Lisa Vellinga just stopped dead in the doorway, and I was tempted not to go through myself. It was like Brigadoon, or the forest in that movie *Legend,* in which a young Tom Cruise cavorts about, embarrassing himself, and there are leaves and flowers in the air all the time. Often, in my head at least, these Beverly Hills gardens are formal and elegant, staffed by gardeners dressed as playing cards, but this one was nothing like that. Tall, flowering hedges and old brick walls covered with vines formed the borders, which stretched off quite a way before meeting as a curved wall at the far end. Tall shrubs covered in fragrant flowers formed irregular edges in front of the walls, so you felt like you were in a forest glade. Flower beds and lawns were mixed all over, with large, flat paving stones broken up with moss straggling across. Here and there were benches, swings, mosaics set into the grass, ponds, and other things to draw the eye.

Gene came to stand next to me. "It's amazing, isn't it? Like I said, the guy was a set designer, and he told me that he wanted to create the garden he'd been dreaming of since he was a child. He did it, too. He said this was exactly as he'd wanted it, and I think they basically spent most of their time out here." He pointed alongside the house. "And even though it looks somewhat wild and organic, it's actually brilliantly planned, with state-of-the-art irrigation and a little outdoor kitchen over there." He shrugged. "My kids played here constantly, and it's lovely to see other little ones here now." He grinned. "And in a few years, baby Emily, and hopefully a few others, will be dashing about. I am a lucky man, Lilian, yes, I am." And with that, he rubbed his paws together and went off to let in the pizza guy.

It was true, the kids had run yelling into the garden and were beside themselves with joy. Bash was swinging on a rope swing, Annabel was peering into a pond, and Clare was nowhere to be seen. I looked around. Ah, she was talking to Eloise about something. Worms, probably. I wandered over, close enough to hear but not close enough to interrupt.

"But then my daddy died, so I don't have one anymore."

Eloise nodded. "My daddy is dead, too."

Clare looked sympathetic. "Do you still have a mommy?"

"Yes, but I don't see her very much."

"I'm going to stay with my mommy always. She needs help."

Eloise met my eyes over Clare's head. Hers were twinkling.

"Really? She seems very organized and together."

Clare shrugged. "She is, but she's only got one pair of hands, you know, she can't do everything herself."

Eloise's mouth twitched as I died a little of embarrassment, hearing my own complaints parroted back.

"And," Clare added, definitively, "she's not a magician. Or an octopus."

Which was true.

"Aunty Rachel says she needs a boyfriend, but I don't see why. Boys are just trouble."

Eloise nodded. "Some boys are nice."

Clare looked dubious. "Really? I don't know any nice boys."

"What about Bash?"

Clare snorted. "Bash doesn't count. He's my friend." She looked around. Edward was helping Bob carry flats of flowers into the garden. "Edward is nice. Maybe Edward can be her boyfriend."

Oh great. This is the irritating thing about kids. Most of the time they appear to be completely deaf. Ask them to pick something up, ask them to pay attention, ask them what they want to eat, and you're met with the sound of waves breaking in the distance. Speak in a low voice to someone on the phone, and you'd better confidently expect to hear it broadcast through the neighborhood. A good friend of mine had a hysterectomy, and her five-year-old told the assembled company at Baby Gap that her mommy couldn't have another baby because of her rectum. Apparently, the store assistants were all very sympathetic.

Eloise was no longer meeting my eye, so I turned and wandered off. Gene had brought the pizzas out and was busy opening the boxes and wielding an expert pizza wheel. I was hungry, which was just as well, because he'd literally bought a dozen pizzas.

"One each, Gene?"

He shrugged. "Isabel's away for another day, and I'll need something to eat." Ah. Forward-thinking, not wastefulness. Standing around eating pizza, we looked at the spot Gene had picked out for the flower garden. It was nestled between two larger trees, and sort of hidden from the house. He'd found a lovely old bench somewhere, and a pair of small tile-topped tables for either end. The trees met overhead, dappling the Southern Californian sunshine. I imagined Gene's wife would sit there embroidering pillows for the poor of Beverly Hills, but that was just envy. I wanted a bench. Gene had already cleared the soil, or had someone do it for him, who knows, and brought in a load of plants and flowers, which were sitting around in their pots. The colors were all over the place, no great scheme there, but he'd gone for scent in a big way. I only recognized a few of the flowers, but they all smelled wonderful. Lisa ticked them off for me, her mouth full of pepperoni.

"Jasmine, freesia, lavender, sweet peas, alyssum, night-scented stock, scented phlox, clematis of course, and some fancy tuberose." She looked over at Gene. "You picked well. These should give her fragrance for most of the year, in turns. And some nice evening scents, too."

Gene looked pleased. "Isabel grew up with lots of lilacs, she says, but the guy at the garden store said they won't grow here, 'cause it's too hot."

Lisa shrugged. "There may be varieties that would work. I can look into it for you. But remember, you can add and take out plants all year. That's the nice thing about gardening: It's never done."

Rachel turned to me. "Or it's the maddening, frustrating, soul-destroying part of gardening, that it's never done. Either way." She seemed tired, and I thought maybe she should blow this off and go home for a nap. I was about to say so when an old-fashioned bell phone rang, back in the house. Gene set off.

We started moving the pots around, trying different combinations. Edward started explaining that one of the problems with having a lot of fragrant plants was a lot of interested bees, so we were debating that when Gene reappeared, looking freaked out. "She's coming! She's coming! Little Emily is doing great, so she's popping back for a day or two to do something in town — I have no idea what — and then she's going back. That was her, at the airport in Santa Barbara. We only have a couple of hours at most. What shall we do?"

Mike stuffed the last piece of his pizza in, and dusted off his hands.

"Chill, there's plenty of time. Let's plant these pretty ladies and have it all ready when she arrives."

Eloise nodded. "We're almost done arranging them, Gene. It'll only take us a little bit to stick them in the ground."

"She'll never know we were here," added Angela.

Gene seemed a little flustered still, by this turn of events, so we put him in charge of the kids, who followed him off to the ridiculous swing set on the other side of the lawn. Honestly, my first apartment was smaller than that swing set.

It really didn't take more than an hour, seeing as there were seven of us planting and the hardest part was not squashing someone else's work. But Lisa got us organized, and we planted from back to front, and in no time at all we were standing around admiring our handiwork. It looked really pretty, and it smelled amazing. I sat on the bench and closed my eyes. All I could hear was the sound of the children playing, the buzz of about fifty thousand overjoyed bees who'd just realized Christmas had come early, and a random conversation about Sex Wax between Frances and Mike that sounded like it was based on a simple misunderstanding that neither realized had happened. It was heavenly, the sitting and listening part, not the strange conversation.

The scents of the flowers filled my nose, the sunlight was warm . . . Isabel was one lucky lady.

Gene spoke and I opened my eyes. "How is it?"

I smiled. "I was just thinking how lucky your wife is. It's a great spot, and you're a very thoughtful husband."

He went pink, again. "Well, she deserves it."

Then we heard the scrunch of wheels on gravel, and Gene jumped like a hare.

"Shit, Isabel's here already."

We all started giggling, like naughty kids. "Do you want us to hide?" asked Rachel.

Gene looked quizzically at her. "No, of course not. There's no need for that." He seemed about to say something else, but just shot off into the house instead. We stood about and waited, apart from the kids, who just swung and swung and swung, as children will.

After a moment, he reappeared on the terrace. I frowned — was this his daughter? Didn't she just have a baby? The woman was talking nineteen to the dozen, in a strong London accent.

"Honestly, Gene, she is the smallest little treasure you ever saw. I couldn't put her down. I thought Jane was going to wrestle me over her." She laughed, her face lighting up. She was beautiful and had one of those vivacious faces that you just want to watch and watch. But honestly, she couldn't have been any older than I was.

Suddenly she spotted us all, and shrieked. "Blimey, Gene, you didn't tell me we had company." She basically rushed down the steps and held out her hands to us all. "Hey there, I'm Izzy! I'm going to guess you're the gardening class. How lovely of you all to come and visit. Did you hear I'm a grandmother?" She laughed, a wonderfully loud laugh, and was among us, shaking our hands and hugging the children. Up close, she was even cuter, with smooth skin and shiny blond hair piled on her head. Her blue eyes sparkled with naughty good humor. I looked at Gene, but he was looking at her and smiling like the cat that got the cream.

Suddenly she shrieked again. "Gene, you naughty bugger, what's all this?" She'd found the bench and threw herself down on it. "Ooh, it smells lovely." She looked up at him as if he were a movie star instead of a sixty-year-old retired banker. "Did you put this here for me?" We all swiveled to look at him, and were rewarded by seeing him blush like a hot pepper. Mike burst out laughing and slapped him on the shoulder.

And then we were all laughing.

Isabel was actually the one who cleared it all up for us.

Rachel, Frances, Angela, and I were sitting on the grass near the swing set, watching the kids and eating pizza, when she wandered over and joined us.

She grabbed a slice from the box in front of us, and spoke up.

"So, which one of you has the balls to ask me the obvious question?"

Rachel never needed asking twice. "So, how is it that you're clearly so much younger than Gene but have grown children?"

Isabel laughed. "Well, that's one of the obvious questions, although I was thinking you were going to ask me how a brainless tart like me had caught such a shiny fish." I looked at her closely; she wasn't joking. She thought Gene was a prize, and hey, maybe he was. But she was explaining.

"I met Gene ten years ago, when he was fifty and I was twenty-eight. His first wife deserted him, did you know that?" We shook our heads. She took another bite of pizza and talked around it. "Yeah, she left him when his two daughters were young, around the ages yours are now." She looked at me. "And he raised them himself. The silly cow disappeared, you know, she just went off one night and never came back. He spent months hunting for her. The police and FBI were involved. They thought she'd been kidnapped or something. Gene had lots of money, an important job, but there was never a ransom note. It was dreadful, a real nightmare. And then suddenly, out of the blue, he gets a call from her that she'd had enough of being a mother and a wife, and needed to find herself. She'd spent the previous months bumming around India, without a second thought for those she'd left behind, and now she wanted a divorce so she could marry this guy she'd met in an ashram, or some such nonsense." Isabel's eyes were glittering. "When I met him, the kids were in high school and he'd done an amazing job, but he was so lonely, you could see it across the room."

She dusted off her hands. "I snapped him up before you could say Jack Robinson, and I make him very happy, if I do say so myself. And I, of course, thank my lucky stars every day." She looked over to where Gene was sitting on the grass with Mike, drawing on a piece of paper and clearly explaining something. "He likes that young guy a lot. We should have him over for dinner." She leapt up and went over, presumably to invite him.

I swallowed my pizza and found my voice.

"Well, I, for one, am utterly in love with her, but I don't know about the rest of you."

"She's awesome." Rachel nodded. "I was expecting a woman in sensible slacks, not a foxy blond MILF in tight jeans and a T-shirt, but hey, life's full of surprises."

"I'd do her," confirmed Frances, airily.

How to Grow Zucchini

Zucchini likes warm soil, so wait until early summer at the very least. Planting in midsummer might be even wiser, as you avoid vine borers, and other pests with names like cartoon villains.

- Zucchini need full sun, moist, well-drained soil, and lots of verbal encouragement.
- Mulch plants to protect their shallow roots and retain moisture.
- Water deeply once a week, applying at least one inch of water. Make sure the soil is moist at least 4 inches down.
- If your zucchini blooms flowers but never bears actual zucchini, or it bears fruit that stops growing when it's very small, then it's a pollination issue. To produce fruit, pollen from male flowers must be physically transferred to the female flowers by bees. If you do not have enough bees, you can manually pollinate with a Q-tip. Awkward.

CHAPTER 14

Another Monday. They kept coming around with irritating regularity, and none of them were any easier than the last. How about we start on a Tuesday just for once? No? Fine.

I'd never used a headhunter, seeing as I'd had this job forever, but one of my old college friends, Melanie, had gone into that business, so I'd called her the day Roberta had let us go. Something had come along, apparently, because my phone rang and there she was. The headhunter, not Roberta. Roberta was too scared of Rose to show her face.

"Lilian! Thanks for *reaching out!*" That's how Mel talks, all exclamation points and italics.

"Hi, Melanie, how are you?"

"I'm *fantastic,* but more importantly, how are you? The news just got out about Poplar, and I am so excited!"

"I didn't know there was anything to be

excited about."

She laughed. "You're kidding, right? There is nothing, *nothing,* that happens in publishing in L.A. that I don't know about. It's not like New York, with publishers all over the place."

"Really?"

"Noth-ing." She was actually nearly yelling. Who knew the intricacies of publishing were so compelling? "You're a hot commodity right now, which is superlucky in this economy, right?" She goes up on the ends of her sentences, too, like a teenager, but it's OK. Optimism is a key requirement for her job, I imagine. "Two companies are already interested in talking to you, which is fabulous! Do you have your calendar in front of you?"

I actually had a blank piece of paper in front of me, but seeing as I had nothing planned for the rest of my life, same same. I could actually meet with one of the companies that afternoon, and the other the following week.

"So the one today is another niche publishing house, but they don't do textbooks. They do something else." She paused. "I can't read my assistant's writing here. It looks like *esoteric,* which doesn't make a lot of sense, but anyway, some kind of books.

They need an illustrator — do you have a portfolio with you?"

"Nope, but I can run home and get it before the interview. It hasn't been dusted off in a while."

She clicked her tongue. "Well, then, after your meeting this afternoon you should spend some time going through it and updating. You'll need a revised résumé, of course, and maybe a head shot. Do you still look like you did in college?"

"Skinny and pale and wearing a Duran Duran T-shirt? No."

"Did you get fat?" My God, she was blunt.

"No. I just had two kids and lost my husband."

She sighed. "Yes, I remember. Very sad. But presumably you lost weight?"

Now I sighed. She was focused on her product, and seeing as her product was me, I should try and be a little more helpful. "Mel, I still basically look the same, but older. But why would anyone want to see a photo of an illustrator or graphic designer?"

"No idea," she replied airily. "But if you'd won the Nobel Peace Prize, I'd mention it, too, and you used to look like a model, so we should use whatever we have that will make you stand out from the crowd, right?"

Right. "Well, I don't have a head shot, so

we'll just have to muddle through somehow without it."

She was not thrown. "Well, if we don't find you a job quickly, we can always get some taken. Don't worry, Lili, we will get you a *great* job *really* soon, OK?"

Super.

The interview that afternoon was actually not very far from my office, which would have been convenient except I had to run home to grab my portfolio and get changed. I had one nice suit, which, miraculously, still fit me, and I put a *Cat in the Hat* T-shirt under it, because I am A Funky Person and an Artist, and because it was clean. Now that I was being forced to change jobs, I found myself wondering a lot about what kind of work I actually wanted to do, and something a little more unusual than textbooks would be good. I was almost excited . . . and only thought about Edward every third minute. Every second minute or so I spent feeling guilty about Annabel, which left me only one minute in three to be excited.

The company was in a slightly older building than mine, which was nice. More windows, less cubicles. Big open spaces with desks scattered around, a nice fancy coffee machine, and cool images on the walls.

My meeting was with James Peach — my new favorite name — who was their creative director. He turned out to be young and good-looking, which wasn't his fault, and he gave me a slightly appreciative look when he met me in the reception area. So far, so good.

He led me back to his office, and I tried to pay attention to what he was saying and check out the work space at the same time. It didn't seem very busy. Nobody was running around yelling, and everyone who caught my eye smiled as I passed.

His office was simple but stylish, and all in all, the whole place was giving me a cool vibe. I was starting to think whatever the job was, I wanted it.

James sat down and smiled. "So, have you worked a lot in porn before?"

"I'm sorry?"

He kept smiling. "Erotica. Have you worked in adult books before?"

Erotic. Not esoteric.

I cleared my throat, willing myself to stay calm and not blush. "I'm not sure what you mean. For the past ten years or so, I've worked at a textbook publisher. We did a wide variety of titles, mostly for the school and college market."

He reached up to a bookshelf behind him and pulled down some hardback books. "We do titles for the college market, too, but they're not really textbooks. Although, they do have instructional value." He laughed, but not in a filthy-pornographer way. Maybe I was mishearing everything he was saying. I looked at the books he'd handed me. He was still talking.

"Most of them are erotic fiction, although some are more hard-core than others. Our niche, which is a very successful one, is illustrated texts. Somehow pornography becomes erotica when it's illustrated rather than photographed. And we catch the graphic-novel audience, too."

I had opened *Tale of Six Titties* at random, and was looking at three women licking each other. In pen and ink, mind you, and done with great attention to detail. I flipped open *Come with the Wind* and discovered that some people had been fiddling while Atlanta burned. I wasn't really sure what to say.

Mr. Peach had stopped talking. I looked at him. His mouth was twitching.

"I'm going to guess you had no idea what kind of job this was, am I right?"

I nodded.

"And you look a little shocked, to be honest."

I got my voice back. "I'm not shocked because I think there's anything wrong with it. I'm just surprised because it's unexpected." I held up *The Mound and the Furry*. "I didn't know this kind of book existed. I didn't even know people wanted marmots to do this stuff."

He held up his hand. "No marmots were actually involved. That's the nice thing about this type of book." He sighed. "I started this company because there was a lot of money in pornography and, as a result, a lot of exploitation. I felt there must be another way, and there is. We create fantasy, that's all. You would not believe what our writers dream up, and a lot of it is informed by what our readers tell us they want to see. There's a whole alien subgenre, for example, that would be ridiculous in photographs but which takes on a magical aspect in illustration." He looked disappointed. "I guess you're not interested in the job?"

He had handed me an alien book, and I was looking at a beautiful illustration of a creature with three multitasking appendages. It was lovely work, technically, but not for me.

"I don't think it's really my style. I'm sorry."

He shook his head. "Don't be sorry. For those of us who work here, it's a dream come true. I want everyone here to feel the same way." To which there is no adequate response.

We stood up and shook hands, and I walked back through the office, looking at things a little differently. No wonder everyone was smiling at me. They were all horny.

I called Melanie. She needed to get a better assistant.

But at least I knew that if all else failed, I could get a job where my previous experience with whale penises might actually come in handy.

Angela called early the next morning, which was a pleasant surprise. "Do your kids have today off school?"

"Yeah, it's some kind of holiday, right?"

"Who knows? Anyway, I was thinking that I would take you up on your playdate offer, if it still stands?" I was lounging in the kitchen, enjoying the small fermata between emptying the dishwasher and reloading it. It's a glamorous life.

"Of course, that would be great. In fact, Rachel was planning on coming over to hang out after work, and we'd talked about going out to dinner. Why don't you come over in the afternoon, and we can leave the kids with my babysitter and grab an early dinner somewhere. It will be fun." I hung up, pleased to have a plan.

The kids were thrilled to show Bash the fairy house. Despite the fact that they had grown up in different environments, the three kids got along flawlessly, proving yet again that children are our future. Angie, Rachel, and I let them lead the way by sitting in the kitchen drinking coffee while they played in the garden.

Angie did her best to get details about Bob out of Rachel, but she underestimated her.

"I've got nothing to tell," Rachel insisted. "There's really nothing going on. We've had one dinner, and I've had about seven filthy dreams, but that's it. At dinner, all he talked about was rotation farming. I don't even know what it is, although presumably it involves rotating in some way." She turned up her palms. "Sorry, but I don't think he likes being objectified for his looks."

Angie snorted. "That's right, men hate it when you think of them as sex objects. It makes them feel all anxious and small inside."

"It belittles their spiritual side," I added, "and crushes their dreams."

Rachel raised her eyebrows at me. "Did I walk into some kind of Wiccan anti-men coven?"

I shrugged. "Look, don't try and change the subject. We're not mocking men. We like men. We're mocking you."

Angie nodded. "You're the only one here who has any kind of romantic life." She turned to me. "Although I might be wrong about that. Sorry for making an assumption, Lili, and we need you to share details."

"It's not just an assumption. It's a fact." I pointed out the window. "Did you meet my birth control?" Rachel knew I didn't want to talk about Edward with anyone, least of all someone who actually knew who he was, so she stayed quiet. With every day that passed, it was getting easier to pretend that the kiss in the kitchen had never happened.

Angie laughed. "I know. It's not that I'm not occasionally interested in romance, or even just sex. It's just that the chances of my interest coinciding with opportunity and, more important, physical energy are very remote."

Rachel frowned. "You guys make it very hard for us single women to look forward to having kids."

Angie and I spoke in unison. "Good."

Maggie appeared, having let herself in. Frank stood up to greet her, his tail going a mile a minute.

"Nice guard dog you have, Lili." She looked at Angie and grinned, sticking out her hand. "Hi, I'm Maggie, Lili's sister-in-law, recently arrived from Italy, where my husband is having an affair."

Angie paused for just a second, then went with it. "Hi, I'm Angie, a friend of Lili and Rachel from gardening class, recently arrived from South Central L.A., where my ex-husband is doing something I couldn't care less about."

"Nice to meet you."

"And you."

Maggie sat, then immediately stood to get herself some coffee. "You know," she said, "when I moved to Italy, Americans were all drinking Folgers, and now you guys are drinking better coffee than the Italians. What gives?"

The kids came bursting into the kitchen.

"I broke my fairy's wings!" Clare was distressed.

"We can fix it," Bash said, calm and confident. "My mom is a nurse."

Angie took the tiny fairy from Clare and examined it. "Hmm. I think we're OK. A little glue should do it."

I fetched the glue and she expertly performed the repair. "You guys go back out and play. The glue will take a few minutes to dry. I'll call you when it's ready."

Bash took Clare by the hand and led her away. "You can play with my fairy, Clare."

We all watched them. Maggie sighed. "At least Clare found a nice guy."

Angie sniffed. "It'll be fine until she doesn't turn into a fighting robot with laser vision, then he'll lose interest." She looked at me and shrugged. "I have to be honest."

"No, that's fine. They're doomed to failure anyway. The divorce rate among the elementary set is brutal. Most marriages don't even make it to recess."

However, Clare, Bash, and Annabel played peacefully until suppertime, and then, when Leah arrived, settled down to watch a movie on the sofa. We'd decided to just make it a sleepover, so we could stay out later, and this had been thrilling news to the kids.

Feeling like a TV show, the four of us got dressed up a bit and headed out the door.

"No strip joints this time, OK, Rachel?" Maggie sounded firm.

Angie raised her eyebrows. "I missed the strip club? That's not fair."

"You didn't really miss anything. What do

we all want to eat?"

"Italian."

"Sushi."

"French."

"Burgers."

We stood on the street and looked at each other. "Come on, ladies, let's work together here." I put on my best Mommy voice. "I'm sure there's something we can choose that will make us all happy."

"I'm suddenly very hungry," warned Rachel, who'd wanted burgers. "And I need to eat soon or I will get cranky."

I put up my hand. "How about this? How about we just go to the Grove? There are lots of options for eating, and then we can see a movie, or wander around the bookstore, or whatever." The Grove is a big outdoor mall. It's got a fountain and a movie theater and all that good stuff, and is a harmless way to spend time. And money.

"Good plan," Angie responded. "I've never been there."

"Although," Rachel said, not sounding so into it, "it can be supercrowded."

I looked at my watch. "At 6:00 P.M. on a weeknight? You think?"

Maggie was already heading off. "Let's just go see. Honestly, the worst thing about a girls' night out is the endless agreeable talking. Come on!"

As it happened, The Grove was showing off for the tourists. A band was playing on the grassy area, and the fountain was doing its fancy fountain tricks (jets of water shooting high into the air, colored lights, that kind of thing). It was pleasantly busy, but not crowded, and we got a table right away at a French place with a huge menu. Rachel ordered a burger, I ordered spaghetti, Maggie ordered a BLT, and Angie ordered French onion soup. Everyone was happy. See? Mommy was right.

"So, Angie," Maggie said, "what's your deal? You said you have an ex-husband, and I met your son, but do you have a boyfriend or something?"

Angie shook her head. Maggie persisted. "Girlfriend?"

Angie shook her head.

Rachel leaned over. "Are you interested in Mike?"

Angie smiled. "I like Mike, don't get me wrong, but we couldn't be more different."

Maggie was confused. "Who's Mike? Am I supposed to know?"

I shook my head. "No, he's someone from our gardening class."

I raised a hand to ask for coffee, while Rachel persisted. "Yeah, you're different, but sometimes that's interesting. Do you find him attractive?"

Angie laughed. "Of course, don't you? He's gorgeous."

There was a pause. Rachel and I looked at each other. Mike was nice-looking, but he was not in any way gorgeous, in my humble opinion. Rachel answered for both of us. "He's cute, but he's no Impossibly Handsome Bob."

"Really?" Angie looked genuinely surprised. "Huh. I think he's totally hot."

We let the subject drop as we consulted the dessert menu. Four pieces of chocolate cake later, we stumbled out of the restaurant and went to sit down on the grass for a bit. To digest.

It was nice, sitting there. I was zoning out when I noticed a man gazing at Rachel with all the concentration of a puppy watching a toddler eat ice cream. I nudged her. "That guy is checking you out."

She looked over. "He looks familiar." She met his eye, and he spoke up.

"I'm sorry to stare, but aren't you Rachel Anderby?"

She smiled, but it was clear she didn't remember him. "Yes, have we met?"

All of us were riveted, of course. He was

cute, and we were hopeless romantics. A repressed widow, a young divorcée, and a brokenhearted professor? You couldn't ask for a better audience.

He was blushing a bit as he stood up and came over to sit with us. He was tall, which she would like, and dark haired, which she would also like. He was casually dressed, check; high-cheekboned, check; apparently clean, check, check, check. I leaned back on my elbows to watch. He seemed a little nervous.

"Yes, we met, sort of, but it was a while ago. You gave a talk about international importation law to my company, and I saw you. It, I mean. The talk. I was there."

Rachel looked amused. "At the talk?"

"Yes."

"You were there, then."

"Yes."

"Which company was it?"

"Bugler, Arthur and Barnes."

She raised her eyebrows and looked dubious.

"They're a law firm. I'm a lawyer. We're lawyers."

Her face cleared. "Oh, yes! I remember." She paused. "Wow, it must have been a good talk. That was over a year ago."

He smiled and seemed to recover his

301

composure a bit. "It was. It was a very good talk."

I looked at Rachel to try and gauge her reaction. She looked very calm and, luckily, totally gorgeous. The evening sun was managing to catch the highlights in her hair, her face was as clear and lovely as it always was, and all in all there was nothing for an older sister to worry about. I couldn't tell, though, if she thought he was cute, which was unusual. Normally she gets a little giggly when she's interested. Oh well.

"Do you specialize in international law?"

He shook his head. "No, I actually do very boring corporate law, but I saw you before the talk and kind of followed you into the conference room."

She frowned at him. "You mean you weren't interested in the subtleties of cross-border jurisdictions?"

He smiled. "Once you started talking, I was completely engrossed."

Angie, Maggie, and I tried futilely to pretend we weren't listening, but we were. They didn't seem to care. Rachel was probably aware of our scrutiny, but she was a cool cucumber.

"So, do you like being a lawyer?"

He shrugged. "Sure. I would rather be acting, but wouldn't everyone?"

She shook her head. "Not me. So you're the classic Los Angeles lawyer-actor hyphenate?"

He looked abashed. " 'Fraid so. Clichéd, right?"

"Well, you could have been a waiter. That would have been more traditional."

He made a face. "All the good waiter jobs were taken, and I had this law degree . . . I know it's not the usual path, but hey, I'm a rebel."

"A tort rebel?"

"Rebel without a subclause."

"Hmm. So corporate attorney by day, actor by night?"

"Yes. The law is what I do for money, and pursuing an acting career is what I do as a futile, soul-destroying hobby."

Rachel smiled. "So it's going well, then?"

He smiled back. "It's fantastic. I get to meet lots of strange people who explain what's wrong with me and then send me away. It's made being turned down by women seem quite pleasant in comparison."

"I imagine you don't get turned down all that often."

"You'd be surprised."

"You're very handsome."

"So is everyone else here."

"That is a true story."

After this positive flood of conversation, they fell silent.

Angie had had enough.

"I'm going to the bookstore. Anyone with me?"

Maggie got up, too. Rachel smacked herself on the forehead.

"My God, I'm so rude. I totally didn't introduce you to my friends."

"You don't know my name."

"That's true. What is it?"

"Richard."

"Richard, this is my friend Angie, this is my sister, Lilian, and this is her sister-in-law, Maggie."

"Doesn't that make her also your sister-in-law?"

I shook my head. "No. She is my sister-in-law, and Rachel is my sister, but they are not sisters-in-law, because Rachel is not married." I paused. "Not right now." That was awkward. Maggie was ready to make it worse, though.

"And, Richard, are you married?"

He smiled. "Not right now."

"Do you have a girlfriend?"

He shook his head.

Maggie sighed. "Then you can carry on talking to Rachel." She raised her hand. "I'm sure you're a lovely guy, and a straight arrow, but many men are scum-sucking, bottom-feeding cheat machines, and I don't want Rachel to get hurt."

There was a pause. Angie cleared her throat. "OK, then, how about that bookstore?"

The three of us headed off, leaving Rachel and Richard to chat. Assuming she could get past the cheat-machine thing. I looked back — they seemed to be doing just fine. Then I paused and asked the others to wait. I went back, pulling out my phone as I went. I tapped on Richard's shoulder.

"Full name?"

"Richard Byrnes."

I typed it into my phone.

"Address?" I put it in, too.

"Social security number?"

He told me that, too, the idiot.

I tsk-tsked. "Haven't you ever heard of identity theft?"

He grinned at me. "How do you know I didn't make it up? I didn't, but I'm guessing you're protecting your sister." He looked at her. "She's a grown-up, you know. I've seen her in action."

I narrowed my eyes at him, but nodded. "Yes. She's a grown-up, and she's a black belt in Judo, but I was raised to trust but verify. If I get back here and she's not here,

I will contact the authorities and dox you on the Internet."

He whistled. "Man, you're mean."

Rachel touched his arm. "She's also lying about the black belt."

I drew myself up to my full height, which isn't all that full. "I, sir, am her big sister. In my day that meant something."

He smiled up at me. "I have a big sister, too, and she would be just as protective as you."

"A likely story. Have fun, I'll see you in an hour or two."

And I left them to it.

Ten minutes later, I got a text: "Going to dinner. I'll call you tomorrow."

I texted back: "You already had dinner. How do I know this is really you, and not him, stealing your phone and kidnapping you?"

She replied: "I'll eat more. When you were twelve you kissed the neighbor's dog, with tongue, on a dare."

This was true. No wonder Clare was so free with her affections. It was genetic.

I texted again: "OK, but be safe."

She signed off: "Bite me."

Definitely her.

HOW TO GROW CELERY

Many gardeners believe celery is the trickiest vegetable to grow. To improve your chances, start the seed indoors, 8 to 10 weeks before the last frost, and make regular sacrifices to the celery gods.

- Work organic fertilizer or compost into the soil prior to planting.
- Harden off seedlings by keeping them outdoors for a couple hours a day and speaking to them harshly.
- Transplant seedlings 10 to 12 inches apart, direct sow seeds 1/4 inch deep. These will need to be thinned to 12 inches apart when they reach about 6 inches high.
- Mulch and water directly after planting.
- If celery does not get enough water the stalks will be dry and small, and it will be no one's fault but your own.

CHAPTER 15

Of course I was counting the minutes till I could call and find out how it went. Three seconds after nine the next morning, I called.

"Well?"

She sounded tired.

"Well, what?"

I made an exasperated sound. "Rachel. Don't mess with me. We have a reciprocal agreement to dish any and all dirt as soon as possible."

"Is it in writing?"

"It's in blood. Spill it. What happened? Did you actually go to dinner?"

"Yes. Although it turned out that he had also eaten already, so we just got more dessert."

"What did he order?"

"You're weirdly obsessed with that, you know? We ordered an ice-cream hot-fudge sundae and shared it."

"Very high school. OK. Then?"

She sighed.

"Then I had him drop me at home and didn't even kiss him. I have to say, though, that the temperature in the car was more than steamy, and it took every last ounce of self-control I have not to invite him in."

Apparently, I had missed a memo.

"Why didn't you invite him in? Were you sick?"

She sighed again. "No. I'm not sure. I think it's because I really do like him, and I don't want to mess it up by sleeping with him right away."

I goggled. No, I mean it, I goggled.

"Who are you and what have you done with my sister?" I demanded.

"Very funny. No, honestly, from the moment I clapped eyes on him, I knew I was in trouble. I mean, I like him, or maybe I don't like him but think I like him, or maybe I do like him but think that I don't . . ." She was gibbering like an idiot.

"OK, calm down. Are you free for lunch?"

In our lives before my husband died, Rachel and I had gone different ways when it came to relationships. I got married and had kids, and she'd shown no interest in doing either. Maybe having been repeatedly told by our mother that men would always value her for her looks had planted the idea that that was all they would value her for. The one brief marriage (spit on the ground) doesn't count. She tended to have light-hearted relationships with funny, interesting men, and broke it off when they wanted to be exclusive. It was always friendly, though, which says a lot about her. She had never — I repeat, never — hesitated to go to bed with someone she found attractive. Until now. Either she was getting old, or something unusual was going on.

I saw her across the restaurant as I walked in and could tell, even at a distance, that she had her underpants in a bunch, metaphorically speaking. She looked distracted, which she never is, and was wearing lipstick, which she never does. I sat down.

"I ordered us both burgers and shakes. Does that work?" Her voice was a little loud, and pitched a little higher than normal. Please note, this was an Italian restaurant.

"They had that on the menu?"

She looked around. "Oh. Uh, I guess they do. I just said it to the waiter when I sat down, and now I realize why he seemed surprised, but he said OK and went away."

"I imagine they've sent someone out to McDonald's for us."

"Possibly."

310

I looked around. The waiter was standing at the back, looking nervously in our direction. Probably scared we were going to ask for sushi next.

"So what the heck is going on? Did Richard call you this morning?"

She shrugged. "Yes. He left a message. I didn't want to pick up. I don't know. I feel totally weird. After Dan died, and you went crazy, did you know that you were going crazy?"

My turn to shrug. "I don't remember. Are you saying that having dinner with this man was as traumatic to you as seeing your husband die? Because if it was, you might not want a second date."

She looked at me, and suddenly I saw her snap back into herself. She reached for my hand and squeezed it.

"Shit. I'm sorry, Lili. I didn't mean that at all. Honestly, my mind's totally gone. I confused two shipments this morning, and a customer who's expecting an Etruscan vase is going to be somewhat taken aback when he unpacks a stuffed Galápagos tortoise instead."

"Not to mention he's going to have a hell of a time putting flowers in it."

She sighed again, which was making me wonder if she had a respiratory infection. I mean, seriously, how much oxygen does one girl need?

Our waiter approached. He carefully put down two plates, which appeared to have regular burgers on them — with a side of spaghetti, true, but burgers nonetheless. He also gave us our shakes, and then backed away.

We took a bite. And looked at each other.

"This," she said, "is the best burger I've ever had in my life."

I nodded. "Well, you know what they say. Trauma is the best salsa."

Rachel plowed through the burger, and it appeared to do her some good.

"I hadn't realized how hungry I was. I couldn't eat this morning."

Huh. This really was serious. If Rachel got trapped under a fallen refrigerator, she would try to open it to see if there was something to snack on while she waited for help to arrive. Rachel loves to eat.

"I'm confused," I said, confused. "If you like the guy, what's the problem? You've dated guys you've liked before, right? And you just met this one. He might be an ass-hole by the weekend."

"Sure. But in every relationship I've had, and this is going to sound weird, I've felt a little bit secure, do you know what I mean?"

I shook my head. "No, not at all. What do you mean?"

She squirmed about on her seat. "Like I could walk away. That they liked me more than I liked them. Like I had some control over it. For some reason, Richard makes me nervous. Not scared, just nervous. I feel like he sees through to my insides or something like that."

I took a drink of my shake, which was also outstanding, and pondered.

"Are you sure it's not just that slightly nauseous feeling one gets at the beginning of every relationship?" I reached over and put my hand on her forehead. "Maybe you're coming down with something."

"I don't know. I never had this before. I've been totally into guys before, of course, and keen to see them and sleep with them and excited about the whole thing, but always in a kind of playful way." She looked at me. "Honestly, I thought maybe there was something wrong with me. I saw how you were with Dan, how you could argue and disagree and keep going, and how you turned to each other for support, and I wondered if I was missing something. I always kept my independence." She took another bite of her burger and was silent for a moment, chewing. "Look, don't take this the wrong way, but when Dan died, I thought maybe that was God's plan, or the universe's plan, or whatever. That I stayed single precisely so I could help you get through that. If I'd had a husband and family of my own, I wouldn't have been able to step in like I did."

Jesus. Now I reached for her hand.

"Rach, I will never forget what you did for me, for the kids. If you hadn't been there, I don't know what would have happened. They would have taken my kids away, probably. You saved all of us. You are my hero."

She smiled. "Am I the wind beneath your wings?"

I grinned back. "You are. But you can relax now. If you want to fall in love with someone and get married and have babies, it's OK. Maybe that's why I'm still single, so I can help you."

She laughed, shakily. "I'm not saying I want to get married and have kids."

I looked at her. "But maybe you want to fall in love."

She said nothing, just looked down at her plate. A tear plinked down. I reached over and ruffled her hair, just like I have our whole lives.

"Look, it's OK to be weirded out by a new guy." I had a thought. "Are you worried he doesn't feel that way about you?"

She shrugged, keeping her face down. "I don't know. I honestly don't know what to feel. We talked and talked for hours, about everything. About what happened when Dan died, about his parents, about our parents, about everything. He's funny and smart and kind, and he scares the crap out of me because he's honest about what he's feeling. I think he likes me, too, but what if he doesn't?"

"Of course he likes you. He could barely speak at the beginning." I felt bad for her. Like I said, she's always been a tough cookie. I think I've only seen her cry over a guy one time, and that was when he'd made her so angry that she kicked a wall and broke her toe. This was ever-so-slightly different.

I signaled for the check.

"Look, honey, you're probably very, very tired. You didn't sleep. It sounds like you had an intense evening, and you can't possibly think straight without getting some rest. Why don't you blow off work this afternoon and go home."

She nodded. "I think you're right. Maybe I'm coming down with something and I'll wake up totally OK again."

"Uh, maybe." I signed the bill, and we got

up to go. I took her arm as we left, and felt her lean on me.

My turn.

When I got home, my photos of Dan and the kids had arrived. I'd included our wedding photos, Annabel's and Clare's birth photos, anything and everything. And for some reason now, going through them, I didn't feel like my heart just got ripped out and stomped on. I just felt happy that we'd had that time together. A few of them made me tear up again — a picture of his face as he held Annabel for the first time, a photo of him standing in the street with his arms out as she ran into them, and one, strangely enough, of him and my sister. They were just standing together on a hillside in Italy, grinning for the camera, all of us there for Maggie and Berto's wedding. They were both so young and happy, and both looking at me with such affection, that I suddenly realized what we had all lost when he died. It wasn't just me, it wasn't just the kids, it was everyone who'd been a part of our lives together. Rachel had said this very thing the other night, at Pink's, but as I looked at the photos, I could finally feel it for myself.

Here was one of an enormous group of family, gathered together for what must have been Thanksgiving or something. His family, my family, Annabel on my mother's lap, teeny-tiny Clare on his mother's shoulder — yes, the Thanksgiving just before he died. Clare was only a month old, and my dad had been taking the picture, I guess. Berto was there with Maggie, looking ridiculously Italian and wearing a pink sweater in the way only European men can. Dan was sitting at the far end of the table, wearing a paper Pilgrim hat, goofing about. He had been so funny, so silly, and so had I. The two of us would riff about anything, trying to keep everyone laughing. Making each other laugh had been the thing that brought us together in the first place. After he died, it was a while before I laughed, maybe months, and the first time I did, I started crying immediately, like those videos of deaf people hearing their voices for the first time. Delight, followed by tears. Yet since then every laugh got easier, and now laughter was the thing that held me together, sarcastic comments and stupid jokes.

I did something bold. I called my mother, unconsciously curling into a ball on the sofa as I dialed the familiar number. Just in case.

"Hey there, old lady."

"Hello, dear, are you in jail?" She sounded sober, for once. Maybe the liquor store had finally cut her off.

"No, but I wanted to tell you that I love you."

Long pause. I mean, really, a long pause.

"Are you there?"

"Yes, I'm here. I'm just worried you're dying of cancer."

"Because I said I loved you?"

"Yes. You hardly ever say it anymore, you know. You said it when your dad died, and you said it last Christmas."

"You can remember specifically when I said it last? That's sad."

"Yes." Her tone was as dry as ever. "You were never the most affectionate of children. Your sister is positively cuddly in comparison."

I started to get annoyed, and took a breath. "Well, I realized just now that we all lost Dan when he died, which I realize is stunningly obvious, but still. And that you lost Dad, too, and I never really talk to you about that, about the fact that both of us are widows."

She caught her breath. "Oh, my God, you are dying of cancer. You did always have weird breasts."

I closed my eyes, resisting the urge to wrap the phone cord around my own neck and tighten it until I lost consciousness. She was still talking.

"Please tell me it's you and not one of the children."

For some reason that struck me as funny, and I started to laugh.

"Mom! Pull it together. No one is dying of cancer, for crying out loud. I am trying to tell you that I love you, that I empathize with your loss, that I want to share my feelings with you, and, as always, you are making it totally freaking impossible." I was still smiling, though. "We've always done this, made fun of feelings and not talked about shit, and we're too old. We need to get it together."

Another thoughtful pause. "And you promise you're not going to give me terrible news. It's not me that's dying, is it?"

Tempting. I sighed in exasperation. "Mom, quit it. You're as bad as I am."

"Well, maybe that's where you learnt it from."

"Doubtless."

"I miss your dad, you know. He was always so good at talking to you all. He could tell you stuff I wanted to, but couldn't. Since he died, I feel like every time I open my mouth, I put my foot in it. Thank God he was still here when Dan died, not that I didn't manage to mess that up, too.

I'm sorry."

"I know you are, Mom. We made up about the funeral thing, remember? I miss Dad, too. Why don't you come over more?"

"Why don't *you* come over more? I'm all alone in this big house, rattling around like a seed in a pod. I'd love to have the children here."

"Oh, come off it. Every time we come over, the kids break something and you say something inappropriate. I don't want them to get anxious around you."

"Like you and your sister, you mean?"

I paused. We were actually doing better than I had thought we would, talking, and I didn't want to put her back up. But I plunged on, regardless.

"Sure. Like me and Rachel. We love you so much, but you say hurtful things sometimes."

"You know I don't mean to."

"Actually, I don't know you don't mean it. I know you can't help it, but that's different. Look, let's just try a bit harder? I don't know that we can reverse a lifetime of weirdness, but I don't want to go on like I have been. I can think about Dan without bursting into flames. You can tell me you love me, if you want to. I can not react to everything you say as if I were still fifteen.

Rachel can fall in love."

She laughed. "Let's not go crazy."

I agreed. There'd be time for that later on. I wasn't really sure why my feelings about all this had suddenly changed, but I felt better than I had in a long time when I hung up the phone.

Then the kids got home from school, with Leah trailing behind them. They burst through the door and flung themselves at me, chattering away as always. I realized that I must have been chatty like that with my mother, too, and I wondered how many years it had taken for that flood to slow to a trickle. One small stone at a time, I expect, and before you know it you have a dam. The kids dropped their bags and papers on the floor and took off for the garden, presumably to play with the fairy house. I picked up a picture they'd dropped and looked at it. Clare had drawn the garden, and I was impressed to see we'd acquired an apple tree, a lake with ducks, and a tiger in a dressing gown. Nice. Still no bench for me, though. I thought of something, and went to find the sketchbook I had given to Annabel. I flipped through until I got to my picture of the garden. Aha! A bench! I knew I'd put one in. And there was Dan, sitting on my bench, just hanging out.

I sighed and went to make dinner.

The kids found the photos hysterical. Oh, how they laughed — Mom was so funny-looking! And Daddy was so funny-looking! And Aunty Rachel was so pretty! And Grandma was wearing a bikini! It was all such a revelation, and I felt shitty I'd let nearly four years slide by. I realized I had been cool and self-absorbed in the same way my mother had been. And I get it, that's how she was raised, and her parents before her, yada yada, but enough already. Seeing my sister cry shouldn't have been an epiphany, but it was. News flash! Other people have feelings, too! I could have beat myself up about it, but I decided that was over, too. At least I didn't tell the kids they had weird breasts.

As we stuck pictures in the album, I went and got the camera. I snapped and snapped, and then picked up the sketchbook and drew. This was a new beginning, and I wasn't going to miss any of it.

I had Leah for the evening, so I decided to go nuts and head out, alone, to Target. I needed to get something, probably, and what better place to get something than Target. I remember once reading a study about toddlers, or three-year-olds, or some other unpredictable group like that, in which they diagrammed the movements of the children between other children and tables with activities on them and things like that. Basically it looked like a spiderweb, as they wandered about the room. If you did the same for my life, it would be a square: the house, the school, the office, and Target. And with the office going away, it was going to be a triangle any minute now. Perhaps I could start haunting the gas station or something, just to keep myself quadrilateral.

Anyway, even the smell of Target made me feel happy, and when I was first out of the hospital, I spent a lot of time there, just wandering around waiting for school to let out. I couldn't work for a while, just couldn't stay focused long enough to remember what I was drawing, so I had very little to do between drop-off and pickup. Target was close, there was plentiful parking at 9:05 in the morning, and no one thought twice about a spacey woman leaning on her cart handle, humming the *Sesame Street* theme song and making her fourth pass through car care.

Often I bought nothing, but sometimes I would throw things in my cart with manic enthusiasm, filling my kitchen cupboards with doughnut makers and ice shavers and little fake Christmas trees that smelled like real Christmas trees. I bought clothes for the kids, clothes for Rachel, and clothes for Frank. I bought myself socks because my feet stayed the same size, even as the weight continued to fall off me. After Dan died, I lost forty pounds and my periods stopped. Eventually, my grief therapist threatened to put me back in the hospital unless I started taking care of myself. I went on a strict four-Snickers-a-day diet and regained some weight. Not just the Snickers, just to clarify, them *in addition to* regular food. I can't eat them anymore. They remind me too much of that first year. Snickers, my kitchen floor, the smell of rain, Converse high-tops, broken glass, rubbing alcohol on cotton wool, that Sheryl Crow song about having fun, my husband's shaving cream, the taste of blood in my mouth. None of them are as enjoyable as they used to be.

My phone rang as I cruised through the pet section, debating getting Frank a stuffed duck to chew on. He much preferred dirty laundry, but maybe he'd appreciate the thought. It was Rachel.

"He officially likes me."

"No hello?"

"I'm being efficient. Hello."

I moved from pet supplies to DVDs and books. I knew none of the writers and very few of the new releases. I needed to get out more.

"How do you know he likes you?"

"He told me. No hello back?"

"Hello. When was this?"

"On the phone, just now. Where are you?"

"Target. So, did you tell him you liked him, too?"

"I did. I actually did. Can you get me a packet of Sharpies?"

I wheeled the cart in the direction of stationery, cards, and craft accessories. I could see several other people aimlessly propelling carts while talking on their phones. Somehow we managed not to cause a ten-cart pileup in the middle of small appliances, although there was an awesome mime-opera of raised eyebrows, half smiles, mouthed sorrys, and near misses.

"Well, that's good, then. You've known each other a day and a half, and you both like each other. Super."

"Are you laughing at me?"

"Not at all. I assume when I get out of the store there will be airplanes filling the skies with 'Rachel Likes Richard' in big puffy clouds. I imagine you've already changed your status on Facebook."

"I don't use Facebook."

"I know. I was laughing at you. So what happens now?"

"No idea."

"I have your Sharpies. Black, presumably?"

"Yes."

I also grabbed her a complete set of colors, what the hell. I could never resist a brand-new set of markers. My kids literally had buckets of them. She hung up, and I headed to underwear. I paused, considering a purchase. Was it time for new panties? Just buying them didn't mean I had to show them to anyone, right? I spent twenty minutes picking out pretty, lacy things in pale colors and dark colors, in black and fawn . . . and then handed them to the cashier at checkout. "I've changed my mind about these," I told her, and honestly she could not have cared less. Then I watched her ring up the Sharpies, the printer paper, the T-shirt with a cat, the T-shirt with a whale, the three pairs of slipper socks, the duck for the dog, and the jumbo container of peanut butter and tried to work up the nerve to change my mind back again. Honestly, it was ridiculous. I used to wonder what other people thought of me, then I wondered what other people thought of my children, and now I just hope I can attract someone's attention if I catch fire.

Finally she was done, and then, miraculously, she smiled at me and said, "Are you sure about the underwear?"

I said, "Actually, no. I want it after all. Thanks for asking."

She grinned and pulled it from under the counter. "Good for you," she said, as she scanned the tags. "It's nice to treat yourself once in a while."

She was right, of course. And now the underwear is sitting at the back of my drawer and may never see the light of day, but hey, baby steps, right?

How to Grow Strawberries

Strawberries can be planted as soon as the ground can be worked easily.

- They are sprawling plants, sending out runners to cover the ground.
- Plant them deeply and widely enough to accommodate the entire root system without bending it. However, the crown should still be right at the surface. Sometimes gardening is a precision science.
- Give them lots of room and plenty of sunlight. Raised beds are particularly good for strawberries.
- Don't plant them anywhere that recently had tomatoes, peppers, or eggplants growing in it. It freaks them out, don't ask me why.

CHAPTER 16

Speaking of new beginnings, the next day I had another job interview. This time I quizzed Melanie in detail.

"It's a children's book publishing house, so you have the right kind of experience. They want someone who can do a variety of styles, which you can, and it's a contract job."

"Which means?"

"It means they have a stable of artists and illustrators that they use, and they want to expand it. I don't know if they want you to come in and do work in-house, or if it's just freelance."

I frowned. I wanted health insurance. Mind you, I also wanted a holiday home in Aruba, but I doubted that was on offer. I climbed into my suit again (Thompson Twins vintage T-shirt this time) and was twenty minutes early.

The vibe at Rubber Ball Press was a little

bit different from the erotica place. To start with, there were two people in reception arguing fiercely.

"You're totally wrong. He's an octopus."

"Squid. It's in his goddamned name!"

"But count his legs!"

"He's a cartoon, not a textbook. It doesn't matter how many legs he has."

They were talking about *SpongeBob SquarePants,* of course. The debate about whether Squidward Tentacles is an octopus or a squid is a fascinating one, and ultimately unanswerable. I weighed in.

"I hate to interrupt, but I think he's been described as both on the series."

They turned to me, and rather than being weirded out that a total stranger had interrupted their argument, seemed open to input.

"But he has only six tentacles."

I shrugged. "While it's embarrassing to admit this, I heard the guy who made the series on NPR, and he said it was just easier to draw six. Ten made him look like he was going to trip any second. Just too many."

They nodded. I was willing to bet they were illustrators, too, because we're weird.

The receptionist was smiling at me. I told her who I was, and she seemed to be OK with it and suggested I take a seat. I looked around. No nudes, but lots of bright colors and toys. It kind of looked like my house, but neater, obviously.

After a little bit, a woman about my age appeared, looking harassed, and said my name in the form of a question.

Her office was not very big, and the resemblance to my house was much closer. There were photos and toys and pieces of paper everywhere. Her computer was covered in Post-its, and I counted three coffee cups on her desk. She and I were obviously sisters under the skin. Her name was Betty. As in Boop, she said. I told her I was Lilian. As in . . . I had nothing.

"Mel explained you're leaving Poplar because they're closing the department?"

I nodded. "They've decided to outsource the illustration overseas."

She made a face. "Well, we tried that, too, and the good part of it was we discovered some freelancers over there who we still use, but it ended up that we always needed some folks in-house to do faster-turnaround stuff, or to do fixes on the overseas stuff, so in the end, we backed off it. Poplar may do the same."

I turned up my palms. "I'd be happy to freelance for them if they need it, but I have kids, so I need a real job."

"We aren't looking for full time. Didn't Mel tell you that?"

My heart sank. "She wasn't sure."

She frowned a little. "I don't want to waste your time. We only have one or two people full time in-house, and the rest of the work gets done by a dozen or so illustrators who work from wherever they want. However, we are able to offer a retainer, which is a guaranteed amount of work." She pointed up at her shelves, which were loaded with books. "We've been lucky. Our Squirty Squirrel character took off, and we produce a couple of titles for him each month. We also do the books for several kids' cable networks. You know, those irritating books based on the episodes?"

I nodded. She was right. They were irritating, but still, work was work. She had pulled down a couple and handed them to me.

"They annoy the crap out of me, personally, when I read them to my kids, but the kids eat them up."

"How many kids do you have?" I looked for photos but couldn't see any under all the clutter on her desk.

She smiled. "Just two, but they keep me busy. Eight and six. Girls."

I smiled back. "Me, too. Seven and five, also girls."

"Well, then, you know exactly what we do, because your daughters are the target for most of it." She reached for my portfolio and started flipping through it. Silence descended.

"You're very good, but I guess you know that."

I made a face. "Not really. It's been a while since I did my own style, so I don't really know what it is anymore."

She flipped the portfolio around. She had it open to a page of little pen-and-ink drawings of my kids. I had put it in there just to fill the portfolio out, actually. I did these little doodles all the time, but don't really consider them work.

"These are great. Unusually quirky and fun, but they still communicate a lot, do you know what I mean? I mean, I see what these kids look like, but I also get a sense of their natures. That's the real skill. But anyway, I need artists who can be flexible and do a variety of styles. Do you write at all?"

I shook my head. "Nope, I'm not a writer."

She closed the portfolio and handed it back. "Well, we have a stable of writers, too, so maybe if I come across something that I think would be good for you, we can put it together. We've had a lot of good fortune

333

with our own titles, and your quirky little pen-and-inks aren't like anything else we do right now. I'll give it some thought."

Was the interview over? I was suddenly confused. Luckily, Betty was still on top of it. Her harassed air apparently hid an organizational maven. No wonder she ran the joint.

"So, I'd love to add you to our roster. How it works is that a job will come in, you'll stop by the office to get briefed, and often meet with the writer or editor on the book or series, and then you can work here if you want, or at home if that's what you prefer. We do flat fee, not hourly."

I was feeling slow. "I'm sorry . . . did I get the job?"

She laughed. "Yes, if you want it. I have two projects I need to brief out tomorrow. Can you take them on? One is a series-episode book, and one is a new series for us with an established style to copy. I'll send you home today with samples, if that works?"

She stood up, and so did I.

"In theory, I'm still working at Poplar until the end of the month."

"Well, then you take one of these jobs, and I'll give the other to someone else. Once you have more time, I'll ramp it up." She suddenly grinned an enormous grin. "I'm stoked! You're really talented, and I think we'll have fun." She led me out of her office. "You should bring the kids over, too. We have a whole play area downstairs."

Oh, my God, I was in heaven. This couldn't get any better.

"It's right next to the espresso machine."

Sigh.

Well, obviously I was beside myself with excitement. Work! Fun work! Work I could do at home if I wanted, so I could see my kids. Maybe work doing my own illustration. I still needed to figure out health insurance, but if I had enough cash, I could afford to do COBRA for a while and then see what happened. I felt calm and peaceful and optimistic, which made a nice change from feeling like a paratrooper in mid-drop. I smiled at the children when they came home, I smiled at Leah, I did gentle stretches and a breast exam in the shower (they're really not weird), which made me feel both yoga-tastic and responsible all at once, and I actually put on nice pajamas for lounging around the house.

Rachel was thrilled about my new job. She actually danced around my kitchen. I wasn't dancing, because I was emptying the dish-washer.

"You see? I knew it would work out. You'll become a rich and famous children's book illustrator, and I'll get to meet George Cloo-ney."

I raised my eyebrows. "Does George have a lot of interest in children's books? He doesn't even have kids, does he?"

"Details, details," she replied airily. She was doing better, having finally given in and slept with Richard. I knew it had been great, because she wouldn't tell me anything about it. Normally I got diagrams.

"Are you seeing Richard later?"

"Nope, he has a work dinner."

"So, are you eating with us?"

"I thought you'd never ask."

"I didn't think I had to."

I finished unloading and started reload-ing, which is, of course, the reason why housework is so depressing. You do it and undo it and redo it all day. You pick up the crap from the kids'-room floor and then the little bastards come along and throw every-thing down again looking for the tiny prin-cess figure you just secretly threw away. You drink a cup of coffee and put the empty cup down on a bedside table and plan to grab it on your way back to the kitchen, but you don't. Next time you make coffee, you grab another cup and leave that one in the bathroom because you're drinking it while you're getting ready for work, but the dog throws up in the hallway, so you leave it there. Before you know it, the whole house is a coffee-cup graveyard and you feel bad about it, but not bad enough that you remember to take the cup back to the kitchen in the first place. Still, better a cluttered house than an empty head, that's what my dad used to say, not that he ever cleaned in his life.

After dinner, I went out to evaluate my garage as a possible studio space, while Rachel played with the kids. I opened the doors and just stood there, regarding the accumulated crap. Dan's bike. Dan's skis. Dan's suitcase. A big dollhouse that the kids might actually play with now. A horse on springs my parents had given them long before it was safe for them to play on, and which I had totally and completely forgotten. Several boxes of mystery items. A clothing rack of winter coats you can never wear in Southern California. Ski clothes, which I don't need, on account of the fact that I can't ski. Shit, I can barely walk down the street without tripping, the last thing I want to do is go somewhere slippery and strap shiny pieces of high-tech polymer to my feet. I'd rather just break both ankles with a pool cue and save on the airfare.

But as I looked around, I saw potential. The garage had been built at the same time as the house, and had some nice details. It had ceiling beams, for example. And two nice windows. The floors were dry, the walls were dry, and there was already electricity out there. I felt something strange in my tummy . . . What was that? . . . Oh, my goodness, it was excitement.

"What do you think?" Rachel had apparently completed her ninja training and had come up behind me on little pussycat feet. I leapt about eighteen feet in the air.

"Jesus H. Christ, don't do that! I've had kids, my pelvic floor can't take that kind of shock. I thought you were playing with the children."

"They fired me. Can I have those skis?"

"Sure. I forgot you skied. I was thinking of making this into an office."

She made a considering face. "That could work. I like the windows."

"Me, too. I can put my desk there."

"It's pretty big, actually." She stepped in and started poking about.

"Bigger than my office at work was."

"You could rent it out." She pulled out a

lamp I honestly had never seen before. Maybe complete strangers had been creeping in and storing stuff in my garage.

"That's true. Maybe I'll see if Sasha wants to share it." Although, as I said it, I wasn't sure if I wanted to share. It would be nice to have a space of my own.

"You'll need help cleaning it out."

"Are you volunteering?"

She shrugged. "Of course. I love to throw stuff away, you know that. Can I have this lamp?"

I nodded. "I'm hoping we can give a lot of it away to charity."

Her voice floated back from behind a stack of boxes. "That's good. Otherwise, I'm just going to take half of it to my place, where I have no room for it. Where are you going to put the bouncy horse? If you throw it away while they're in school, they'll never know."

"That's a great idea, because I have no idea where to put it."

"You can put it in our room," a tiny voice piped up. I closed my eyes.

"And the dollhouse can go in the living room," added another small voice.

We turned around to see the kids and Frank standing there in a row, tallest to smallest.

So much for that plan, then.

The next day I had an appointment with Dr. Graver again. God, they seemed to be coming around so frequently. I said as much.

"We haven't changed the frequency at all, Lili. Maybe you just have more things to talk about."

"Or not talk about."

"What aren't you talking about?"

"Wouldn't you like to know?"

She laughed, which was one of the things I liked about her. She didn't take me all that seriously. "I would like to know, actually. You're paying me for my expertise in analyzing and commenting on your life experiences. It would be helpful if you actually shared them."

I felt chipper but slightly on edge. "Why don't you guess?"

She looked at me. "I would say you're feeling exposed and vulnerable because being interested in someone, sexually, has reminded you of Dan. You feel guilty for wanting to move on, and subconsciously angry because your overdeveloped sense of guilt won't let you do it."

I hated it when she was accurate. "I don't think my sense of guilt is overdeveloped.

I'm just not ready."

"I think you are ready. You just aren't ready to be ready."

"Again, in English?"

She looked at me with deep patience. "There is something comfortable for you in the life you've built, even though you're deeply sad still, and lonely. It's a rut, but it's your rut, do you know what I mean? Additionally, you're going through enormous change all over right now. You're leaving the job you had when Dan was alive. Your sister is getting into a relationship. Your sister-in-law is getting a divorce, from a marriage that predates your own. Your eldest child is coming to terms with the loss of her father, and part of that process means talking about him more frequently. She and her sister are also growing, as children will, and as they get older, your relationship with them changes, too, of course. You're trying to talk to your mom without either of you slamming the phone. You are deeply attracted to someone and trying to pretend he doesn't exist. It's a lot to handle."

"Wow. That is a lot of stuff." I stretched, making myself big and tall. "I'm impressed with my ability to remain calm in the face of it all, aren't you?"

"Yes. I am."

"You realize I could fall apart at any second, like a spineless book in a strong wind?"

"Yes, of course."

"I'm holding on by a thread."

"I realize that."

"I'm totally broken on the inside."

"Completely."

I curled up on the sofa and cried for the rest of the session. Thank God she knew I was a nutcase, or she would have thought I was totally insane.

How to Grow Peas

Peas are easy to grow, but they have a very limited growing season and only stay fresh for a day or two after harvest. If all else fails, don't forget they're easy to find in the frozen section.

- Believe it or not, sprinkling wood ashes on the soil before planting peas is helpful. To the peas, that is.
- Peas are finicky about temperature. They don't mind snow, but they do mind low temperatures. However, if the temperature gets above 70 degrees Fahrenheit, they don't like that, either. Honestly, they're small, but whiny.
- Plant 1 inch deep (deeper if soil is dry) and 2 inches apart.

CHAPTER 17
THE FOURTH CLASS

The next day was Saturday. Gardening class. Edward was friendly but a little distant; maybe he was finally losing interest in me in the face of my apparent lack of interest in him. Which, of course, sucked, because I was interested in him, just not interested in, oh never mind. It was all too complicated.

I have to say our vegetable garden was looking pretty damn leafy. It was time to plant the squash in my Three Sisters garden, which I did, feeling very in tune with nature, and then I shock-and-awed the caterpillars for a while. Mike and Gene were in charge of the salad bed, and it looked amazing. A thick carpet of curly edged leaves, all in miniature right now, but verdant with promise and good health. Angie and Rachel had grown berries, and Eloise and Frances had beans and peas. All of it was growing energetically, and even Impossibly Handsome Bob seemed impressed. I couldn't tell you why just seeing the garden filled me with peace and happiness, but it did. I would have felt like an idiot, except the entire rest of the class felt the same way. After we'd all weeded and fiddled a bit, we started going around admiring each other's areas, which sounds dirty but wasn't.

Rachel's little lavender bed was the least impressive, in that it had been plants when it went in, but there had been growth, and it looked pretty, and goodness knows it smelled nice.

"Are you feeling any better?" I asked her, keeping my voice low because she was being so private about the whole Richard thing. Also, I wasn't sure where Impossibly Handsome Bob fit into this whole picture.

"Yes, actually. It was so good just hanging out with you the other night and being with the kids. It calmed me down. Whatever happens with Richard, I still have my family, you know?" Her voice sharpened. "But if you pick another piece of my lavender, I'll stab you in the ear."

I paused my hand in midreach. "I thought you were feeling all grateful for family."

"I am, but keep your claws off my flowers."

"OK, you nut job." I wandered over to

Angela, who was about to unleash a pod of praying mantises into the garden. *Pod* might not be the right word, but it's what comes to mind.

"I am Shiva the destroyer," she intoned, loudly. "I am the ender of worlds." She shook the little muslin bag and several long, scary-looking insects fell or clambered out. "I am . . . the Mantis of Vengeance!"

I looked at her, my eyebrows raised. She shrugged. "I learned it all from him." She indicated Bash, who was actually looking a little like St. Francis, holding a ladybug gently on his fingertip. "It's amazing how scary even a piece of Lego can be if you give it the right name and sound track."

"Are we going over to your house after class today?"

She shook her head. "No. I thought about it for a while, but I've decided I'd rather move and save all of you for working on an actual garden, if I'm lucky enough to find a place that has one. Fingers crossed, right?"

"Did Bash's dad come around?"

She crouched down, the better to see her mantises wreaking havoc, presumably. "Maybe. I talked to him the other day. He's got a new girlfriend, an actual real, grown-up person. He seemed more open to the idea of my moving." She looked over to where Bash was carefully weeding in his garden plot, next to my kids. He was quietly focused, and the three of them were chattering away. She straightened and stretched. "Being in nature seems to chill him out a bit. I might move a little out of the city, try to find somewhere cheaper, that has a bit of space. But isn't too far from school, for me." She sighed, but then she smiled. "It's nice to see him so mellow, though, makes a change from the human tornado he usually is."

Eloise came up to us. "The kids look happy." We all watched them for a minute. "Hey, week after next is the last class, and Frances and I were thinking of cooking the big celebration meal at our place afterward. I think lots of things will be ready, the salad for sure, some of your tomatoes and corn, the berries . . . what do you think?"

"I think it would be lovely," I said. "Shall we all bring something?"

She shook her head. "No, I think Frances wants to show off. She was a home-economics teacher, you know, back when she started. Public schools don't really teach home economics anymore, sadly. For God's sake don't ask Frances about it. She'll go off on a tirade about the pointlessness of graduating young people who can't boil an egg."

Edward called the class together.

"As you can see, looking around, Mother Nature has been kind to us. Plentiful sun, healthy soil, and the right amount of water have meant that all of your plants have sprouted. We have two more weeks of class, by which time you will all see more substantial growth. The botanical gardens have agreed to let us keep the class area open for the summer, so that your plants can get big enough to transplant to your own gardens, if you wish. I'm also going to teach the class again in the fall, and you're welcome to sign up once more, to deepen your knowledge and enjoyment of gardening." He really did talk like a dork, although my Dutch was nothing to boast about. I gazed at him, remembering that one kiss and wondering if he wanted to kiss me again. Would we ever sleep together? Would we ever even have lunch again? And then I wondered why everyone was looking at me.

Annabel came to my rescue. "Edward was asking if we were going to do the course again?"

"Oh." I blushed. "Maybe. Can I get back to you?"

"We'll do it." Clare was confident. Her

people were going to make it happen.

"We'll discuss it."

Edward smiled at me, and I felt my tummy tighten. I felt adolescent, completely vulnerable and scrutinized, and suddenly it occurred to me that I was going through super-early menopause. Maybe all this hot and cold was just hormonal. I could have all this *plus* hot flashes, memory loss, and vaginal dryness. Fan-fucking-tastic.

At the end of class, we all stood about for a bit, trying to persuade Angela to let us come over to do some planting on her balcony. She had to be firm.

"No, it's not ready for you yet, and I don't have any plants to put out there anyway." She looked around at us all. "What about Mike's place? We haven't been there yet."

She was right. We all swiveled to look at him. He laughed and put up his hands. "Dudes, put down your weapons. I don't have a place, actually."

Gene didn't look surprised, so I guess this wasn't news to him, but the rest of us were taken aback. Rachel spoke up. "What do you mean?"

He turned up his palms. "I mean I'm a rolling stone, bro. I live in a trailer attached to my car, and I move around a lot. One of the reasons I wanted to do this class was to do something I can't do otherwise, which is have a garden."

There was a pause. Luckily for all of us, Annabel has some sense of courtesy.

"Then why don't you all come back to our house for pizza again? Bash wants to see the fairy house, and you can help us clear out the garage to be Mom's office. She got a new job."

"How come you didn't mention that earlier?" Angela was slightly outraged. "I mean, that's big news, right? Are you pleased?"

I nodded, looking around. A retired banker, a pair of teachers, a surf bum, a working single mom, an importer of rare artifacts, and three small kids. A mixed lot, that's for sure, but we were all happy to be together, and somehow we had become friends. My gaze settled on Edward, who smiled gently at me. I smiled back.

"Yeah, I'm really pleased. Please come hang out, if you want to. You don't need to help me clear out the garage, though."

"Sounds like a plan," said Frances. "And while we're there, Mike can tell us how he came to live in a trailer."

He groaned. "It isn't that interesting."

Frances clicked her tongue. "We'll be the judge of that, young man."

■ ■ ■ ■

As it happened, Mike did the easiest thing and drove his trailer over to my house. Angela was somewhat sarcastic.

"OK, *bro,* I have to say that your idea of living rough is different from mine. That trailer is bigger than my parents' apartment, and there are two families living there."

He looked a little abashed. "Well, OK, but I meant that I didn't really have a fixed address. I go where the mood takes me, or, more important, where the surf is."

His trailer was one of those cool silver things, shaped like a loaf of bread and about twenty feet long. It was attached to a very old Jeep, and the whole thing shouted *California dreamer here!* It could have been the long boards on the top, or maybe the bike rack on the back, or the skis attached to the sides. It was a Sports Chalet store on wheels.

Needless to say, the kids were astonished. Clare just kept going in and out, and laughing at all the tiny furniture, and Annabel set up at the table inside, coloring. This was cute for ten minutes or so, and then it got annoying because it meant someone had to stand out front and watch them. So we dragged them out and distracted them with the fairy house.

Edward and I found ourselves alone in the kitchen.

"How are you, Lilian? I have been thinking about you, of course." I looked at him and realized I was making him unhappy.

"I'm fine." I put the coffee on and made my voice calm. "I'm sorry things didn't work out. You should probably give up on me."

"Like you have?"

I frowned and turned to him, but he was already halfway out the door to the back garden. I finished making the coffee, and found my hands were shaking. I pulled it together and carried the tray out to the garden, ready to be distracted by Mike's trailer tale.

Surprisingly, the story of the trailer itself was kind of boring. It had belonged to his parents when they were young hippies, and they had given it to him as a gift. However, things picked up after that.

"Did you go to college?" Frances was determined to find a story.

He shook his head. He was wearing ripped jeans and an old Bee Gees T-shirt, presumably ironically. "Not so much. Well, yes. Sort of."

Frances clicked her tongue. "Did you or

didn't you?"

He looked embarrassed. "Well, yes. But I went early and not for the whole four years."

"You dropped out?"

"No, finished early." He gazed at his Vans, probably because they weren't grilling him about his personal history.

Rachel had gotten interested, despite herself.

"Michael."

"Yes, Rachel."

"Did you attend an institution of higher learning?"

"Yes."

"Where?"

"In Cambridge, Massachusetts."

"Harvard?"

"MIT."

"Now we're getting somewhere. You're a geek?"

He cleared his throat. "I'm a nerd. Geeks bite the heads off chickens."

"Sorry."

"That's fine. It's a common error." I noticed his surfer attitude was melting away somewhat. I hadn't heard a *bro* in several minutes.

"And how old were you when you went to MIT?"

"Fifteen."

"I see. And did you graduate having completed a degree?"

"Yes. In computer science."

"And when was that?"

"When I was seventeen."

"I see. So you are a surfing hippie nerd genius?"

"No. A genius is someone . . ."

"Michael." Her tone was a warning.

"Yes, then. If you must have a label."

We all sat and looked at him differently, as you do when someone has revealed something unexpected. The sound of mental gears clashing filled the air. Mike sighed. "Now you're all going to look at me differently."

We all shook our heads. Apart from Angela, who, for some reason, looked a little pissed off. She leaned back on her hands and tipped her head to one side. "I am, for sure. I thought you were a hippie dropout, and now I think you're a hippie burnout. Here's my guess: overeducated because you were supersmart, sent away to college before you were really ready, rushed through it because you could and because you were overwhelmed by all the big kids who were as smart as you, then two years hiding in your parents' house trying to get your shit back together, then giving up on the whole thing and driving around from beach to beach. And you take courses like this one because your brain can't stand to be idle for too long." She regarded him coolly. "Am I right?"

We were all looking at him, and I think we all saw the same thing. His first reaction to this somewhat damning narrative was anger — a reasonable reaction, seeing as no one likes to be judged. And then he grinned.

"You couldn't be more wrong, Miss Leapy Conclusion-son. Here, I'll tell you what actually happened, then you really will look at me differently, I'm afraid, and then I'll tell you *your* story."

She nodded. I looked at Edward, who was already looking at me, it turned out, which was awkward, and then I looked at Rachel, who shrugged. I started to feel a little worried that this was going to get messy, but what can you do? One minute it's all happy in the garden, pass the pizza, and the next minute it's *Lord of the Flies* meets spin the bottle. But shit, they'd always had a somewhat prickly relationship, those two.

Mike lay back on the grass and folded his arms on his chest. I flicked a glance around. Everyone was interested except for the kids, who were just playing, and Gene, who was having a moment with Frank. I looked back to Mike, who was apparently reading something printed on the sky.

"Yes, I was supersmart as a kid, and so I went to college early. However, I graduated early because I came up with a way to change how the military processed information from troops on the ground, and the government asked me to go and implement it. My parents are dyed-in-the-wool Berkeley pacifists and weren't having it until I graduated, so I finished my degree early, went to the Middle East, and implemented my system, which made things safer for our troops, most of whom were only a few years older than me. That was great. Then I got blown up in a truck with five other soldiers, three of whom died, which was less than great.

"They shipped me home with a shattered leg, and I spent a year in rehab in San Diego. That's where I got into surfing. My parents gave me the trailer so I could travel around, surf, and work on my Ph.D., which is about the real-time processing of military intelligence." He leaned up on his elbow and looked at Angie a little defensively. "But you were right about one thing. I took this course because my brain likes to be fed new stuff. And because I realized as I was lying in the hospital that life is too short to be lived entirely in your head."

Well, there you have it. Not just a hippie übernerd but a supersmart war-hero nerd. I was clearing my throat to offer sodas to the shocked troops on the ground, so to speak, when he continued.

"And here's my guess about you, Angela. Also supersmart but undereducated because of the crappy public school in your neighborhood, knowing you could do better but not being able to find a way. Maybe one teacher saw your potential, but too many others just looked through you, too tired to care. You met a confident guy with a plan of escape, and you accidentally got pregnant. Bam, there goes college for a while. Broke up with the dad because" — he looked over at Bash and saw that he could hear, although he was playing, and lowered his voice — "because, let's face it, he wasn't as smart as you, and then taking care of a baby and doing school was too hard, so you dropped out. When Bash got a little older, you put him in day care, or left him with your mom, got a job, got your GED, and enrolled in nursing school because you couldn't afford medical school. Now you're just trying to get qualified so you can get out of the 'hood and start building a better life. You're fearless and determined, and I think you're

357

totally amazing and gorgeous, but the chance of you ever going out with someone like me seems like, approximately, fourteen million to one. Against." He smiled at her, crookedly. "Am I right?"

I swear to God, we all held our breath.

She hadn't changed her expression, but she waited nearly a full minute before replying. "Yes, and no. You're scarily right about my life, which I suppose is reasonable, seeing as it's as predictable as it gets, but you're totally wrong about the other thing. I would love to go out with you."

We all burst into applause, because, honestly, how often do you see romance like that played out in front of you? It was like being in the studio audience. The kids had no idea what was going on, but they cheered, too, which is one of the nice things about kids. They're always up for a party.

After everyone had left, Rachel helped me put the kids to bed. They were still obsessed with the fairy house, in the way kids form deep obsessions from time to time. They carried all the fairies inside and washed them in the bath, drying each one carefully with a facecloth and cotton buds. Lining them up on their bedroom rug, they rearranged and named them all about five times. They wrote everything down, very carefully. There was much discussion of internal relationships and family trees. It was like an anthropology lecture.

Once that was sorted out, they consented to go to bed. Annabel looked up at me from her pillow, her pink face relaxed. "Is Bash's mom going to go out with Mike now?"

Remember how I said kids pay attention when you don't know they're doing it? Here was another classic example. I swear to God, they weren't even close enough to hear what was going on, but apparently Annabel had gone back over the transcripts. I gathered half a dozen soft toys from the top of the bed and moved them to the bottom. If they wanted to smother her, they'd have to work for it.

"Maybe," I said. "It's too early to tell. People often like each other but don't end up together, and that's totally all right."

"Like you and Edward?"

"That's different."

"Why?"

"Because I'm not really ready to go out with anyone, but Mike and Angela both are."

She looked at me thoughtfully, her face still calm. For once this conversation wasn't worrying her, which felt like progress. It was worrying the shit out of me, but hey, like I said, baby steps.

"You can have a boyfriend if you like. Daddy wouldn't mind."

I tucked the sheet in around her. Rachel was on the other side of the room, reading a story to Clare, but I could tell she was listening. Clare could, too, and suddenly tapped on the book.

"Hey! You just read that bit wrong."

Rachel fought back. "How do you know? You don't even read."

"I mostly read. And I know this book." She recited the entire paragraph from memory. "You said 'brown bear,' when it's actually 'honey brown bear.' "

Rachel frowned. "That's a pretty minor detail."

"Not to the bear."

I turned back to Annabel, hoping this had distracted her. But no, her eyes were still on me. Since when had my little kid turned into the Spanish Inquisition? Nobody expects that.

"OK, time to go to sleep." I bent down and kissed her.

"Can we talk about this tomorrow?"

I stood up. "No, there's not really anything to talk about." Without waiting for an answer, I went over to Clare, gave her a kiss, and left Rachel to finish the story and turn out the light.

I started making more coffee, despite it being nearly nine. For some people, stress leads to drinking, or saying the rosary, or meditating. For me, it's pulling out a filter paper and filling it with coffee grounds. To each his own, and at least I'll be awake for whatever disaster is coming.

Rachel came in and exhaled loudly.

"Remind me, if I should ever be foolish enough to have kids, that I should keep them secluded from all human interaction. A closet, maybe. Or a convent."

"Convents are full of humans."

"Humans dressed as penguins, though, so not quite the same."

"These are executional details. You haven't said why yet."

She sat down on a kitchen chair and immediately got up again to get herself some water. "I was freaked out by Annabel grilling you. I didn't realize those little balls of poop and tears became people with opinions they are happy to express."

"They do. Plus they also still poop and cry." I poured some coffee.

"It's scary."

"And then, just when they wear you down completely and have you hanging on their every word, they piss off to college and never come back." I sat across from her. "What's going on with Richard?"

"Nothing. It's good. It's all good. Some of it is even great."

"Are you going to introduce him to Mom?"

She laughed. "I said it was going well. Why on earth would I want to risk ruining it? Besides, it's early days. Eventually experience will destroy the illusion that I'm a functional adult, but why rush it?" She pulled the sleeves of her sweater down over her hands and shivered.

I sighed. "Mom and I had a nearly normal conversation on the phone the other day."

"Are you sure it wasn't a wrong number?"

"Pretty sure. She knew a lot of details for a complete stranger."

"Fair enough. Well, I'm not introducing him to anyone just yet. He may still turn out to be a psychopath."

"You're so optimistic."

We went into the living room, and I began my previously described evening ritual of corralling toys.

"Do you get bored of your life?"

I looked up from the Fisher-Price Little People bucket and gazed at Rachel. "Which part?" I threw a horse into the bucket. "The tidying-up-toys part, the making-endless-meals-that-get-ignored part, or the continuous-whining part?" I sat back on my heels, pondering. "Although, before you clarify, none of it is actually any more boring or more interesting than any other part. Until you have kids, you work for yourself, so you can minimize the really boring stuff, and then you have kids and you work for them. It's more boring, but it's boring with a purpose, if you get what I mean."

"I think so." She started helping me tidy up but quickly got distracted by the dollhouse, which I'd brought in from the garage. I crawled over and sat next to her. After I'd pulled the house out of the garage, I'd found a huge plastic tub full of little furniture, which had blown the children's minds completely. Now Rachel and I sat side by side and set up the house. Her rooms were more eclectic than mine, I'm not afraid to say. For example, she made a table out of two Playmobil horses and a ruler.

"You're very creative," I said.

"Only in miniature," she replied, airily. "Look, can I ask you something?"

"Sure." I started arranging tiny throw cushions. Poorly.

"When you first met Dan, how did you know he was the right one?"

This was a surprising question. She had essentially been there for the whole relationship; we'd all agreed Dan was awesome. As if reading my mind, she continued.

"I mean, we all knew he was great, but there are lots of great people in the world. How did you know he was actually The One?"

I shrugged. "Well, first of all, you're assuming there is only one, rather than several. I don't think there is only one."

She looked at me. "Then why aren't you interested in dating anyone else? I think he was your one, and you don't think anyone else comes close."

I thought about it, as I put very small cutlery in a very small drawer. "No, I'm just not ready yet. Think about it this way: If you break a leg, you give it time to heal, and you don't run on it right away, right? Well, I'm still healing, and I'm not ready to run, that's all. It doesn't mean I won't go out with other people in the future." My back hurt, so I moved to the sofa. "Why do you ask, anyway? Is this about Richard?"

She nodded, still working on the house. "Yeah. I feel differently about him than I ever have about anyone else."

"So maybe you're ready. Maybe it's not him, but you."

She laughed. "It's not you, it's me?" She apparently changed her mind about the location of the bedroom, because she suddenly removed everything from two rooms and started over. She was really giving it some thought.

I curled up on the sofa and got comfortable. "Exactly. Here's what I think: I don't think there is just one person for everyone. I think there are actually lots. But think about how many people you meet, and how many people you *don't* meet. Hundreds of people pass you on the street every day, and somewhere among them might be one you could fall in love with, have children with, or just live with in peace and harmony for your whole life. But what if they turn the corner before you do, or go back to get something they forgot, or take one minute longer to get coffee at Starbucks . . . you might never meet. And then what if you do meet but for some reason you're having an off day, or they are, or they just broke up with someone, or they're coming down with a cold, or whatever, so for whatever reason you don't click right away. It's amazing anyone hooks up at all, really."

She was gazing at me. "You realize that in no way answers my question, right?"

I was disappointed. "It doesn't? It felt so

wise as I said it."

"Sorry. Can you just answer the question: How did you know Dan was the right person for you, at that time, at that point in space, regardless of the astronomical odds against anyone ever finding true love?"

I shrugged. "I don't know. He just smelled right."

She grinned, suddenly. "Now, that is actually helpful."

"It is?"

"Yeah." She regarded the dollhouse happily. "That makes sense to me. Richard smells right, too." She looked over at me, slyly. "And Edward doesn't smell good to you?"

I laughed. "Actually, he smells great to me. Maybe my brain is just slower than my nose."

"You know, if we stick to your earlier metaphor, then you can only strengthen a broken leg by using it, not by staying off it."

"You're really annoying, did you know that?"

"Yes. I'm going to take out all the rooms you did. Is that OK? They don't go with my overall vision for this house."

And with that she started disassembling everything I'd put together. I let her. I could always rearrange it when she was gone.

I thought about what she'd said. Maybe I should give Edward a chance, even though the thought of it made me break out in a cold sweat. It was the thought of it, though, not the actual reality of it, and maybe I should listen to my nose while I walk on my leg . . . Jesus, the whole metaphor thing was so tiring. I lay back on the sofa and drifted off, listening to Rachel rattle on about the dollhouse's feng shui.

How to Grow Cabbage

Start cabbage seeds indoors 6 to 8 weeks before the last spring frost, assuming you know when that is.

- Put them outside a week before you want to put them in the ground, to harden them off and get them excited about the wider world they're about to inhabit.
- Put them in the ground 2 or 3 weeks before the last spring frost, so they're good and settled before it comes and startles them.
- Plant 12 to 24 inches apart in rows, depending on size of head desired. The closer you plant, the smaller the heads.
- There are many, many ways to prepare cabbage, most of them delicious. If you think cabbage is smelly, it's because you've been overcooking it. Cook it for too long and it produces hydrogen sulfide, presumably as a comment on your cooking skills. Sorry, but that's how they roll.

CHAPTER 18

I continued clearing out my desk at work. It was amazing how much crap had accumulated, simply mind-blowing. I wish I was one of those people who clean as they go, who are models of organization and clarity, but I'm just not. If I find myself with a piece of paper in my hand, and I'm unsure where to put it, I lay it down on the nearest surface and hope it folds itself into a paper plane and flies wherever it's supposed to go. While optimistic, this approach has obvious flaws and irritated the office cleaner almost to apoplexy. She would pile the paper up every night, neatly squaring the corners, removing obvious bits of trash, doing her best, and every morning I would throw it all over the desk again looking for whatever it was I needed. In the end, we started leaving notes for each other:

Me: "Thanks so much for clearing my desk. Although it looks messy, it is in fact very organized. Please feel free to leave it as it is. Thanks."

Her: "It is my job to clean your desk."

Me: "Thanks so much for cleaning my desk. Please don't worry about it any longer."

Her: "It is my job to clean your desk. If I don't leave all the desktops clear, I get in trouble."

Me: "I have put a big cardboard box under my desk. Please sweep any papers into it, then we'll both be happy."

And that worked. She would throw everything in the box, I would rustle through the box and find what I needed, and my desktop was clear. Everybody wins.

It's possible, of course, that I was following this paradigm in my own life, too: sweep it under the desk, keep the surface clear, no one will notice. It had worked for a very long time at work, but now I was dealing with years of accumulated paperwork and discovering that most of it was no longer needed. I sighed and ignored the obvious symbolism.

While I was mid-purge, the phone rang. It was Edward.

"I know you've made it clear you're not interested in dating, but I'm near your office and I wondered if you'd like to have lunch?" He coughed. He was nervous. "Just lunch. Maybe more milkshakes?"

My first reaction was to frown. But then I remembered the whole leg/nose conversation with Rachel, and realized I was hungry.

We went to the diner, ordered burgers and malts, and sat there smiling vaguely at each other. Edward was wearing a suit, strangely, and looked a little tired.

"My son broke his ankle, skateboarding, and I was up early this morning talking with his mother on Skype. He's fine, and apparently broke his ankle in front of a huge crowd of friends, performing some daring feat, and didn't cry, so he has become a temporary playground hero."

"How old is he again?"

"Twelve."

"A good age to be a hero."

Edward nodded. "His mom is thinking of getting married."

I paused, fork in midair. "Did you know that was coming?"

"Yes, she's been with the same man for the past several years, he's someone we've known a long time." He sighed. "She probably should have married him in the first place. They're much more suited to one another. He is a good father to my son. It's all fine."

He didn't elaborate. I didn't push it.

"Do you always dress up to talk to your wife?"

He was confused for a moment, so I pointed to his suit. "I haven't seen you in a suit before." He looked fantastic, to be truthful. Men in suits are just so . . . dapper.

He made a face. "I rarely wear one. I had a board meeting. My family is vaguely irritated I am in America, but it doesn't stop my sister from asking me to attend the occasional boring meeting on her behalf."

He took another sip of milkshake and smiled at me. "Ex-wife."

"I'm sorry?"

"You said, 'wife.' She's my ex-wife."

"Right. Ex-wife."

We ate in silence for a moment. "Are there more of your family over here?" I asked. "Or are they all in Holland?"

He shook his head. "No, I have a younger sister in college over here, but on the East Coast. I see her even less than my family back in Amsterdam."

"Is she studying horticulture, too?"

"No, Mandarin and political history." He smiled. "She plans to run the United Nations at some point. She's at the age when everything and anything seems possible."

He was really so handsome, his smile was so lovely and warm, and suddenly I was inspired, or possessed, or temporarily insane, or something. "Would you like to come to dinner on Friday night? At my house? My mother is coming, and Rachel . . ." I trailed off, losing confidence. I hadn't actually invited anyone yet. It had just come to me. He looked surprised.

"I'd love to." He paused. "I wasn't sure if you . . . I mean, I know you're . . ."

I smiled at him. "I have no idea if I . . . or if I'm . . . but I just thought it would be nice. Although I warn you, my mother is a piece of work." I swallowed. "Besides, you can check on the garden."

He smiled at me. "Yes, what a good idea."

He and I both knew it had nothing to do with the garden. But if it made it easier to say that it did, then we were going to go with it.

Rachel did her level best to avoid coming to dinner, but in the end I threatened to post teenage pictures of her on Facebook, and she relented. She also agreed to bring Richard, as I pointed out that Maggie was coming, and so was Edward, so there would be plenty of targets for Mom.

"If you're inviting a wolf to dinner, you might as well invite several lambs at the same time, so one or two might survive. Maybe she'll pick on Edward, and Richard will escape with only minor surface abrasions."

"Maybe. Or maybe she'll rip all our throats out and that will be the end of it."

I looked in the rearview mirror. I was driving the kids home from school and had Rachel on speaker. Neither of the kids appeared to be listening. Which presumably meant they were taking notes.

"Let's try and stay open-minded?" I don't know why it suddenly mattered to me to make peace with my mother, but it did.

Rachel sighed in exasperation. "All right. But you must promise to make something delicious and soft, so if I have to fall face-forward into it to cause a diversion, it will be worth it."

"I'm making lasagna."

She cheered. "Perfect. A soft landing *and* a million calories per slice. Win-win."

"I love lasagna." Annabel was listening after all.

"Me, too." And so was Clare.

"And for dessert I was going to make a chocolate cake."

Rachel laughed. "You know she won't eat

it. You're already messing with her by making lasagna. I hope you're also serving a collection of dry twigs for her to nibble on."

"I'm doing a dead-leaf side salad." I turned into our driveway. "Besides, all the more for us."

Our mother had carried two things forward from her modeling career: a cast-iron commitment to sun protection and an unwillingness to eat anything more than ten calories an ounce. She had been one of those mothers who rarely cooked, unless pasta in red sauce out of a jar counts, but had taken us out to restaurants all the time instead. She would eat a side salad, then encourage us to order dessert and watch us eat it. I knew what judgment felt like before I could spell it.

When Friday came, I felt surprisingly enthusiastic about it. I made the lasagna early, so I wouldn't be rushing around at the last minute, and set the table with actual silverware. I bought flowers, I tidied the house, I even wiped the children's faces with the wet corner of a towel — no effort spared. Maggie had come over early to hang out and seemed to be doing better. She'd only broken down in tears once, so hopefully she wouldn't do it again during dinner. I gave everyone extra napkins just in case.

My mom showed up with three bottles of wine and two enormous presents for the kids. Gigantic stuffed horses, one pink, one purple. Clare and Annabel were thrilled, of course, and Mom preened like grandmother of the year as they dragged her to their bedroom to put their new toys with the others. Edward arrived, along with Richard and Rachel, and everything seemed fine, although I got suddenly panicky about the food and bustled around after all, pouring wine, tossing salad, heating that bread you get at Trader Joe's that is already half-cooked . . .

I took the lasagna out of the oven and had to admit to myself that it looked good enough to stick your face into. I listened for the kids and realized my mother and Edward were both in their room. He was unprotected. I put the lasagna down and went to check for casualties.

But when I skidded around the corner, no one was bleeding. Clare had Maggie, Edward, and my mom sitting in a ring on the rug, adults interspersed with those little beanbag animals whose name I can't recall right now, and was holding forth on some topic. My mother was looking at Edward thoughtfully, but not in a hostile or flirtatious way, and Edward was leaning back on his hands and listening to Clare. He looked up as I came in.

"Did you know that the primary source of power in Beanytown is heartfelt love?"

I shook my head. "Heartfelt love?"

He nodded at Clare. "That is what she just told us, and that is the exact phrase she used."

Clare beamed at me. "I saw it on TV," she explained. "I think it means that you love someone and squeeze your chest to make it come out."

Annabel snorted. "It doesn't mean that, you goofball. It just means that you really love something."

Clare frowned. "I'm not a goofball, and it's my game, so it can mean what I want it to mean, Mrs. You."

I told them dinner was ready and went to the living room, where Rachel and Richard were hiding out.

"You realize, I suppose, that both your names begin with the same letter." I poured them a glass of wine. Each. I'm generous that way. Richard grinned.

"Yes, we noticed that early on. We also noticed that if we have a child and give him or her a name that also begins with R that we can say we have the three *R*s covered."

"Wow, and maybe you can all have matching propeller beanies." I was covering the fact I was suddenly excited at the thought of my sister having children. I had accepted it was never going to happen, and it was fine, but a baby is a baby, am I right?

Rachel shrugged. "Why not? How about Rapunzel, or Requiem, or Rumpelstiltskin?"

"Or Random, Rorschach, or Ritalin." Richard liked this game.

"You could go techy and call them RAM or ROM."

"Or medical and call them Rheumatism or Rabies or Rubella."

"Rubella's pretty."

"Actually," my mother said, making an entrance as usual, "Rubella is what we should have called you, Rachel, because you were so incredibly spotty in your teens."

There was a pause, and the thin squeaking sound of air leaking out of a balloon.

"Hi, Mom, thanks for the memory." Rachel gave Mom a hug and turned to Richard. "This is Richard. Richard, this is my mom, Karen."

Richard shook my mother's hand and said, "Well, I can see that despite a possibly spotty youth, Rachel inherited her beautiful skin from you, Mrs. Anderby."

I met Rachel's eyes, and we both did a roll in unison. But it was a good opener, and had the desired effect. Mom smiled her twenty-thousand-dollar smile, the one that had graced the cover of *Cosmo* back in the day, and Richard could be seen thanking his lucky stars for Rachel's gene pool. Which, truthfully, was one good thing about having such a good-looking mother: People were forever commenting on how well she had aged, and how reassuring it was for us, which was true, but didn't really make up for childhood neglect. Or for the problem of bringing home teenage boys who then spent all their time in the kitchen having *Graduate* fantasies. I had hesitated before bringing Dan home, too, but he had met her, been charmed by her, and then told me that pretty though she was, she was nothing compared to me.

"When I look in your eyes," he had memorably said, just before removing my bra for the first time without help, "I see how beautiful your thoughts are, but with her I only see that she isn't really thinking of anyone but herself." And while this was somewhat cheesy, and doubtless motivated by the aforementioned bra removal, it stuck in my head.

We sat down to eat.

"Goodness," said my mother. "This is a tight fit. If you girls end up keeping these men longer than usual, we'll need to get a bigger table."

I let it go, but Rachel has more energy than me. "Are all relationships just opportunities for home furnishings, Mom?"

Mom shrugged. "Mostly, Rachel. Yours don't usually last long enough for furniture, though, do they?" She smiled at Richard, as if that made up for what she'd just said. "Maybe you're a keeper, though, Dick."

"Or maybe I'm just a dick," he shot back, "but hopefully I'm a keeper."

Great. I hadn't even put food on the table and already there was fighting. Please, Dan, I prayed, if you're up there in heaven, have a word with someone and prevent this meal from degenerating. He had always been very good at deflecting battles, and when he and my dad had both been around, there had been family meals that were totally without incident. Thanksgiving '97, for example.

My mother turned to Maggie.

"At least you've lost one, so that leaves more room."

Honestly, she was deadly. Maggie looked as though she might tear up, but she'd known my mom for a very long time and, remembering who she was dealing with, let it go. Edward had been busy seating the kids, and getting them drinks, and generally paying attention to them. Hopefully he hadn't even heard Mom's catty bullshit. He sat, and I brought the lasagna to the table. The children did their usual "whoo" noises, which I love. They're very supportive and impressed by large food, and I basked for a moment before putting it down.

"Watch out, it's hot," I cautioned, handing Edward the large serving spoon. "Can you serve the kids for me?"

"Look out, Edward, she's already put you to work." My mom giggled, attractively. I waited for the other shoe to drop, but she didn't say anything else.

"I am happy to help, particularly if it means I get to serve myself a particularly large piece." Edward's voice was like a temple bell or something else one might use for meditation. The counterpoint of the kids' little fluting tones was very pretty, I thought.

"Edward," said Annabel, "do you like the cheese-sauce part or the meat-sauce part?"

He shrugged. "I like the combination of all of it together, Annabel. What about you?"

She shrugged, too, mimicking him. "Me, too, I guess. But I like the meat sauce when it's just on spaghetti, too."

Richard looked over at me. "This is honestly the best lasagna I've ever had, Lilian. I'm not sure how I ever get Rachel to come out for dinner when she could be eating here all the time."

He smiled at Rachel, but my mother answered him. "It's lucky they inherited my good genes, isn't it, Richard? My girls may not have quite inherited my bone structure, but they both got my metabolism. I can eat like a horse and still stay a size one." She smiled. "I worry a little about Clare, though. She picked up her Dad's slightly chunkier build, didn't you, pudding?"

Rachel caught my eye and looked horrified. I was silent, but it was only because I was building up a proper head of steam. Just as I was about to get to my feet and order her out of my life forever, Clare spoke up.

"It's not about how big or small you are, Grandma, you know." She took another bite of lasagna, and talked around it. "It's about being strong and healthy. You need to eat plenty and run around a lot and drink lots of water and go to sleep early, that's what Mom says."

There was a pause. I looked at my mom, who was looking at Clare with the sappiest expression of love and pride, and I suddenly realized she couldn't help being who she was. My kids had inherited some of her genes, but they had also inherited my dad's, and their dad's, and mine, and apparently they could stand up for themselves much better than I had been able to.

"That's true, honey," Mom said, reaching for Clare's little hand. "And you have a wonderful mom, don't you?"

Clare nodded. "She's the bomb."

Rachel took the chance to change the subject.

"So, Edward, you grew up in Amsterdam?"

He smiled. "Yeah, have you been there?"

"Sure. For business and pleasure. I really like it."

"I knew a Bloem in the sixties. Arlette. She was a model, too." My mother likes the conversation to be about her.

Edward nodded. "Arlette is my father's older sister. She gave up modeling before I was much more than a kid, but she was kind of famous in Holland, so I still see pictures of her from time to time."

My mother was delighted. "My goodness, what a very small world!"

Edward's tone was wry. "The world is very big, but Holland is pretty small."

My mother wasn't paying attention. "Oh,

the stories I could tell you about Arlette."

"Please don't, Mom," I begged. "I'm sure Edward doesn't want to hear about his aunt's exciting youth."

Pointless.

"She was a very beautiful girl, I remember that quite clearly. You know, one fashion week in Milan she managed to sleep with all the best photographers, all of them. She had a copy of Italian *Vogue,* and went through, crossing them out. She was like that, very bold and adventurous." She laughed and looked at Edward. "Are you like that, Edward?"

He laughed with her. "Not so much. There are many top photographers I haven't even kissed, to be honest." We all laughed, even the kids, who had no idea what was going on. I hope. "And now my aunt is just an elegant older woman who dotes on her grandchildren and does good things for charity. She would probably love to hear from you, though. I will give her your e-mail address, if you like." Edward smiled at my mom. "I hope when I am older I will have wonderful memories to think back on, too. It must be good."

Mom frowned a little at the repeated use of "old," but he was charming, so she was inclined to let it slide. "I am still making plenty of memories, Edward. Why, next week I am taking a trip with a Venezuelan cattle millionaire. To Caracas."

Richard coughed. "Don't forget your maracas."

She ignored him. It was easy to see which guy she was going to favor. Oh well, Rachel wasn't interested in her approval. I looked at my sister, sitting with Richard and making quiet jokes about Caracas. She was fine. I looked over at my mother and noticed her hand was trembling a little as it lifted her wineglass. She was nervous, too, probably more nervous than any of us. Her jawline was still firm, but that was all. Our house had been filled with pictures of her — magazine covers, famous images — almost all of them retouched beyond what was real even at twenty-two. She had worked hard to keep looking that way, but time is implacable and moisturizer only goes so deep. It's painful enough to get old without constantly being confronted with evidence of how much better you used to look. Whenever I see aging beauties, I imagine heavy garlands of "before" pictures hanging around their necks, like Marley's chains. And . . . we're back to Meg Ryan's face.

Things progressed peacefully for a while, and then Mom turned to me.

"So, Lilian. Rachel tells me you're going to try and go it alone for a while, professionally."

I looked at Rachel, whose face showed me she hadn't really said anything of the sort, but it was OK. My mom could winkle information out of a parking meter.

I nodded. "Yeah. I'm hoping there will be enough freelance, combined with original illustration work, to keep us going. I might have to cut back a bit."

"No more Leah, presumably." My mom had always been a little bit jealous of Leah.

Balls. I looked at Clare, but she hadn't noticed. Annabel had, though. "What? Is Leah leaving?"

OK, Clare heard that.

"Leah can't leave," she said firmly. "Leah is family, and family doesn't leave."

"Uh, we can talk about this later on, guys. Leah's not going anywhere right now."

"But is she going to leave?" Annabel was persistent.

I shook my head. "I hope not, honey. Let's talk about it another time, though, OK?"

Maggie leapt in to help.

"Clare, I hear you've grown some strawberries."

Clare nodded, her mouth full of lasagna. Maggie turned to Annabel, who was still

386

watching me thoughtfully. If I thought the conversation about Leah was done, I was on crack.

"And did you grow fruit, too, Bel?"

She shook her small head. "No, I grew flowers in a pattern. It's a little patchy right now, but it will be all filled in soon." She smiled. "Did you see our fairy house, though?" She beamed at Edward. "Edward brought us a fairy house with fairies and everything. It's in the garden."

My mother laughed. "Nice work, Edward. Mind you, I guess it makes sense to seduce the children if you're trying to bed the mother."

No. She. Did. Not. But yes, she did. Edward looked surprised, but kept his tone level.

"Well, that's one way of looking at it, but I mostly just wanted to make something fun for them to play with in the garden, so they would enjoy being out there. Being in nature is very good for kids, I think."

My mother just laughed, unable to think of anything to say. Rachel had put her fork down and was just gazing at her in horror. Maggie was trying not to laugh hysterically, I think. And then, thankfully, someone banged on the door.

■ ■ ■ ■

I got up, somewhat shakily, and went to answer it. Everyone I knew was there, pretty much, so it was probably the Mormons or something. Maybe I would amaze them by converting on the spot and begging them to take me to Utah, right away.

"Is my wife here?"

Berto. Looking disheveled and badly dressed, which for an Italian man was a clear sign of imminent nervous breakdown. Great, this dinner was now truly a farce. All we needed to make it complete was a naked couple falling out of a closet, and a vicar in his underwear.

"Uh . . . hi, Berto. Hang on, I'll go look." I closed the door in his face, which wasn't very polite, but hey, he was a bottom-feeding cheat machine, so tough titties.

Maggie heard him, of course, because it's not that big a house. She was totally white, and everyone at the table was staring at her.

"It's Berto," I said, unnecessarily. "Do you want me to tell him you're not here?"

She nodded, silently. I went back to the door.

"She's not here. Sorry." I started to close the door again, but he stuck his foot in it. I was willing to crush it like a grape but hesitated one second too long. He leaned on the door.

"Lili, *cara,* please let me in to see her."

"She's not here, Berto. Go away." I pushed back, ready to call for reinforcements if I needed to.

"Her car is parked outside."

Shit.

"I'm changing the oil for her. She took a cab home. Go away."

"I have known you forever, and this is first time you ever indicate you even know a car needs oil. She is inside, and I must speak with her."

I gave him my best haughty frown.

"First of all, Mr. Cheating Bastard, this is no time to be insulting my car-care abilities, and secondly, she doesn't want to talk to you."

He hung his head. "It is true, I have been a bad husband, a stupid man, and a careless friend, but I love my wife and I must talk to her."

He really looked dreadful, which was satisfying. I shook my head.

"Did you just arrive?" He nodded. "Then you haven't unpacked yet, which will save you some time. Go back to Italy, Berto, back to your little girlfriend."

"She is gone. It is over."

I switched over to disgusted frown. "Well. Maggie is not a consolation prize, shithead. She's the trophy, the Pulitzer, the Nobel. The fact that your girlfriend dumped you means nothing. Go home." Luckily, the anger I had been building up for my mother was right there, ready to be used. I was going to kick his butt.

Unfortunately for my catharsis, he started to cry. I would have been touched, but he's Italian. They cry over soccer.

"Lili, my friend, I know that when Dan died, when you lost your lover, you went mad with grief. It was understandable. And now I, too, feel like I am losing my mind, except it is worse, because I am the one who drove her away, who cast her aside."

I wasn't falling for it.

"You're too late, you sorry sack of shit. Maggie has moved on."

He gasped. "She has taken a lover already?"

I shrugged. "More than one. She is a beautiful woman."

He cried harder. "I know it. I have thrown away my own heart, my own life. I am the most wretched soul who ever wandered the earth. I am a destitute man . . ."

He went on like this for a bit. He can't

390

help it. Unfortunately, neither can Maggie.

She came up behind me and threw open the door, nearly making me fall over.

"Berto." Voice like ice.

"Maggie, *cara mia*!" Voice like fire.

He leapt forward to embrace her, but she held up her hand, her face grave. I noticed she'd freshened her lipstick, though. No dummy, that one.

"Back off! I am not going to forgive you, so don't fritter your charm. You broke my heart and sent me flying home like a kicked dog." Maggie was just warming up. "I fled my home, my work, my friends. Every single person we know, our colleagues, our neighbors, knew I had been thrown over for a younger woman and pitied me. I am not to be pitied, Berto. I am a proud and beautiful woman, and I am the one who should be pitying you. But I don't pity you, because you made your own bed. Now go back to Italy and lie in it. Alone."

And then she stepped back, taking the time to grab me as she went, for which I was grateful, and slammed the door.

"Jesus Christ, Mags, that was amazing . . ." I started to say, but she held up her hand to me, too. She had tears in her eyes. She was listening.

For a moment, there was just the sound

of weeping from the other side of the door. Then there was an enormous sniff, and the unmistakable sound of someone drawing a shuddering breath. And then he began:

"Why do birds . . . suddenly appear . . ."

With an Italian accent, and the occasional pause for sobbing. Honestly.

"Every time . . . you are near . . ."

I looked at Maggie. The tears were running down her face.

"He's singing our song," she whispered.

"Oh for fuck's sake," I said quietly, and opened the door again.

Thank God for the extra napkins.

How to Grow Turnips

Select a site that gets full sun.

- Turnips like the soil to be well worked, loose, and easygoing, and mixed generously with compost.

- Scatter turnip seeds and then lightly cover with a thin layer of delicious fresh soil.

- Once seedlings are 4 inches high, thin "early" types 2 to 4 inches apart and "maincrop" types to 6 inches apart. Do not thin if growing for greens only, obviously, as that would sort of defeat the purpose.

- In many ways, turnips are the unsung heroes of the root crop universe. They don't have the ad budget potatoes have, or the glamorous appearance of carrots, but they shouldn't be underestimated. They're high in vitamins and minerals, low in sugar, and taste delicious roasted, caramelized, or mashed with a pound of butter. Pliny the Elder considered the turnip the most important vegetable of his day, because "its utility surpasses that of any other plant's." Say what you want about Pliny the Elder . . . he was a man who knew his vegetables.

CHAPTER 19
THE FIFTH CLASS

The next day it was drizzling lightly when we all gathered for class. The mood, despite the rain, was good-natured. Rachel regaled everyone with the story of our bizarre family dinner.

"That sounds very romantic and wonderful." Frances beamed.

Gene frowned. "Once a cheater, always a cheater, I'm afraid."

I kind of agreed with him, but shrugged. "Who knows? Maggie didn't go back to the hotel with him, and she's moving forward with divorce proceedings. She's no pushover." I did wonder, though. It's hard to be single after being happily married, and, as with childbirth, you tend to gloss over the painful parts as soon as possible. Thus, multiple children and the many marriages of Elizabeth Taylor.

Bash came flying up just as the rain was stopping, and I looked over to see that Angie was crossing the grass toward us in the company of a man I hadn't seen before.

"My dad is here!" Bash was beside himself. "Look!"

Everyone else turned to look, including Mike, who presumably had a heightened interest in the matter. I knew he and Angie had hung out some in the week, but I hadn't had a chance to find out much more. Judging by his expression right then, he didn't consider Angie's ex a threat, which either meant that he wasn't interested in her, or he wasn't worried. Or neither. What the heck do I know?

They reached us, and Angie introduced him. "Everyone, this is Matthew; Matt, this is everyone in the gardening class."

Matt was not particularly good-looking, but the sun broke through the clouds right then, burnishing him with a golden glow. He had a great smile, and I could see Bash in his face. He also had that relaxed self-confidence that makes regular-looking guys attractive and handsome guys irresistible. I could easily see a teenage Angie falling for him.

"Hello, everyone. I wanted to see for myself the wonderful group of people my son raves about. This class is his favorite thing in the world right now. It's great."

He knelt down and addressed my kids. "And you two beautiful young ladies must be Clare and Annabel. Sebastian talks about you a lot."

"Who's Sebastian?" Clare wrinkled her nose.

"I am," Bash said.

"Why didn't you tell us that before?"

He frowned. "I don't know. You can still call me Bash. My mom calls me it. My dad calls me Sebastian."

Clare clasped her hands to her chest in the manner of a silent-movie star. "Oh, but Sebastian is so glamorous." She smiled blisteringly at him. "I shall call you Sebastian." The little boy looked shy. "And you can call me Princess Clare."

Matt laughed. "You have your work cut out for you there, dude." He stood up and smiled at Angie. "So, shall I meet you later?"

She shook her head. "No, I'll drop him at your mother's, is that good?"

"Sure." And then he leaned over and kissed her on the mouth, casually touching her butt as he did so. Possessively.

It was kind of shocking, and Angie clearly wasn't expecting it, because she pulled back right away and opened her mouth to say something. But then she looked over at Bash, who was watching them with interest, and just smiled tightly.

"Bye, Matt, we'll talk later on."

He grinned, waved at the kids, and walked off. She watched him go, silently, and then turned to look at Mike. For a moment he said nothing, but then his mouth turned up at the corners. "Asshole," he said, softly.

She grinned, relief flooding her face. "Exactly."

I was sitting on the ground a little while later, randomly pulling weeds out of the herb bed, when Edward came over and crouched down next to me.

"Are you aware that you're pulling out perfectly viable plants?" He kept his voice low, presumably to protect me from public ridicule.

I coughed. "Uh, no. I thought these were weeds."

He smiled. "No, but you're being consistent in your pursuit of rosemary. Clearly, you hate rosemary."

"I've got nothing against her, I assure you."

"Well, she's gone now, so she can't contradict you."

I frowned at him. "Shouldn't your English not be good enough to allow you to make plays on words like that? Shouldn't I be able to outcolloquialize you?"

He stood up and raised his palms. "The Dutch educational system is superlative."

"Yeah? Well, my kids know that worms are hermaphrodites, so there."

He sauntered off, not bothering to comment. It was all very relaxed. I could hear Sebastian and my kids chattering away.

"My dad is a cop," Bash said. I was surprised. When Angie had said, back at the beginning of the course, that maybe someone would shoot her ex-husband, I had immediately thought it would be because he was involved in something shady. Honestly, I needed to get out more.

"He chases bad guys and protects people." Bash clearly had a great deal of pride in his father, and who can blame him? This is yet another problem you face as a single parent — you want to protect the opinion your kids have of your ex, and yet life would be easier if they were as irritated by them as you were. If you could all agree that things would be better if Daddy stayed under a rock, then things would go swimmingly. But no, you have to agree that Daddy is a great guy, a wonderfully brave man, and dodge the implicit question of why you no longer want to live with the aforementioned great guy. It's a tough exercise in double-think.

Again, I think maybe it's easier to be a widow than a divorcée. The kids and I are in total agreement that life without Daddy sucks.

I sat back and looked around. Only one more class after this, and people were tidying industriously, pimping their patch, so to speak. Rachel was the exception, of course. She was just sitting in the middle of her lavender, reading. I had to admire her follow-through. She'd had an idea, she'd made it happen, and now she was enjoying it. She felt me watching her, I guess, because she turned to look at me.

"Enjoying your lavender?"

She shook her head. "No. Worrying about random shit. How about you?"

I laughed. "Isn't that my job? What are you worrying about?"

She held up her hand and folded her fingers down one by one. "Richard. Maggie and Berto. My butt. My skin, particularly my neck skin. My job, and will I ever have the balls to leave it. You and the kids if I move to Paris."

I was surprised. "Are you planning on moving to Paris?"

She shook her head. "No, but what if I did?"

I turned away. She was obviously beyond

help. I could see Mike sitting next to Angie, chatting away, laughing. I realized that he was one of those people, to me at least, who keeps revealing new sides of themselves in a never-ending unfolding of niceness. Everything I learned about him made me like him more. Based on the way Angie relaxed around him, I was far from alone.

Nearby Frances and Eloise were bickering gently over something, and Gene was shoveling manure onto an empty patch of earth. He caught my eye, and I waved and called out.

"Salad not enough for you, Gene? Expanding your base of operations?"

Eloise and Frances looked up.

"I hope you're not planning on annexing our area, Gene." Frances was jokingly stern. Gene shook his head.

"No, just helping out a bit. I like it." He pulled off a glove and wiped his brow with his sleeve. "Hot work, though." He was dripping sweat, but it didn't seem to bother him. Made a change, I guess, from yelling "Buy! Buy!" and "Sell! Sell!" for forty years.

I checked on the kids again. Annabel was lying on her back, which freaked me out for a second, but then I saw her sneaker bobbing up and down in time to the tune she was singing.

"All right there, Bel?" I called over.

"Yeah, just watching the clouds and stuff." She carried on singing, happy as a little clam.

On the other side of the kids' garden, Lisa was helping Bash and Clare transplant more strawberries into their plots, presumably to jump-start their crop. Clare suddenly stood up and whirled around in big circles, her arms out, and then plonked back down again. I shook my head. Honestly, who knows what that was about? That kid didn't just dance to her own tune; she'd hired her own orchestra.

I was just turning idly back to my own planting when I heard a cry and looked up. Everyone but me was on their feet and moving. Mike and Angie were scrambling, Eloise and Frances were stooping down, and Edward was turning and running toward the main entrance of the park. I stood up as Rachel shot past me toward the kids. I was confused, alarmed, and then I saw what was going on.

Gene was lying on the ground, his shovel next to him. He was totally still. Totally pale. And totally in the hands of Angie, who was pulling open his shirt and starting to perform CPR.

I froze. I had often wondered, in the years

since Dan's accident, whether I would react better the next time someone died in front of me. I cannot tell you the number of nights I've dreamt about saving my husband, about running out and pulling his body from the crumpled car, of lifting a truck off him, of pulling a crying baby from a burning house, of leading frightened horses to safety — you name it, I've rescued it. In my dreams. Now that I was faced with another emergency, it turned out I was even more useless than last time. If God had been watching from above, or from the Goodyear blimp (assuming he could get a ride), He would have seen two points of stillness: me, one, standing about twenty-five feet away from Gene, two, who was lying exactly the way you'd expect a dead body to lie. Around the two of us people moved like ants around a doughnut: busy, busy, busy. Rachel had led the kids away to look at something else, although Annabel kept turning back to look. Eloise and Frances were forming a shield, while Mike and Angie were taking turns performing CPR. The sun shone. The birds sang. Trees waved, uncaring. I could just see one of Gene's shoes, loosely tilted to one side. I stood very still. If I moved, I would shatter any chance he had.

Suddenly Edward blew past me doing about ninety. He was carrying a case, and it wasn't until Angie pounced on it that I realized it was one of those portable paddle thingies you see all over the place these days. The thing where the doctor yells "Clear" and the body jumps up and down. I still didn't move. I realized tears were dripping down my face. I should go to my kids. I should call 9-1-1. I should start digging a grave.

"Clear," yelled Angie, and I saw Gene's shoe jump.

A pause.

"Charging." Angie's voice wasn't her usual voice. It was a working voice.

"Clear," she yelled again, and again Gene's shoe jumped.

I heard running behind me and realized the ringing in my ears had been sirens. Show's over. Nothing to see. I sat down slowly on the ground and waited to be taken away.

Rachel touched my shoulder.

"Come on, babe. Time to get out of the way, yeah?" She knelt and looked me in the face. "He's going to be fine. We need to take the kids home now, OK?"

I shook my head. "He's dead."

She shook hers back at me. "No, Angie

403

brought him back. Edward got the paddles, Mike did CPR, and Angie shocked him back to life. He's going to be fine."

I looked up. The EMTs had loaded the body onto a gurney and were bumping it across the ground. As I watched, I saw Gene raise his hand to Mike, who was grinning down at him. Not a body. A person.

Reality snapped back into place with the roar of an earthquake in a drum factory, and I got to my feet. Rachel was watching me closely.

"You're OK, Lili. You're OK, too." She was holding my hands and squeezing them, I realized. Edward came up, and they exchanged glances.

"Are you all right, Lilian? That was very shocking."

I looked at him. "You saved him. You knew what to do."

He grinned, obviously still a bit freaked out himself. "Actually, the city of Los Angeles saved him. You can't teach a course on city land without taking a CPR course. I knew we had paddles, and I knew where they were."

"Wow. *And* they taught the kids about worms."

He and Rachel both laughed, apparently relieved I wasn't about to go nuts.

Speaking of the kids, they were suddenly there, too. I pulled them into a hug.

"Gene fell down!" Clare was amazed that she wasn't the only one to whom these things happened.

"Gene had a heart attack, Clare," Annabel informed her, little M.D. that she was.

"*And* he fell down. How unlucky is that!"

Bash was there, too, watching his mom follow the gurney toward the ambulance. His expression was clouded.

"Are you OK, Bash?" I knelt down next to him.

He looked at me, and his eyes were brimming with tears. "My mommy saved him, didn't she?" I nodded. He smiled. "That's even cooler than chasing bad people."

"It's totally awesome," said Clare. "And that is even more awesome." This was because the ambulance had pulled away, sirens and lights screaming.

She turned to me and Edward and Rachel, and put on a very serious expression.

"You know, I thought gardening class was going to be a little bit boring. But it isn't at all! It's better than TV!"

HOW TO GROW CORN

Plant seeds outdoors once a few weeks have passed since the last frost. Corn likes warm soil.

- Plant them 1 inch deep and 4 to 6 inches apart, in rows 30 to 36 inches apart. See, your mother was right: Math did turn out to be useful after all.
- Water well after planting.
- Harvest when tassels begin to turn brown and the cobs start to swell. Pull ears downward and twist to take off the stalk. (The corn ears, not your ears, silly.)
- Corn cobs lose their sweetness very quickly after picking, so eat or preserve them immediately.

CHAPTER 20

Once Isabel showed up at the hospital, Angie and Mike headed over to my place to pick up Bash and calm down from the excitement.

When Angie walked in, we all cheered — the whole class had come to my place and were waiting for the inevitable pizza, the shorter ones among us with less patience than I would have liked.

"Mom! You're a hero! You saved Gene!" Bash ran up and threw his arms around her.

She hugged him hard and looked around at us. "It was a team effort, Bash, like always. Edward and Mike helped to save him, too. None of us could have done it alone."

Bash looked like he was going to argue the point, but the doorbell rang just in time. Yay, pizza.

"Isabel was amazing," Mike said, giggly, probably with delayed shock. "She burst into the emergency room, yelling for Gene and taking no prisoners." He laughed. "Gene heard her and yelled back. It was like Romeo and Juliet." He shook his head.

Angie was grinning, too. "We just backed away and left them to it. He's in good hands, and seems pretty stable for a guy who was dead for two minutes this afternoon."

"Was it just a heart attack?" Edward said.

Angie nodded. "They think so, but they're running tests. He's got some residual problems. Basically, as he himself said back when we all met him for the first time, he's in pretty bad physical shape, and he was shoveling shit, literally, in the hot sun."

Edward frowned. "I should have been paying closer attention. He seemed fine."

Angie shook her head. "He was fine. And then he was dead. That's how it goes."

Several of them turned and looked at me. I turned up my palms. "She's right. That's how it goes. In my experience, that's the only way it goes."

"Well, hopefully, you'll have a long, lingering death, with plenty of time to prepare." Rachel squeezed my arm. "That didn't come out right, but you know what I mean."

I grinned at her. "Actually, I totally do. And thanks. I hope your death is long and lingering, too."

She held up her hand. "Nope. I want to go quick, laughing my ass off, sudden aneurysm and immediate ruination of whatever dinner gathering I was at."

Eloise looked at her and raised an eyebrow. "You are officially uninvited to my party."

"Oh, come on. A young and lovely body like mine has years to go."

I said nothing. I'd seen a young and lovely body get squished like a bug, but this probably wasn't the time to mention it.

Although I felt fine, that night I had a nightmare for the first time in ages. I was standing in the street outside my house, and it was totally empty. I could hear cars coming, and then they were there, one on either side of me, moving fast. For a second, the street was filled with emergency vehicles and people staring, but then it was deserted again and still the cars were coming. I could see Dan's face, and the girl's face at the same time. She wasn't paying attention, and Dan was oblivious, as he must have been to get hit so hard, and head-on. I yelled and shouted and screamed, but they weren't listening. I tried to pull my feet out of the asphalt, but they were buried to the ankle, as if it were mud. In the next instant, the cars were crashing around me, the sound battering me even though the twisting metal and smoking engines and scalding gasoline were bending around me, leaving me untouched. From where I stood, in excruciating slow-motion, I saw Dan's arms fly forward and hit the windshield, his hands crumpling like paper, his wrists snapping instantly, his forearms shattering, bones bursting through his skin, tugging their tendons with them. His head snapped down and back, and I saw blank terror in his eyes, an animal in a slaughterhouse. The dashboard rippled like silk, the airbags unfurling like giant obscene mushrooms, and then I saw the piece of metal, something from behind the airbag, piercing it, a harpoon straight to Dan's chest. He never saw it, but I did, and reached for it. I grabbed it as it came through the bag, but it ripped through my hands, leaving them like ribbons of raw meat, fluttering tentacles at the ends of my arms. I screamed again, this time in horror for myself, forgetting about Dan in my own fear, and when I looked over again in the dream, he was gone. Edward had taken his place, the harpoon sticking him to the seat, so tightly wedged that three firemen had to pull on it to get it out, and bits of Dan had come out with it when it finally wrenched free. And then it was Clare and Annabel, huddled together, pinned like butterflies, dead and terrified, and my shredded hands were useless to help, all slippery with blood, and I screamed and then it was over.

Dr. Graver made space for me the next afternoon. Her room never changed, the sun slanting in across the bookcases, the dust motes moving gently, supportively.

I was distressed, on the verge of hysteria. I'd held it together all morning, with the kids, because it's not like there's a choice, but the minute I stepped away from them, my throat had tightened and I'd basically run to Graver's. "I dreamt about the accident again, and it was just like it used to be, seeing it happen and not being able to do anything about it, but this time it was Dan and then it was Edward and then the girls."

"Is it ever you?"

I frowned. "How do you mean?"

"Is it ever you, in the driver's seat?" Her dark bob was always perfect, her stylish, slightly ironic retro suits elegant. She was the most contained person I'd ever known, and I wondered if she ever freaked out, ever, about anything. Now she was regarding me calmly but with interest, as if we were discussing the importance of a gluten-free diet, rather than my potential readmission to the loony bin.

I thought about it. "No. It's always Dan, or the kids, or Rachel. Edward was new, but that's because he is new. To me."

In classic psychiatrist mode, she said, "What do you think your dreams mean, Lili?"

I sighed, my tears dry now. "That I want to be able to save everyone? That I feel powerless to protect the people I love?"

She nodded. "That's the obvious interpretation, right? It makes perfect sense. We're all afraid of it, actually, unless we're sociopaths. You have a concrete example and experience of a time when you failed to prevent something bad from happening, so you frame everything in terms of that one traumatic event. But what's interesting is you're never scared for yourself, and that's actually what worries me. It's like you don't exist in your own subconscious."

It struck me differently, and I said so. "Maybe I just think I'm invincible."

She looked at me, hard. "Or maybe you're worried you'll be left behind. Dying in an accident might be the easier option, right? No afterward to deal with."

412

I nodded, slowly. "I'll be the last one standing."

She pointed at me, half-irritated. "Why standing, Lili? Why always standing? You always frame your response to disaster in terms of strength, but actually what happened after Dan died was you fell apart. And that, I think, is what really terrifies you: Not losing someone, but being weak again. You're scared that if you fall in love, you run the risk of losing that love and going crazy again, and that is really terrifying." She sat back and put her palms up. "But yesterday something bad happened and what did you do?"

"Nothing."

"Right. You stood there and waited for it to be over. You protected yourself. You survived it. You lived through it without losing your mind. It's no wonder you dreamt again last night. Your subconscious is freaked-out."

I was totally confused. "But is that good or bad? Isn't it OK to be scared of going crazy?"

She nodded. "Of course. If you weren't scared, you'd probably already be mad."

I laughed, suddenly. "You're very strange, do you know that? You're making me even more unclear than I was when I walked in."

She laughed, too. "And that, dear Lilian, is how you know you're alive. Welcome to the real world." She stood up. "Now, carry on. You're doing great."

"You mean apart from the nightmares and the back-and-forth about Edward and everything?"

"Yeah, apart from that. Go take care of the kids. They're probably freaked-out, too."

I actually went to visit Gene next, because Graver's office was next to the hospital. Isabel was there, sitting silently by the bed. Now she looked her age. Gene was sleeping, attached to machines that occasionally beeped in time with one another, then drifted out of phase. Nurses came in and out, not looking at anyone, just communing with the machines. Tending them, and by extension, Gene.

"Hi, Isabel," I said softly, not wanting to surprise her.

"Hi, Lilian," she replied, obviously completely unsurprised.

"Gene looks very calm," I said, pulling a chair up and sitting next to her.

"Looks are deceptive." Her ebullience had faded. She seemed terribly depressed.

I took in the stillness of the bed, those perforated cotton blankets folded at the foot, the superwhite starched sheets, the pale gray cords everywhere like bloodless arteries. "What do the doctors say?"

She still hadn't looked at me, just kept watching Gene's face. "They say he's not out of the woods. They say his heart is very damaged. And they say he may not survive a surgery, even though that's the only option. I think they're saying he's going to die, but I'm not sure." She leaned forward and squeezed his hand. When she let go, the fingers stayed stacked for a moment, then drifted apart. Wherever Gene was, he was apparently not home.

I sat silently. After a moment, she went on.

"So I have decided I will simply believe that he's going to live, and I will sit here until everyone else is as sure as I am, and then I'll go home."

"And what can I do to help?"

She shook her head. "Nothing. I'm fine."

I knew from experience that that wasn't even slightly true. I looked around for clues. A tray of food sat nearby, untouched.

"Isabel, have you eaten?" She shook her head. "Are you hungry?" She shook her head again. "Look, if you don't eat and drink, you'll get weak and they'll make you move. If you want to stay next to Gene, you need to eat and drink."

She finally turned and looked at me. "Your husband is dead, isn't he?"

"Yes. Very dead."

"How did you deal with it?"

"Badly. I went temporarily insane, and I'm still not a model of mental health. But Gene isn't going to die, because you're going to sit here and make sure of it."

Tears filled her eyes, but didn't fall. "Do you think I'm mad? For thinking I can keep him alive?"

"Nope. I totally get it. But I'm going to be a pain in the ass about the food thing. I'm going to go and get you a sandwich and a drink, and then I'm going to sit here and watch you eat it. While you eat it, I will tell you all about my dead husband, and after you've eaten it, you can tell me all about your alive one, OK?"

She smiled, faintly. "Were you always this pushy?"

I smiled back, getting to my feet. "No, only today, and only for you. So if you want to be supportive, you'll let me do my thing." I headed off to the cafeteria. Isabel could sit there and keep Gene alive, and I would sit there and keep her alive.

For two days, she sat there, and I stayed until their daughter showed up, and then she and I took it in turns, and then they did the surgery. Amazingly, Gene pulled through, but then there were more days of sitting and waiting until he woke up. It was boring and terrifying and frustrating and gross, as these things always are.

And what was everyone else doing while Gene hovered between life and death? Well, of course, they were carrying on with their lives, in that insulting way the living do. Mike moved his trailer over to Gene's driveway and was helping out at his place, running errands and getting the house ready for Gene's return. They set up a bedroom downstairs. They got a fancy hospital bed, which my children loved and which they nearly broke on the first day, riding it up and down. Gene's other daughter was coming up once Gene was out of the hospital, for a week or so, and the one with the baby was coming up once her sister had left. All in all, there was a pretty good support system being set up.

I was still going into work, of course, finishing up what I needed to finish up, and helping Sasha. Not that she needed help. She'd gotten a great job in about two days, working for a company that made graphic novels, her dream job. I don't know why we didn't both quit earlier. If we'd known these great jobs were out there, maybe we would have. Al was still employed as a fact-checker, and Rose had simply refused to be fired, and had eventually been moved upstairs, where, presumably, she was causing trouble in a variety of satisfying ways.

Roberta King wandered into the office toward the end of the week, grinning. She'd relaxed quite a bit since firing everyone. Maybe it was just the push she needed to get her into jeans.

"Hey, Bloem sent the first part of the encyclopedia content. I hope you haven't taken on too much freelance work."

I looked at her. How was it possible that she and I were wearing basically the same outfit — jeans, sneakers, and a sweatshirt — and yet she looked like a preppy college freshman and I looked like I'd parked my shopping cart in the ladies' room? Despite this wandering through my busy little mind, I managed to shake my head at her. Multi-tasking queen, that's me.

"Nope. I've got room on my plate for vegetables, so to speak."

She perched on my desk. Oh, the casual-ness. "In addition to individual vegetable varieties, there will apparently be illustra-tions of various gardening techniques, tools, and that type of thing." She kicked her feet. "I'll e-mail you the first section when I get back upstairs. We have a call with their editor tomorrow to go through it and decide what to illustrate and how."

"Are we starting with artichokes and asparagus?"

"Actually, no. They sent us *P* first. Parsley, parsnips, peas . . ."

I raised my eyebrows, pushing my chair back so I could lean. "Wow, how long is this all supposed to take?"

"A year or so. Should keep you busy."

I thought about it. I hadn't expected vegetables to become such a major feature of my life, but that's the thing with plants . . . they grow to fill the available space. I realized she was still talking to me.

". . . and then they send you samples, or photos, I guess."

"Why don't they just use photographs?"

"Tradition, they said. I asked the same thing." She pushed herself off the desk.

"You look very relaxed, Roberta."

She grinned. "I only got dressed up for you guys. Now I can just be myself."

I laughed at her. "But we hardly ever saw you."

She laughed at herself. "Yeah, but I could hear you all down here, breathing. Any minute I might have been called on to settle a dispute and look managerial."

"You're joking. We had Rose. She was judge and jury on everything."

She stopped laughing. "I know. She sits outside my office now, and scares the living crap out of me. She stares at me angrily from the minute I get off the elevator until I get back on at the end of the day."

"Doughnuts. Baked goods will set you free. Get in before her every morning for a week or two and leave something on her desk. You'll be old pals before you know it."

She thanked me and wandered off. I stretched and looked around the mostly empty office. This had all worked out pretty well. A long-term freelance project from Poplar, the kids' stuff, my own stuff . . . I was a one-woman art factory. Apart from the nightmares, everything was great.

How to Grow Radishes

Plant radishes a month or so before the last frost, and work plenty of fertilizer into the soil first.

- Sow the seeds 1/2 inch to an inch deep and 1 inch apart.
- Don't crowd them! They need sun. If they don't get enough sun they will retaliate by focusing their energy on growing leaves, and you'll have to go buy radishes and lie about your horticultural prowess.
- Plant every two weeks while the weather is still cool so you can have a continuous harvest.

CHAPTER 21

I decided to go visit Dan's parents, and took the kids with me. They lived in Pasadena, only about half an hour away, and we usually went over once a month or so. Paul and April were über-grandparents, best in class, possibly best in show. Dan's mother, April, made cookies, wore aprons, was pleasantly round-faced and apple-cheeked, and watched *My Little Pony* so she could discuss it intelligently with the kids. Dan's dad, Paul, built toy rockets and blew things up in their huge backyard. Seriously, it was a dream house, and they were fairytale people. You'd never know that they'd both recently retired from the Jet Propulsion Laboratory, where they'd programmed satellites.

Maggie was out when we got there, presumably with Berto. April confirmed this.

"Yes, she's allowing that shitbird to talk to her." She said this as she pulled a tray of brownies from the oven, sprinkling M&M's

over the top to get all melty and ridiculous. "That fuckhead."

I was surprised. "Maggie?"

April shook her head. "No, of course not. Dirto."

"Dirto?"

She shrugged. "I'm sure you've found the same thing: When someone hurts your child, you become very immature and angry about it. I changed his name to Dirto, and Dirto he will stay until he cleans up his act." She put the brownies on the cooling rack and turned off the oven. I had spent probably months, over the years, in this kitchen, and very little changed. Wooden love spoons hung above the counter, April's collection of blue and white china stood on a rack above an original Welsh dresser, a cat slept on top of the microwave. Presumably the cat had changed over the past dozen years, but as they always had ginger cats, it was difficult to be sure.

I pushed my coffee cup away, hoping to make room for a brownie. "He seems repentant . . ."

She shook her head and sat down across from me, folding her hands on the table. "No, he seems regretful, which is a totally different thing. He regrets doing it because it didn't work out. It doesn't mean that he

423

wouldn't do it again. Repentance, real repentance, would mean he knew what he did was wrong and learned from it." She stood again to cut me a brownie, having finally realized that my frequent glances in that direction meant I needed sugar. "You realize these are too fresh to cut, and that you run the risk of burning your mouth and making an enormous mess?"

"Yes."

She slid a plate across. I could hear Paul, out in the garden, encouraging Clare to strike a match. I should have been worried, but I wasn't. Sometimes it's better for them to learn how to do dangerous stuff properly, so they don't panic and hurt themselves when they inevitably try it on their own. Besides, he was a rocket scientist.

There was a pause while I took a bite and then immediately had to breathe hard to cool it down. April just raised her eyebrows at me.

"So Maggie tells me you're dating someone?"

I choked on a crumb, and a distressing moment ensued with April having to get me a glass of water and bang me between the shoulder blades.

Eventually I was able to shake my head. "No, I'm not. I met someone, but I'm not

424

ready to date yet."

She frowned at me. "We've talked about this before. You know Paul and I want you to be happy. I really believe Dan would want you to move on with your life, and not have to raise the children alone."

I shrugged my shoulders. "Well, he's not here to ask, and I miss him so much still." I paused. "Don't you? I can't imagine how much harder it is to lose a child than a husband."

She was silent a moment. "For the first year, I thought I might die every day. I didn't want to be alive, but I had to keep going, for Maggie, for Paul." She looked sharply at me. "I imagine you felt much the same. I know when we visited you in the hospital, you were as deeply sad as anyone I've ever seen, not including myself." She shook her head, subtly, and got up to refill her mug of tea. "I feel bad for not visiting you more, but I worried if our twin planets of sorrow got too close, they might cause a black hole we'd never get out of."

From the garden, there was a giant whooshing noise followed by a simply enormous bang and the sound of cheering. We waited for the ceiling to fall in, but it didn't.

"Let's do it again!" Clare's voice was

several octaves higher than normal, and I could hear Annabel chiming in.

Paul answered them thoughtfully. "I'm not sure we have enough of the rocket engines. Let me go look."

He came through the kitchen door, and April silently pointed to the larder.

"Third shelf down, cardboard box." He bustled in and out, fistfuls of rocket engines in his hands. I liked the fact that they stocked Estes rocket supplies along with the cat food. What could possibly go wrong?

April was silent for a moment, thinking. "Do you still get mail for him?"

I nodded. "Mail and e-mail, all the time. He's qualified for an incredible amount of credit since he died, which is hard to believe. It's possible Visa is accepted in the afterlife, I guess, but you'd think they'd send the bills there." I carefully blew on another bite of brownie. "Lots of fishing catalogues, because he bought a rod one time, lots of consumer electronics . . ." I looked at her. "Do you?"

"Sure. We always got mail for him, ever since he went to college. Once a month we'd forward on anything that looked important, and then once you and he were living together, he got mail there instead, and we'd only get the occasional thing. But they still come."

"It sucks, seeing his name. And I can't face calling these people and telling them he's dead. Especially as they often tell me he was the only authorized user and therefore the only one who can cancel the account." I took another bite, this time without burning myself. "I think I'm still paying for his cell phone." I also kept his Facebook page alive, and other social media crap. I expect "the cloud" is full of ghosts.

She nodded silently. Then she said, "But it gets a little better, as the years go by. At first, every memory was painful, even agonizing, but eventually I was able to think about him with joy again, remembering all the wonderful things about him. He was a wonderful son, a wonderful father."

"He was," I agreed. "He can't be replaced."

She looked at me calmly. "You're not trying to replace him, Lili. It's acceptable to go in a new direction and let him stay as he was. It's not a betrayal, it's not a rejection. I can take pleasure in Clare and Annabel, and in Maggie, and in Paul, and it doesn't take away from my sadness about losing Dan, or the joy I can now feel when I remember him." She reached across the table and took my hand. "It's not even related, you must understand that." She stood up. "He didn't leave us on purpose, honey, but he did leave, and that's all there is to it." She headed toward the back door. "Now, I'm going to make sure Paul is setting his trajectories correctly. Sometimes his math gets a little sloppy."

I sat there alone and watched the cat, who was industriously washing his tail. He curled it tidily around his paws and assumed the loaf-of-bread pose for which cats are so rightly famous. For a moment, I envied him his comfortable spot, his simple life. But then I put the last piece of gooey brownie in my mouth and stood up to go outside and watch the fireworks.

COMPANION PLANTING

Dill and basil planted among tomatoes protect the tomatoes from hornworms, and sage scattered about the cabbage patch reduces injury from cabbage moths.

- Marigolds are as good as gold when grown with just about any garden plant, repelling beetles, nematodes, and even animal pests. They also look dandy tucked behind your ear.
- Some companions act as trap plants, luring insects away from your precious vegetables. Nasturtiums, for example, are so favored by aphids that the devastating insects will flock to them instead of other plants. Psych!
- A glass of wine placed between a gardener's fingers improves most planting situations. Replace often, especially in warmer weather, or on Fridays.

CHAPTER 22
THE LAST CLASS

The following Saturday was the last class, and the Grand Harvest.

I was hoping for sheaves of wheat, giant draft horses pulling plows, and all that good pastoral stuff, but that wasn't how it went down. Instead, we all picked and pulled and dug, and ended up with a mountain of stuff. It was pretty impressive, actually.

I had about twenty ears of corn, two large baskets of pattypan squash, and three baskets of green beans. Blue Lake green beans, to be precise, each one as long as my palm and then some. Biting into a freshly picked bean is a lot juicier than I had suspected, and more delicious. However, the big surprise, for me at least, was how awesome fresh lettuce is. Picked, washed, and eaten, it's a whole different leaf, as it were. Honestly, you could eat handfuls just on its own — or I could, at least. Eventually Mike threatened me with a trowel. Because

Gene was still in the hospital, Mike was harvesting their salad bed alone, and I nipped back in and stole more when he wasn't looking. Just like Peter Rabbit, but without the little blue jacket.

Gene was doing better, possibly due to Isabel's control of the forces of nature, and would be allowed to return home in a month or so. Angie and Mike had been to see him the evening before, and reported to the class.

Angie was holding Mike's hand. "Gene's going to need a lot of nursing support and rehab, so Mike is going to park the trailer there for a few months, and Bash and I are going to move into their guest house." She grinned at her son. "I think Isabel and Bash put this plan together, to be honest, because I can't tell which one of them is happier about it."

"Isabel says I can go on the swing whenever I want." Bash seemed amazed at his own good fortune, and Clare narrowed her eyes and muttered, "Lucky," under her breath.

"We can go visit them, honey," I reminded her.

"We'd better." Honestly, she'd turned into a Mafia don all of a sudden. I couldn't keep up.

Rachel had brought Richard to help with the harvest, and the two of them were laughing with Frances and Eloise. Richard had a piece of lavender tucked behind his ear, which made him look like a cute village idiot. Rachel was relaxed and happy, wearing no makeup and smiling a lot. You think you know someone better than yourself, but then it turns out there's a whole other side you never guessed about. Rachel had always seemed tough, competent, unreachable, and now was sweet, soft, and vulnerable. I liked Richard so far, but if he hurt her in any way, I was going to slam his dick in a drawer. Just saying.

I went to finish gathering the tomatoes, which had produced in such an overachieving way that I kept finding more and more of them hiding under leaves. The two rows of plants had also grown impressively, creating a hidden green corridor between them. I sat on the ground and closed my eyes for a moment, relaxing and taking in the scents and sounds. I heard rustling and opened them again to see Edward, who was just sitting down to join me. It was a tighter squeeze for him, but he managed it. We sat there, cross-legged like a pair of kids, knee to knee in the tomato patch.

"I like your hiding spot," he said. "It's very green."

I nodded. "It smells nice, too."

"You missed one," he said, leaning forward to point it out. He was so close, and impulsively I ducked my head as well, kissing him and putting my hand on his cheek. I felt him hesitate, so I slid my hand into his hair and pulled him in tighter, making it clear I wanted this, wanted him. There was less recklessness than in the kitchen; more control, and after a few seconds, even more heat. As the kiss got deeper, Edward slid his hand down my arm, twining his fingers with mine, and I felt an increasingly familiar desire. This wasn't a kiss. This was foreplay. We were going to be lovers, and I couldn't wait.

"Ew," came a small, disgusted voice. "I found them. They're hiding in the tomatoes and kissing! Like caterpillars!"

We pulled apart and looked up. Clare was peering at us through the leaves, and after a moment the rest of the class appeared, their heads looming into the greenery, one by one.

Edward cleared his throat. "Class dismissed," he said firmly, before leaning forward to kiss me again.

■ ■ ■ ■

Eventually we were all done, and we stood and posed for a photo with our baskets of produce displayed in front of us, like a county-fair brochure. Total? Four big baskets of salad; my corn, beans, and squash; five giant baskets of tomatoes, both cherry and regular; a sack of lavender; three baskets of English peas; and eight baskets of berries. Ridiculous. We could have opened a farm stand.

But instead we threw a party.

Frances and Eloise headed home, with Mike and Angela assisting, to create a meal out of our pickings. They didn't take it all, actually. Much of it was left, and the kids and I took it to a community kitchen. They were happy to have it, and the kids were all puffy-chested and proud. Clare borrowed my cell phone to call her grandma. I only heard one side of the conversation, of course:

"Hi, Grandma, guess what? I gave food away to hungry people, food I grew myself." (Big emphasis on that last part.)

(*Pause*)

"No, not on the street. In a place."

(*Pause*)

"Yes, I went into the place."

(*Pause*)

"No, Mommy and Annabel came, too."

(*Pause*)

"No, nobody touched my bottom." (At this point, she frowned and looked at me, and I took the phone. Honestly, my mother could suck the joy out of Christmas.)

Frances and Eloise lived in a nice part of the city, one that was quiet and residential. The crappy economy had made it possible for them to get a house, proving, yet again, that all clouds have a silver lining, although presumably not for the people who sold it to them. It was small but cute, and the garden was wonderful, surrounded by tall hedges, with wild flower beds filled with California poppies and other colorful flowers I can't even begin to name. Mike and Frances were discussing the building of a raised bed for vegetables, and maybe a chicken coop. We were all going a little nuts.

There was loads of food set up on a large picnic table just outside the kitchen door. Potato salad with green beans. Sautéed squash with onions and garlic. Tomatoes on their own, or stuffed with cream cheese, or with rice and peppers. Bowls of salad, dressed and undressed. Fresh bread. Berry pie, berry cobbler, berries and cream. Pretty much everything had been grown by the class, and it was enormously satisfying to eat it all. Buckets of ice and soda sat around, and people popped beers and just hung out and talked. It was great, and I knew it wouldn't be the last time we were all together.

I turned as someone chimed a fork on a glass. Edward.

"Can you all hear me? I'd like to say something."

We all quieted down, apart from the kids, of course, who were chasing one another around in their usual way. God only knows what would happen once the chickens arrived.

Edward began to speak.

"Teaching this class has been a wonderful experience for me, and I'm glad you've all signed up for the next session. The botanical garden has extended their agreement with my company, in return for some very rare plants, and next semester we'll have twice as much room."

"More worms!" cried Clare.

Edward smiled at her. "Actually, we're going to set up a larger vegetable garden to supply two or three local soup kitchens. It's going to be great, and we will all need to work hard to make it happen."

He looked at me. "In addition, I want to create a book about this course, and about the community garden we're going to build, and I am hoping we can all persuade Lilian to illustrate it. The proceeds will go to support the garden."

My goodness, I wasn't going to have a free moment. But what the hell? I raised my glass. "I'd be honored."

Annabel came over to me. "We'd better get started on the garage, then," she said seriously. I hugged her.

"I don't think there's that big of a rush, honey, We've got all summer to get ready for next semester."

She looked doubtful. Summer, in her limited experience, seemed to always fly by.

Rachel stood up and raised her hand. "Hey, everyone, ssh a minute. I have a toast."

We all went quiet. She has charisma, there's nothing you can do.

"I'd first like to propose a toast to Edward, who taught us to look more closely at what we're stepping in, and to have more respect for the humble worm."

We all laughed and raised our glasses.

"Then I would like to propose a toast to Gene, in absentia, who taught us that while it is never too late to take up a new hobby, it's best not to shovel shit too exuberantly."

Again our glasses went up.

"And finally, I'd like to propose a toast to Mother Nature, who grew our vegetables for us, put color in our berries and our cheeks, made several of us fall in love, and both took away and returned a good friend to us. To Mother Nature!"

This time we cheered and drained our cups.

"You know what, though," piped up a little voice, "I don't know that I could have any more respect for worms than I already did."

A pause.

"They're awesome."

Rachel and Richard came back with us to my place, and when we got there the kids suddenly got all strange and giggly.

"We got you a present," Clare said, grinning.

"You did?"

Rachel smiled and asked me to close my eyes.

"Are you going to break an egg on my head?"

There was a pause. "Did I ever do that before?" Rachel sounded intrigued.

I shook my head. "No, I don't know why

that occurred to me. Sorry."

Richard raised his eyebrows. "You two are really weird. Lili, close your eyes. We've got a pleasant surprise to share with you, OK?"

I shut my eyes, and the kids led me through the kitchen and carefully down the back steps, into the garden.

"Is it more fairies?" I asked. Honestly, they were taking over.

"Nope," Clare replied, letting go of my hand, "although you could put fairies on it, I suppose."

"Open your eyes now," commanded Annabel, tugging at my hand.

I did. And there, under the tree at the end of the garden, was a bench. A perfect, simple, wooden park bench.

"Look," said Clare, dancing around, "it has your name on it!"

I walked slowly over and traced the carving with my fingers.

TO MOMMY, it read. THE BESTEST MOMMY IN THE WORLD. FOR SITTING ON.

I turned to Rachel. "Does that mean the bench is for sitting on, or that I am for sitting on?"

She laughed. "Clare wrote the inscription, and we approved the ambiguity." She pointed to the bench. "So sit!"

I sat, and the kids piled on top of me.

"See?" Clare was thrilled. "Now you can sit on the bench and we can sit on you!"

Richard grinned. "I don't know if you've noticed, but you don't sit down very much."

"Really?"

He shook his head. "No. You're always getting someone something, or rushing to pick something up, or doing something else." He looked at Rachel. "Rachel does all the sitting for both of you."

She punched him in the arm, but didn't deny it. In fact, she joined us on the bench. Despite the tight squeeze, it was comfortable.

I thought of the sketch I'd done, of Dan sitting on a bench in this same spot. Was it wrong for me to be happy here without him? But then I looked at the kids and realized that because of them, he was always there. And, knowing him, he would argue that to make him happy, I should make them happy. And the best way to make them happy was to be happy myself, because I was the bestest mommy in the whole world. Even if only for sitting on.

I rested my head on Rachel's shoulder for a moment, and just let it all sink in. Of course, Frank picked that moment to scoot across the garden, his butt making an actual divot in the lawn.

"Worms!" announced Clare.

"Mom!" said Annabel, exasperated.

"I know, I know," I said, "I'll take care of it."

And, once I'm done sitting for a bit, I will.

■ ■ ■ ■

Readers Guide:
The Garden of
Small Beginnings

ABBI WAXMAN

■ ■ ■ ■

DISCUSSION QUESTIONS

1. The Anaïs Nin quote at the start of the book expresses the challenge facing Lilian. Have you experienced a situation where staying in place was as painful a choice as moving forward?

2. As the story begins, Lilian is deeply sad, but comfortable in her sadness. She resists people's encouragements to move on, and is quite verbal about it. What impact does her position have on the other people in her life?

3. Lilian's children experienced the loss of their father differently. How have you seen your own family or friends deal differently with grief, or other losses? Is there a "right" way?

4. Does Lilian find her work as a textbook illustrator fulfilling? Is she as stuck in that

job as she is in her personal life?

5. What are the similarities and differences between the way Lilian and her sister, Rachel, process emotions? How did their childhood impact their approach? Both have a tendency to use humor to diffuse stress, or make light of personal struggles. What do you think are the strengths and weaknesses of that approach?

6. Are the differences between Lilian and Rachel similar to the differences between Annabel and Clare — how does each pair of sisters relate to each other?

7. Lilian takes the gardening class because her boss asks her to, but it ends up being a transformative experience for her. Has that ever happened to you, where something that started out as a chore instead became something wonderful?

8. Gardening turns out to be relaxing for Lilian, despite the hard physical work involved. What do you enjoy about gardening, and why do you think it's so helpful for Lili?

9. Lilian is often surprised by the distance

between her first impressions of people and what she subsequently learns about them. Do you think that's a common experience? Do you think the first impression you give people is an accurate expression of who you really are? Is that even desirable?

10. A theme in the book is unexpected events and their consequences — how have unexpected events affected your life?

11. Do you think Edward and Lilian will end up together? Is Lili ready for a new relationship?

ABOUT THE AUTHOR

Abbi Waxman is a chocolate-loving, dog-loving woman who lives in Los Angeles and lies down as much as possible. She worked in advertising for many years, which is how she learned to write fiction. She has three daughters, three dogs, three cats, and one very patient husband.